LOCKED

ELLA FRANK
BROOKE BLAINE

Also by Brooke Blaine

Standalone
Flash Point

L.A. Liaisons Series
Licked
Hooker

Sex Addict
Co-authored with Ella Frank

PresLocke Series
Co-Authored with Ella Frank
ACED

Dedication

To all of you who have been dying to know what Ace & Dylan's

next step would be...

Go ahead and let go of that cliff!
And thank you for being patient little f*ckers.

1
TO HELL IN A HANDBASKET

"ACE, THE MANAGER'S here."

I was vaguely aware of Dylan's voice behind me and the hand he had on my shoulder, but as I stood at the floor-to-ceiling window of Syn's presidential suite overlooking the Las Vegas Strip, I couldn't seem to turn my gaze away from the press that had gathered at the hotel's entrance far below. It seemed more were streaming in every minute, and as I watched the crowd grow larger, the panic I'd been feeling morphed into utter numbness. How was it possible that life could change so drastically in the span of a few minutes?

"Ace?" Dylan said again. "I think maybe you should sit down."

Surely all those people aren't here for me. Word couldn't have spread that fast.

But even as the thought crossed my mind, I knew it wasn't true. Images flashed through my head—the paparazzo standing in the middle of Dylan's suite, disguised in a bellhop uniform; the *click click click* of his camera as he stole our private moments; Dylan running after him in nothing but a towel draped around his waist; me, pulling him back inside as my world collapsed in mere seconds.

Resting my forehead against the cool glass, I closed my eyes and tried to slow the rapid beating of my heart.

"Just give him a second," I heard Dylan say as his hand left my shoulder. I knew I needed to turn around and face the reality of what had just happened, but doing that meant I was ready to deal with the fallout I knew was coming. Somewhere in the hotel my cell was ringing, and it was an easy guess who that could be. Roger, my manager, or Martina, my publicist. Hell, probably both of them on speakerphone.

The secret I tried so hard to conceal, gone to such great lengths, like this entire getaway weekend, to protect...

I shook my head against the glass. What would this mean for my career now? Sure, the world knew I was gay, but they'd never actually had a visual to go along with that. According to Roger and Martina, and even my parents, my career wouldn't survive if I flaunted a relationship in the faces of moviegoers. And unfortunately, it looked like I was about to find out whether they were right in that prediction or not, because there was no way I could deny the man I'd come to need in my life.

"Ace?" Dylan's voice was gentle, as though he was coaxing a skittish mustang, and I couldn't blame him. I knew he thought I was about two seconds away from bolting. I took in a much-needed breath of air and then finally turned to face the music.

Dylan was standing only a few feet away from me, dressed in his jeans and t-shirt, and it was right then, with his eyes locked on mine and the earnest expression on his face, that I knew the first thing I wanted...no, *needed* to do, was lay his fears to rest.

Not the fear of what was to come, because honestly, I had no idea what nightmare would soon unfold around the two of us. But I needed him to know that the reason for my withdrawal, the reason for my panic, wasn't steeped in regret for being with him.

"Ace, the manager—"

"Can wait a minute," I said, and took the three steps it required to bring me toe to toe with him. I brought my hands up to his face and trailed my thumb along his lower lip. "Everyone else can fucking wait a minute."

Dylan's hands came up to circle my wrists, and his eyes were full of compassion as they roved all over my face, trying to ascertain if I was okay. I wasn't, and I knew that much was obvious. But before any misunderstandings made their way between us, before we were descended on by people who would have very strong opinions one way or another about us and our relationship, I wanted Dylan to be one hundred percent clear that any opinions expressed were *not* mine.

I swallowed, trying to find the words to explain all the emotions that were racing through my mind. But before I could get any out, Dylan lowered my arms and wrapped them around his waist. He nuzzled his face in against my bare shoulder and neck and asked, "Are you all right?"

I tightened my hold around him, thinking if I didn't keep him close he might somehow get pulled from my grasp and I'd never have this opportunity again.

"No," I said. "But this is the first time my heart has slowed somewhat since you opened that door and everything went to hell in a handbasket."

"And may I just say, on behalf of the hotel, how unbelievably sorry we are for the intrusion," Charles Toth, Syn's assistant manager, said, coming forward. "We've already called the local authorities, and rest assured we'll get to the bottom of this. It's almost impossible for anyone to have access to this floor, so I'm not sure how—"

"Almost," Dylan said, lifting his head from my shoulder. "*Almost* impossible? Somehow, a man was able to steal not only one of your employee uniforms, but also the private access elevator keycard, as well as a separate entry card to my room. How fucking lax do you have to be, *especially* considering the kind of guests you have staying on this floor?"

Oh hell. Dylan was pissed, and even through the shitstorm swirling around us, I couldn't repress the small smile that twisted my lips at his possessive tone.

Charles blanched and began wringing his hands. "I guarantee we'll—"

"Don't bother making promises you can't keep," Dylan said, facing the man turning Casper. "Have you bothered looking outside yet? Even from forty-five floors up you can see the swarm of people. What are you going to do about that? About the damage that's been done already? About Ace's future?"

My hand went tight on Dylan's waist so he wouldn't take a step farther. With the flush that was creeping up his neck, I didn't trust that he wouldn't strangle the man he had literally shaking in his polished Gucci loafers, and the last thing we needed to add to the field day was a murder.

"I...uh...we have full faith in the authorities—" Charles said.

"Who can magically erase the pictures that are probably going up all over the internet right now?" Dylan said. "Right."

"I appreciate you trying to help, but could you give us some privacy for a few minutes?" I asked Charles, and the fact that I was kicking him out seemed to surprise him.

"Of course," he said, walking backward to the front door. "I'll just...guard the door until you... Right." Then, as he shut the door behind him, I steered Dylan toward the couch.

"Okay," I said, "let's just run over the choices."

"Should you answer your phone first?" Dylan asked over the insistent ringing of my cell, and when he finally took a seat, I went to the back bedroom to grab my phone. Ten missed calls already, from both Roger and Martina, along with more than a handful of texts. As I stood there staring at the screen, I had an overwhelming sense of déjà vu. A little over a year earlier, there'd been the same frenzy, the same phone calls, the same feeling of despair. Only that time there hadn't been pictures. Shayne's matchmaker boss from hell had leaked my secret to the press, but before things had gotten too out of hand, Shayne had covered for me and things had slowly died down.

As I headed back to the main room and caught sight of the stunning man sitting on the couch worrying his hand through his brown hair, I realized too that I had been alone the last time.

"Dylan…" I said as I went to his side and took a seat. He angled his face so he was staring at me, and I couldn't stop myself from reaching out and drawing a finger down his jaw.

"Please, don't worry about me. God," he said, shaking his head. "You have enough to worry about."

My lips pulled into a thin line at his words, because while he was right, and I had a million and one things to worry about, my brain and thoughts kept zeroing in on him—and wasn't that an eye-opening moment, to realize that Dylan was my number one concern here.

I cleared my throat and reached for one of his hands. When he entwined his fingers in mine, I realized how his were shaking, and wanted to ease him somehow. But that was going to be difficult considering my own were trembling.

"Okay, so," I said, and then sighed. "We have to work out what we're going to do next. What *you* want to do next."

"Me?" Dylan said, his eyes widening. Then he squeezed my fingers and gingerly let go. As he stood and started to pace in front of me, I could see the wheels turning in Dylan's head. His face closed off, his expression became unreadable, and then he stopped and looked down at me, and I had a feeling whatever he was about to say was going to cut me straight to the core.

"Ace…look, I'll say whatever you want me to say. Or nothing at all, if that's the case. I can hide in this room until everyone leaves. Whatever. But the way I see it, if you leave here by yourself and deny it, then for a while this would have to end. Maybe forever—"

"No," I said, getting to my feet. That was the one thing I was sure I *didn't* want. "That's not going to happen." I placed one of my hands over the ones he was twisting in front of himself, and shook my head. "*This*, what's happening between us, is not ending. Not unless you want it to."

Dylan chewed his lip as he held my hand in almost a death grip. "I…I…"

"I know this is a lot to take in. Shit, I haven't even taken it all in. But if you want this, if you want me, then I'm ready to walk out that door with your hand in mine and tell the world to fuck off." And as soon as those words were out of my mouth, I knew they were the right ones. When it came to Dylan, there wasn't a choice to make. It'd been made from the first day I saw him, and if he was willing do this, to stick by me and weather whatever came our way, then it didn't matter what anyone else had to say. He, and my decision, was non-negotiable.

* * *

MY MOUTH FELL open. *Holy shit*, I hadn't been expecting that at all, and when the phone on the couch began to ring again, I asked, "What about your team? Won't they have an opinion on that?"

"I'm sure they'll have many opinions, but the only one that matters right now is yours."

"You can't be serious. But all those people—"

"Don't mean a fucking thing right now." Something in Ace's tone told me he was dead serious, and I clamped my mouth shut. Then he continued, his voice softer this time. "This is going to be a nightmare. I'm not about to sugarcoat it and tell you otherwise. If you stay with me, you'll be followed. Everywhere. Your picture will *be* everywhere, and not the hot billboard or magazine ads, either. They'll catch you at the grocery store. Getting gas. Leaving my house. Leaving yours. Hell, there will probably be helicopters over my neighborhood for the foreseeable future, and I need to know…"

As he trailed off, his gaze dropped to the floor, and I reached for his face and brought his mouth to mine, needing to reassure him that I wasn't going anywhere. And when I pulled back, I whispered against his lips, "At least then we won't have to hide…"

Ace's brilliant blue eyes met mine, and he seemed to search for something. "But when you realize what being with me now entails, you might want to."

"No," I said, shaking my head firmly. "Don't try to scare me off."

"It's not *me* I'm worried about."

"Don't worry about them either. So they'll follow us. So they'll post shit in the papers—"

"Untrue shit."

"I can handle it. But can *you*?"

And that right there was the real question. Yeah, Ace had dealt with the price of fame for most of his adult life, but I knew what it could cost him to come out of hiding and show the world who he was…and whom he was with. Plus, being gay was still something he was coming to terms with. He'd only been out for a year, for God's sake, and he'd never even been in a relationship before. I'd had three decades of living as a gay man, and I knew the kind of hate that could get thrown our way. And in his line of work? It could—and would—get brutal.

Ace sighed and rubbed a hand over his eyes, and when he looked back at me, there was a weariness there that I'd never seen before. As though he'd already lived out the way this thing was going to go. But there was determination there too, and it was in that moment that I knew there was no turning back.

Ace reached for my hand, and as he brushed over my knuckles with his thumb, he said, "If you're with me, I think I could take on anything."

"That's the sweetest thing that's ever come out of your mouth. Not something I'd have thought *the Ace Locke* would ever say," I teased. Inside, though, his admission made every part of my body thrill.

"Hey, I can be sweet."

"Yes, you were very sweet this morning. And last night," I said, and planted kisses along his jaw, his nose, his forehead.

"Now if *that* gets out, it might ruin my reputation."

"Or it might open up a whole new world to you. Ace Locke in romantic dramas. Ace Locke in quirky indies. Ace Locke in a Disney animation—"

"Okay, okay, let's not get crazy. Ace Locke in action thrillers suits me just fine. At least for now."

"Then the world will just have to get on board. Besides, who wouldn't fucking love you?"

Ace quirked an eyebrow at me, and when I realized what my words had implied, my face went hot. That just made the small grin on his lips grow, and I rolled my eyes and shoved him away playfully before something *else* decided to come tumbling out of my mouth.

As Ace's cell went off for the upteenth time, he said,

"I should probably figure out a game plan with my team if you want to go get your stuff ready to go. Grand Canyon next time?"

"Next time," I said, relieved there'd even be a next time, and as Ace sat on the couch and brought the phone to his ear, I gave him some privacy and went to the adjoining suite to grab the bag that had started this whole mess. If I hadn't left the damn thing in there last night, I wouldn't have opened the door, and then there'd be no half-naked paparazzi shots, no exit plans being made. But I couldn't think about that. Refused to take the blame for the havoc they'd caused. Those assholes would've gotten a picture somehow, someway, no matter whether it was here in Vegas or sneaking around back in L.A.

At least that's what I was trying to tell myself.

Heading back into Ace's suite, I went behind the couch as to not distract from the heated conversation he was having, and as I did, I paused by the window and looked down. The crowd outside the hotel's entrance had more than doubled in size, and it made my heart thump harder in my chest as I backed away.

Would *all* of those people follow us? At least we'd be going out the back private entrance, the same way we'd come to the hotel, but what happened when we got to the main road?

Yeah, okay, that's not intimidating at all, I thought, and headed toward the bedroom to pack our bags.

2
I WANNA HOLD
YOUR HAND

"I'M SO SORRY, Mr. Locke, and if there's anything we can do—"

I slammed the door in the manager's face, annoyed at the endless apologies he'd been making while standing in my suite's doorway for the last ten minutes. The police had also come and taken our statements, but since nothing appeared to be missing—and the fucker had gotten away—there wasn't anything they could do.

Is it too early for a damn drink?

"So? How'd it go?" Dylan asked as he headed into the main room with our packed bags and dumped them on the armchair. "Did you guys come up with a game plan?"

Before the unnecessary conversation with the head of Syn, I'd had a long, drawn-out powwow with Roger and

Martina about what should or shouldn't happen next. And since neither could seem to agree, as was always the case, I'd decided on my own damn plan.

"I'm gonna say fuck 'em," I said.

"Fuck 'em? Which means…what, exactly?"

"It means we're already all over TNZ now, and since Martina doesn't think at this point that we can deny, then there's no point in hiding anymore. Is there?"

"I guess not."

"So we'll go out the front and let them get the shots they need."

"Wait, what?"

"It's either that or the alternative, and I'd rather the images that show up on the front of the rags not be the shots of us in our towels."

Dylan stared at me and then shook his head as though he'd heard wrong. "So…you want us to leave here and go through all those people down there? Together?"

As I paced in front of the couch, it wasn't lost on me that this had been the moment I'd been trying to avoid for so long. The fact that it was here now had a swirling mix of emotions flowing through me. Anger. Frustration. Resentment. Resignation. Sadness. But somewhere underneath all those things, I also felt the first taste of freedom, and that was what had solidified my decision.

"Yes," I said. "If that's okay with you, then I think what you said about facing them head-on with our middle fingers held high is the best option."

Dylan let out a surprised laugh. "So literally go out there flipping off the press. Right. Good plan."

"Okay, so maybe more your hand in mine, but the sentiment is the same."

The amused expression on Dylan's face dropped, and he looked down at his faded jeans and plain green t-shirt. Before he could say anything, I told him, "Don't even think about changing."

"But...I'm a hot fucking mess. I can't go out there like this."

Strolling over to him, I let my eyes rove down his body. "Pretty sure you're just fucking hot."

"I think I'd prefer the pictures of us in the towels."

I fingered the hem of his shirt and then let my fingers slip underneath to feel the smooth, warm skin of his stomach. "You look perfect."

"You're crazy."

"Probably."

The side of Dylan's mouth curved, and when one of his dimples appeared, I shook my head. "You have no idea just how magnetic you are, do you? They're going to climb all over themselves for photographs of this face."

"You're slightly biased."

"I thought that even before you were mine." As the words left my mouth, I realized it was as close as I'd ever come to laying out just how strongly I'd felt for him. And it was something that wasn't lost on Dylan, if the way his eyes darkened on me was any indication.

"You did, huh?"

"I did. On my birthday, actually. My first thought was that Russ was stupid for letting you out of his sight. My second was, some lucky fucker is going to make a pass at you before I get a chance."

Dylan pressed his mouth to mine in a sweet kiss, and as his lips curved, he said, "They could've tried, but I was too busy thinking about the birthday boy."

I traced the backs of my fingers down his cheek and asked once more, just to be sure, "Are you positive you want to do this?"

Dylan leaned into my caress and his eyes shuttered closed, his lashes thick and dark against his flawless skin. "No," he whispered, and my heart just about stopped. Then he opened those gorgeous eyes and the expression there shocked me back to life. It was one full of apprehension, desire, and the same emotion I was feeling then—possession. "I'm not sure about any of this. But I am sure about you. I want you, Ace. And *you* come with all of this."

I laid a kiss against his forehead and took a step back, trailing my fingers down his to take his hand in mine. "Okay, then let's do this."

Moving around him to grab our bags, I got two steps away when Dylan tugged on my hand and I looked back at him.

"I don't have to, like…say anything, right?"

I laughed at that. "No. In fact, I think it would be best if neither of us said anything right now. The image of us hand in hand will be more effective than words anyhow. But you may want to put on your sunglasses."

"Why?"

"You'll see."

* * *

I TOOK A nervous breath and shrugged my bag farther up my arm as Ace led us out of the elevator and into the private lobby that had apparently been cleared out for our departure. When it was clear Ace wasn't stopping on his way out the door, Charles jogged up alongside us.

"May I have someone take your bags?" he said.

Ace didn't spare him a glance. "I think you all have been helpful enough."

"We'll be comping your stay—"

"I fucking hope so," Ace said with a disgusted snort.

"If you're leaving now, I'll have a driver pulled around immediately—"

"Actually, that's been taken care of."

The furrows in Charles's forehead deepened. "But there's not a car ready at this entrance—"

"Not going that way." Ace took us left toward the main part of the hotel instead of going right, toward the back entrance.

Oh God, I thought, as the quiet hallway opened up to the bustling, vast casino floor. Ace didn't hesitate as he walked us past the blackjack and roulette tables, even as I squeezed his hand for dear life. *We're doing this. We're actually holding hands…in public…and everyone can see.* But I barely noticed the faces of the people we passed because Ace was not stopping. However, once we passed the slot machines and neared the busy main check-in area, I heard the first murmurs with Ace's name in the mix. And sure enough, as we passed through the lobby, the surprised shouts began.

"Is that Ace Locke?"

"Oh my God, look, I think that's Ace."

"Ace! Can you sign my shirt?"

"I didn't know Ace was gay—"

"Is that his boyfriend?"

"Ace, can I take a picture with you?"

Ace moved us through as if he hadn't heard a thing, and as we came to the entrance, Ace's grip tightened on my hand. And as we took our first steps outside and the crowd descended on us, I realized why he'd said to wear sunglasses.

Flashes came from everywhere, so blinding that if it weren't for Ace's hand in mine, I wouldn't be able to see where we were going. The shouts were deafening, every photographer and member of the press out there vying for Ace's attention as the hotel's security cleared the path for us toward the idling Town Car.

If I'd thought the crowd looked big from the forty-fifth floor, it was nothing compared to the reality of what awaited us. Bodies pressed in against us from all sides, and combined with the Vegas heat wave, it was a suffocating combination.

Don't pass out in front of all these people, was all I could think, as the driver opened the door and Ace moved aside to let me in first.

"Ace, is this your new boyfriend?"

"Where did you two meet?"

"Is it true you eloped this weekend?"

As Ace slid inside after me, the door slammed shut behind him, and though the roar of the crowd had muffled somewhat, it was still like being in the eye of a tornado. Eerily quiet compared to the maelstrom happening on the outside.

"Are you okay?"

Ace's voice was pitched low as his fingers tightened around mine. I glanced out my tinted window and could see the continued flash of cameras as the paparazzi took photo after photo, all competing for the ultimate money shot.

"Dylan?"

At my name, I turned to face the man seated beside me, and for the first time since we'd met I saw him in a whole new light.

Ace Locke was the real deal. He wasn't just some actor a few people knew here and there. No. The man sitting beside me, with his hand wrapped around mine, was a fucking superstar. And somewhere along the way, I'd forgotten that.

"No one touched you or hurt you, did they?"

Ace's blue eyes were full of concern as he inspected me the best he could. When it became clear that I wasn't capable of actually speaking, he nodded once, satisfied that I was okay, and then leaned forward to the driver. "Take us to McCarran," he said, and then settled back beside me.

As the driver slowly began to accelerate, I could see the throngs of people who'd gathered in front of the vehicle, for a shot inside the car, part like the Red Sea as to not get hit. My heart was thudding wildly and I knew my eyes had to be as big as saucers, because never could I have prepared myself for what we'd just walked through. I didn't think anyone could.

When Ace had said I had no idea what I was about to walk into, I'd stupidly believed he was exaggerating. *Ha*, I thought, *if anything, he totally underplayed it.*

"Hey? Dylan, look at me."

I took in a gulp of air, trying to calm my racing pulse, and then turned my head to face him. Ace's brows were pinched together with worry, and his lips were drawn tight. He looked wary, as though he was worried I was about to bolt, and really, if I hadn't been in as deep as I was with him, I just might have. That was a whole fucking lot to take in.

"Are you okay?" he asked again, and this time I nodded.

"That was... Wow, Ace. That was insane."

Ace let out a bark of laughter, as if he hadn't been expecting that. "Uhh, yeah. I told you it would be."

"But..." I paused, trying to think of my next words.

"It's different seeing it. Jesus, I've never seen so many people in my life. And they all wanted your attention…I just…I guess I forgot who you were for a minute or two there."

As my words lingered between us, I thought for a second I might have offended him, but then he brought my hand up to his lips and smiled before pressing a kiss to my palm. "That's the best compliment I've had in a long time."

I released his hand to draw my fingers under his chin. "You've obviously been hanging around the wrong people."

"Obviously," he agreed, and leaned across to brush his lips over mine. When he pulled back he asked me again, this time leaving no room for misdirection, "I totally understand if you're freaking out right now. If you want to change your—"

"No," I said, shaking my head. "I mean, yes, that was crazy. And yes, I'm okay, but not once did it ever cross my mind that I wanted out…" I paused and then had a horrible thought. "Did it cross yours?"

Ace's eyes held mine, and the sincerity there blew me away as he said, "Not even once."

As the car pulled away from Syn's elaborate entrance and the crowd faded in the distance, it occurred to me for the first time that I was dating Ace Locke. Really dating him. And if the way my stomach was somersaulting at the affectionate expression he was aiming my way was any indication, I had no doubt that I was precariously close to falling in love with Ace Locke.

3
FEAST FOR
A KING

"NO, YOU DON'T need to come over... No, I don't want to make a statement. Roger, look..."

Ace sounded weary as he paced his vast kitchen, and when he caught my eye from across the room, his lips turned up for a moment before he went back to his conversation.

He'd been fielding calls for the last couple of hours since we'd gotten back to his place, showered, and come downstairs for food, and it didn't look like things would let up any time soon. My own phone had been going off nonstop, and as another message dinged, I looked down to see it was from Derek.

Can I say I told you so yet?

"Fuck off," I muttered, as I texted back the same

message. I'd barely hit send before another ding went off, this time from Russ.

Hey... I just saw pictures of you and Ace on the news. Call me.

Nope, wasn't even gonna respond to that one.

Derek: Nice towel, btw. Good to see you're still working out.

Oh, for God's sake.

As my phone began to ring from an unlisted number, I looked over to where Ace was rubbing the back of his neck and I made a snap decision. Powering off the cell, I tossed it on the couch and went over to take a seat on one of the barstools at the kitchen island that Ace was currently wearing a hole in the floor in front of. He was getting more frustrated the longer he stayed on the phone.

"No, I'm not planning to deny anything either. Walking out of Syn was enough of a statement, don't you think?"

Leaning my elbows back on the island, I spread my legs and waited for Ace's attention. Ever since we'd gotten back, it'd been one call after another, and the more it went on, the redder Ace's face got. It was time to unplug and unwind after the never-ending day we'd had, and as Ace turned and headed back in my direction, I bit down on my lip—but he just walked right on by, too engrossed in conversation to notice my open invitation.

Hmm. Maybe he needs something a bit more obvious.

I'd changed into a pair of Ace's workout shorts and a

t-shirt after we'd showered, since I'd only packed an overnight bag for our trip, and when I pulled the shirt up and over my head, Ace's eyes flicked up to the movement. Tossing the shirt on the tiled floor, I gave him a suggestive smile and then resumed my position, leaning back on my elbows with my legs wide. *That* had Ace pausing momentarily, his eyes raking over my body, but then the person on the other end said something that had his focus returning to the conversation.

"Fine," he said, with an exasperated sigh. "We can have a meeting but not tonight... It'll have to be after filming if it's tomorrow... Yes, over here's fine."

Okay, maybe it was time to take things up a notch. There was no way I was letting the outside world invade our private space any more today, so I needed to get Ace's mind *off* the chaos swirling and back on...me.

After glancing behind me to make sure the island was clear, I hopped off the stool, and when Ace's pacing had him facing in my direction again, I turned around and slowly pulled my shorts down. Since there was nothing underneath, Ace was getting a prime view of my ass as I bent over and took my time lowering the shorts to my ankles and then stepping out of them. When I stood back up and faced him, I kicked the shorts away, and my cock was mighty pleased at the look of lust Ace was aiming my way. I could hear the person on the other end of the phone repeating his name, but Ace was too busy looking over my naked body to notice.

Licking my lips, I backed up, and when my lower back hit the counter, I pushed myself up and onto it. Ace's eyebrows shot up, and he swallowed as I laid myself out for him like a feast for a king.

Your move.

"Uh…yeah, Roger. I'm here," Ace said, but his voice was distant and he didn't take his eyes off me, especially when my hand trailed down my stomach to my hips and then took a hold of my cock.

"Fuck," Ace said under his breath. "What? Nothing. Listen I need to go—"

The man on the other end of the line wasn't having that, though, but then again, neither was I. Ace was mine tonight, and I didn't mind doing whatever it took to get his attention, eyes, and hands, back on me.

* * *

I WAS TRYING my hardest to concentrate on what Roger was yammering on about in my ear, but really, if I hadn't lost interest twenty minutes earlier, the sight of Dylan naked and lounging across my kitchen island had made Roger the *last* thing I was focused on.

"I'm hanging up now… No, I said—"

As Roger cut me off for the umpteenth time, I held the phone to my ear and walked over to the edge of the counter. I let my eyes rove from the hand Dylan had curled around his erection, up and over his flawless body to the face that was angled my way, and when he slicked the tip of his tongue along his top lip, I cursed.

"No, Roger. Do *not* come over here now."

The smirk Dylan gave me then was pure sex as he jacked his hips up and shoved his cock through his fist.

Christ, the guy was trying to kill me. It was clear Dylan was after my attention, and there was no way I wasn't about to give it to him. The day had been long and drawn out, and with the sun now set on a day full of pandemonium, I got the impression that Dylan was ready to unwind, ready to tune the rest of the world out. And so the fuck was I.

Unable to resist touching him any longer, I trailed my fingertips down the arm closest to me as I made my way down the kitchen counter. When I rounded the end of it, I aimed my eyes up at the brazen man who was working his length as though he were flat on his back in my bed as opposed to the middle of my kitchen, and that was it...Roger had to go.

"I'm hanging up now... I don't care, Roger. I'm done talking about this. Don't call me again tonight or you will be having a discussion with my voicemail." And before he could respond, I ended the call.

As I lowered the phone to the other counter in the kitchen, I took the moment to readjust my hard-as-hell dick and saw Dylan turn his head on the counter to watch me. His lids were heavy as his entire expression turned carnal.

"Are you quite comfortable, Mr. Prescott?"

Dylan stroked up his length as he bent his far leg and planted it on the island. "Well, you did tell me I could use your kitchen whenever I liked. But—" His words came to an abrupt halt when I flicked the light switch on the wall, plunging the room into darkness. But that wasn't what I had in mind at all, as I hit the switch beside it that illuminated the strip of four halogen bulbs that hung in a direct line above the counter.

Oh yeah, that's better. If Dylan wanted to be the center of attention, I was more than happy to give him a spotlight.

"You were saying?" I asked, as I strolled back to where he now lay, lit up spectacularly for my perusal. Dylan's eyes tracked me, and as they did I dropped my gaze to the fingers he was swiping over the head of his cock before massaging his slick palm down his shaft.

"I was saying," Dylan continued, as I stopped at the end of the counter and looked down at him. "That while it's kind of you to allow me the use of your kitchen, I really think it's past time that *you* used it."

I reached for the hem of my shirt, and as I tossed it down on the shorts he'd kicked out of earlier, Dylan raised his other leg and bent it at the knee to give me a prime view of everything I wanted to suck, kiss, and touch.

"Damn," Dylan said, and pumped his hips up. "I love that sound."

I moved my hands to the button of my shorts and unsnapped it, and as I went to shove them off my hips, I raised an eyebrow at him, waiting for further explanation.

"That growl. You don't even know you're doing it. But *fuck*. It's so hot."

He was right: I hadn't even been aware I'd made a sound, but it didn't surprise me. Dylan made me feel like a goddamn animal. When my shorts hit the floor, I stepped out of them and brought my hands up to Dylan's bent knees, where I then trailed them down his shins to his ankles.

"Spread your legs for me," I said, and when he did, the sight that greeted me had my dick aching for release. As Dylan moved his hand up and down his hard length, I couldn't stop my own hands from grabbing the back of his calves.

My voice was a low rumble as I said, "Gonna need you closer than that," and pulled him to the edge of the counter. Dylan's hands shot out to his sides to brace himself, and it left his cock free for my mouth. Bending down over him, I didn't waste time running my tongue from the thick base of him to his tip, and as I let my lips linger there, teasing him, he pushed his hips up for more.

"You have to ask," I said, lifting my head and giving him an evil grin. "You have my attention now. Is there something you wanted?"

As I kissed down the inside of his inner thigh, Dylan panted and then said, "I want your fucking mouth on me, for starters."

Your wish is my command, I thought, and then I drew his legs over my shoulders and took him all the way to the back of my throat. Moaning at the fullness of his erection, I pulled back to his tip and then went down again. And as I did, a stray thought crossed my mind. There was no way I would ever get enough of this man. How was it possible that I could have him like this whenever I wanted him? That he could have me. I'd had no idea it could be this good. No idea what I'd been missing, what I'd been denying myself for all these years.

As I sucked him deeper, I still couldn't get used to the fact that he was mine. And at that moment, I didn't give a damn who knew.

When Dylan's hips jerked and his breath grew ragged, I lifted my head and shook it. "Not yet," I said, and lowered his legs from my shoulders. "Move back."

I didn't have to say more, because Dylan was quick to scoot back on the counter, and I pulled myself up to join him. And...just damn. His lean body on display below me made me want to get a little closer—make that a whole *lot* closer, and as I dropped down on all fours, I crawled up his body slowly.

Dylan's eyes never wavered from mine—not when I straddled his hips...not when I lowered my body down on his...and not when our cocks grazed against each other in a delicious slide that had my breath catching in my throat.

"This is torture by teasing to get me back from my striptease, isn't it?" Dylan grunted as he arched against me, his throat exposed and waiting, and I obliged by running my tongue up the length of his heated skin.

"I'm glad you got the message."

"Fuck your message," he said, reaching down between us and gripping us together in his hand. The friction of his fist and erection sliding against my dick was almost too much to take, and I cried out before taking his lips in a kiss.

* * *

JESUS, ACE WAS a sexy fucker. *Oh yeah*, I thought, as his tongue sank deep between my lips to rub against mine. His legs were between my spread ones, and he had a hand planted on either side of my head, crowding down over me where I lay on the kitchen island. He was practically doing a damn push-up as he moved his lips over mine, groaning into my mouth as I clenched my hand around our stiff pricks.

"Dylan... Holy..." he said as he dragged his mouth off mine and kissed his way along my jaw to my ear. "Yeah, God. Harder."

I turned my head and kissed his jaw as I squeezed, and his hips punched forward, grazing his length along mine.

"Like that?" I said, taunting him as I did it again, and Ace was right there grinding his hips over me.

"Yes. Just like that."

I moaned at his words, and wound one of my legs over the back of his muscled thighs. He was all strength and

power as the arm by my face bunched and I had an
undeniable urge to lean over and— *Oh, fuck it.* I craned up
and licked my tongue over his bicep, and when I nuzzled
into the crease of his arm he shifted to wrap it around me,
lowering me back to the counter and angling his body half
off me. Then Ace reached down between us and covered the
hand I had wrapped around us and we began to move
together.

His lips were ghosting over mine, his breath warm as
he panted with every grunt and fuck of his hips, and I used
the leg I had anchored around him to propel myself up to
meet him thrust for thrust.

I could feel his fingers digging into the skin of my
shoulder where he held on, and just when I thought he
would crush my lips under his, Ace instead lowered his
head so we were cheek to cheek and whispered in my ear,
"You, Dylan Prescott, are worth every scandalous thing
that's about to be written…"

Ah hell, I was so down for the count when Ace got
like this. When he was destroying my brain cells with the
sinful way he was using my body and the delicious way he
was imprinting himself on every part of my soul.

"And you know why?"

With his voice, low and raspy in my ear, there was
no way words were going to come out of my mouth. So
instead, I bowed up and rubbed my entire length along the
solid wall of his body, and Ace turned his head and planted
a firm kiss on my cheek before saying, "Because with you,

I've found me."

And that was it. Those sweet words, falling from a mouth that moments ago had destroyed me, had me tensing under him. Then Ace sucked my lobe between his lips and said, "Come for me, Dylan. All over the both of us."

He shifted then, and as I lay flat on the counter, Ace began to drive his body over the top of mine in a way that nearly had my eyes rolling to the back of my head. But there was no way I wasn't going to watch this. His arms flexed on either side of me, and I reached down to fist the two of us as Ace brought the friction and I brought the fervor. My hand was working overtime as my climax raced down my spine, and when I felt my balls tighten, and Ace went rigid above me, the two of us came in a spectacular release of both body and mind.

We had been wound so tightly, and this moment was so freeing that I was surprised not to feel tears in my eyes at the relief that, even after such strain on our new relationship, at the end of the day, we were still one.

4
SWEET. TIGHT. MINE.

I NEVER UNDERSTOOD the need for guys to have a bodyguard until I faced the wall of paparazzi waiting outside of my neighborhood's main gate before dawn on Monday morning.

"Oh holy…" Dylan said from where he sat beside me in my Range Rover as the gate opened and the flashes went off like hundreds of lightning bolts striking at once. The effect was blinding, and though the sun hadn't come up just yet, I had to grab my sunglasses from the console to be able to see past them to the main road. And hopefully not hit anybody in the process, though I couldn't say I'd be devastated if that happened.

Invasive little assholes.

I maneuvered the car slowly through the crowd shouting questions at us, and all I could think was, *Why do they bother?* Did they believe I would roll my window down and answer them? *Wasting their breath.*

Out of the corner of my eye, Dylan tugged his hat down over his face, and I felt a twinge of guilt. I couldn't blame the guy at all if he wanted to flee after the last twenty-four hours. God, was that all it had been? Twenty-four hours? It'd felt like an eternity.

Once we were past the mob, I pulled off the sunglasses and then reached for Dylan's hand.

"I'm sorry," I said.

A deep groove formed between his brows. "What are you sorry for? It's not like you asked for this."

"No, and neither did you. I know it comes with the job, but I'm sorry you're getting dragged into it."

"I don't want to hear any more apologies from you, you got that? I'm with you, and they'll all go away eventually. Right?"

Maybe. Possibly. I hope so. Instead of answering him, I asked, "So did Paige get everything you needed from your place last night, or do we need to make a pit stop on the way?"

"No, I've got everything I need until tonight. Tell her thanks again for going."

"Will do." When we'd realized that going back out last night would probably cause a frenzy, I'd called Paige in for a favor. Unlike Shayne, whom the press would've recognized from the year before, Paige had been able to get in and out of Dylan's apartment to grab a few necessities without notice.

The drive to the studio was quiet, as it usually was before the rest of Los Angeles woke up, except for the handful of cars that had been staying on our tail the entire drive over. When we finally drove past the Warner Bros. gate, we were home free. For a few hours, at least.

As I pulled into my parking spot just outside of the soundstage, Dylan released my hand.

"Looks like we're breaking your rule," he said, his lips tipped up. "Didn't you warn me against dating costars?"

"That rule is still in effect. Unless that costar is me." Leaning over the console, I grabbed the back of his neck and pulled him toward me for a kiss. His lips were hesitant at first, as though he were nervous others were watching, but then they softened under mine and he kissed me eagerly.

When I finally let go, I grinned and said, "Have a great day at work, Mr. Prescott."

"Well, what do you know? Looks like Ace Locke has changed his policy on kissing. And, I must say, I approve."

"Smartass," I said, laughing at him throwing my words from when we'd first met back in my face. As Dylan turned in his seat to grab his bag, I popped open my door and hopped out, just as Ron parked his sports car in the space beside me.

"Morning," I said when he stepped out, and then

took an eyeful of his shirt. It said, *Does Not Play Well With Narcissists.* "Nice message this morning."

"Wore it just for you. What's with the shitfest that just exploded all over my phone?"

"That's a long story."

"Well, I'd love to hear it. Please tell me you're not actually dating that—" As Ron's eyes fell on Dylan getting out of my car, his mouth clamped shut.

"Hi, Ron," Dylan said.

As our dumbfounded director looked back and forth between us, his jaw clenched. "Right," he said. "See you boys on set."

Glancing back at Dylan's worried expression, I shrugged. "He'll be fine."

"If he calls me out today, do *not* say anything."

"Yeah, yeah."

"Ace, I'm serious. You open that trap and I'm cutting you off."

I strolled around the front of the SUV and cocked my head at him. "You threatening me?"

"Damn right I am. Now that people know, you absolutely cannot say a thing to defend me."

"And if I do, you'll cut me off."

"For at least a week."

I raised an eyebrow. "A whole week?"

"Okay, maybe a few days."

"I'm sure I could grovel my way back into your good graces," I said, and he rolled his eyes.

Backing away before I could reach for him, Dylan grinned at me and said, "Better head to your trailer, Mr. Locke. Time's a wasting."

* * *

FOUR HOURS AND thirty-five minutes later, I wished I was anywhere but where I was—mainly on set with Ace Locke, my new boyfriend. From the second I opened the door to stage sixteen and stepped inside, things had been...well, weird.

Ron was on a rampage today, and if I'd been worried he was going to take it out on me, I needn't have bothered, because I was not the one in his line of fire. No, that honor belonged to Ace, and Ace alone. From the first line out of his mouth to the one he'd just delivered for the twelfth retake, nothing Ace said, did, or hit made Ron happy, and the tense set of Ace's shoulders and jaw hadn't escaped my notice—he looked close to exploding.

"Cut. Stop. Stop!" Ron shouted as he climbed out of his chair and came out from behind the camera.

Today's shoot had the majority of the cast in close quarters with one another as we stood around Ace, who was addressing his crew in an impassioned speech about overcoming the enemy, and who would stand up beside him. As it turned out, with the odd looks he and I had been receiving all morning, I couldn't help but believe that if an affirmative hadn't been *written* in the script, not one of these men would've volunteered to stand by Ace's side in that moment. *Minus myself, of course,* I thought, keeping my eyes on the ground.

"For God's sake, Locke. That was about as passionate as a wet rag. What the hell's the matter with you today?"

I willed Ace to keep his cool, knowing he wasn't usually the disrespectful type, especially not with Ron, whom he'd told me he enjoyed working with and truly admired. But after everything that had happened in the last twenty-four hours, Ace was apparently at his wits' end.

"What's wrong with me?" Ace demanded, and stormed off set to meet Ron halfway. "What's *wrong* is that you haven't let up since I got here."

The entire cast stood paralyzed as we watched the two powerhouses in front of us going head to head for the first time since production began. And it wasn't lost on me that everyone in that room was well aware that *I* was likely the reason behind the tension and discord this morning. Well, that was the impression I got, as I scanned the curious eyes looking between Ace's rigid back and me.

"If you'd been giving me your best, I wouldn't be on your case," Ron said. "As it is, this is sloppy and unrehearsed. I want to feel like I would follow you to the end of the fucking earth. Not as though I doubt you could find your head from your ass."

Ron crossed his arms over his chest and fumed up at Ace, and that was when I glanced over at the men standing on the opposite side of the podium we were gathered around, and caught Russ's eyes. They were narrowed on me and his lips were drawn in a thin line, and I could feel the judgment in them as I wished to God the ground would open up and swallow me whole.

"Bullshit," Ace finally exploded. The word boomed around the stage and echoed off the walls. *Jesus,* I had never seen Ace like this. "I've delivered that speech perfectly at least ten out of the twelve times you've made me shoot it. This has got *nothing* to do with my acting, and you and I both know it."

Ron's face had turned crimson, and he looked as though smoke was about to come out of his ears as he took in a belabored breath. "Take twenty, get your shit together, and be back on set in thirty," he told Ace, and when Ace brushed by him and marched toward the far exit, Ron turned his attention on us. "The rest of you, get something to eat and be back in thirty also. If you're late, I'm locking the door. Got it?"

As everyone started to break up and head off set, Ron walked to the opposite exit muttering about needing a drink, and I spotted Russ turning to leave.

"Hey, Russ. Wait up!" I called out, jogging after him. He hadn't spoken to me when I'd arrived this morning, but we'd all been in such a rush to get ready for the shoot that I hadn't had time to ask him how his weekend was...or, for that matter, the reason he was looking at me like I was an alien.

He stopped and waved to one of the guys we'd hung out with after work a few times, and then turned to see me coming to a stop opposite him. When it became clear that he wasn't going to be the one to initiate a conversation, I slipped one of my hands into the pocket of my white dress slacks and flashed him a smile, hoping to ease us back into the friendship that had been developing between us.

"How's it going, man?" I asked. "Did you have a good weekend?"

Russ's mouth opened as though he were about to say something, and then he shut it again and turned on his heel to leave. *What the…?* I reached for his wrist and pulled him back around, and when he glanced down to the hand I had on him, I quickly removed it.

"Yeah, might be best if you keep your hands to yourself," he said. "I wouldn't want your boyfriend to get jealous and punch me out. Lord knows Ace Locke could do major damage to someone's face."

I flinched at that and shook my head. "Come on, Russ. You know he's not like that. I want to talk to you for a minute. Want to get—"

"I'm busy," he said, and went to walk off again.

Shiiiit.

I stepped around in front of him and frowned. "Russ."

"I'm busy, Dylan. I called yesterday to talk. You didn't seem to think I was worth your time then so…hey, no skin off my back."

"It's not like that. Yesterday was…it was…insane, is what it was. I didn't have time to talk to—"

"How long have you been fucking him? Locke, that is. Or is it the other way around? I have to say…I'm curious, as is the rest of the world. And aren't you the one who told me you weren't ready to jump into a relationship right now? Yeah…that's obvious."

Russ's question was so blunt and so direct that my words stumbled and stuttered to an abrupt stop. His eyes were locked on mine, and right then I knew this was where our friendship was about to end.

It wasn't as though I'd consciously decided "that's it, we can no longer be friends." But as Russ stood there expecting me to give him details on my relationship with Ace, intimate details, I was aware there was no way I was going to give him shit. And there was no way a friend would act the way he was.

I owed him no explanation. We hadn't been dating; we'd *barely* formed a friendship. But here he was expecting me to what? Explain myself? Gossip? Gloat?

Well, he was in for a vast disappointment. I started to back away from him and shook my head. *Unfuckingbelievable.* "See you around, Russ."

I turned on my heel, ready to go and track down Ace in the lunch tent, when I heard Russ call out, "It was at his birthday, wasn't it?" But I didn't bother looking back.

* * *

A FUCKING DISASTER. That was exactly what this morning's shoot had turned into. Ron had been impossible from the first word out of my mouth, and everything that came after was just another thing he could get annoyed over.

I wasn't an idiot. I was well aware this was his way of telling me quite pointedly how frustrated he was that the most recent press our upcoming movie had received revolved around its main star and his costar, but that was too damn bad. There was no way I was about to let the chance to date Dylan pass me by because it was slightly inconvenient. *Okay, maybe a whole lot inconvenient.* But despite what I'd told Dylan about not being allowed to date costars, the truth of the matter was, it wasn't illegal. It wasn't written in our contracts. It was just…well, frowned upon due to the media circus that often followed—and most certainly had with us.

Yeah, and they are just getting started.

I pushed the piece of plain boiled chicken around the plastic container it had arrived in, and could feel the beginning of a tension headache throbbing in the base of my skull. I needed to get a handle of myself. This was just the beginning of what promised to be a *very* trying few months. It was day two of the press discovering I was seeing someone, and it was only a matter of days—hell, even hours until they put two and two together and realized the gorgeous guy I'd had in my room in nothing but a towel was the same man currently gracing billboards for Calvin

Klein nationwide.

I sure hoped Dylan knew what he'd said yes to…because it was only going to get more intense from here on out.

"Excuse me? Is this seat taken?"

I glanced up to see the man who'd just been on my mind standing beside me with a concerned look on his face, probably wondering if I'd cooled off yet. After the spectacle with Ron I couldn't blame Dylan for being cautious, and considering the wide berth I'd been given here in the lunch tent from the cast and crew, it was obvious they were also waiting to see what exactly was going to happen next.

But was there really any question? Was Dylan actually worried I'd say no, he couldn't sit with me? *Sorry, but not a damn chance.* What would be the point of that? Or any of this, for that matter, if I sent him away? Everyone was already watching and gossiping, if the murmurs now reaching my ears were any indication.

I managed a crooked grin and then indicated the chair opposite me with my fork. "It will be once you sit your sweet ass in it."

The worried expression Dylan had been wearing eased as his lips tipped up in a slow smile.

"Sweet, huh?" he said as he sat opposite me, placing his plate down in front of him. I looked longingly at the steak and fries and nodded.

"Sweet, tight, mine. Take your pick."

Dylan looked from his left to his right before

bringing his eyes back to mine with a raised eyebrow. *Poor guy isn't quite sure what he's allowed to do here. Or what I want him to do. Well, time to rectify that.*

I reached across the table, laid my hand over his, and squeezed it reassuringly. "It's okay to talk to me, you know."

Dylan leaned in and lowered his voice. "That's kind of ironic coming from you, don't you think? Just last week I wasn't even able to look in your direction."

"Yeah, but things have changed," I told him as he turned his hand over and our fingers entwined. "I'm pretty sure most people know you do more than just *look* in my direction now."

I added a flirty wink, and it had the desired effect. Dylan's cheeks flushed and he laughed. "Aren't you worried someone will take a photo?"

"Of what? Us holding hands? This is far less scandalous than you close to naked in my hotel room…" I let my eyes linger over Dylan's body and then back up to see him shaking his head at me. "What?"

"Nothing."

"No… What? Tell me."

"I'm just surprised how calm you are right now, I suppose."

"Calm?" I said. "I'm sorry, but were you not at this morning's shoot?"

Dylan raised his eyes to mine, and his lips quirked. "No, I mean…yes, I was there. I don't mean that. Ron is obviously pissed about this and was taking it out on you. But what I mean is"—once again he scanned our immediate surroundings—"surely you know everyone in here is watching us right now. Talking about us."

Dylan looked so scandalized that I couldn't stop the chuckle that escaped me. "Yes...and? Ashamed of me, Daydream?"

"Oh, please. Who in their right mind would be ashamed to be with you?" My stomach flipped at those words, but then it tightened when he added, "It's just all the speculation they're doing. It's in their eyes every time they look from you to me. Hell, Russ just asked me who fucks—"

When Dylan bit off his words and took in a breath, I didn't need him to keep talking to know what he'd been about to say. Of course that blond asswipe had gone there, and before I could stop myself, I asked, "What did you tell him?"

"Nothing," Dylan said, and then frowned as he withdrew his hand.

Shit. What the hell is the matter with me? I hadn't meant to sound accusatory. And I knew Dylan wouldn't have said anything. My question was just a knee-jerk reaction. Something that had been ingrained in me for so long that it was hard to ignore. "Hey? I'm sorry. Of course you didn't. I just—"

"I get it," Dylan said. "Habits are hard to break. You're used to people running their mouths. But Ace?"

"Yeah?"

"That's not going to be me. I would never do that to you. Hurt you like that."

As I picked up the knife to cut into the bland chicken in front of me, I knew that was the truth. Dylan was actually doing everything in his power *not* to hurt me. He was standing by my side publicly while we dealt with the insanity that had descended on us, when he could have left at the first sign of madness.

I felt like an ass. I hated that I'd let my frustration at the situation make me snap at him, when really all that had kept me halfway sane through my hellish morning was the knowledge that I could openly enjoy my lunch with this man. Everyone else be damned. So I reached across to his plate and stole several of his French fries. Dylan stared at me as I chomped on one, and then he arched an eyebrow.

"Oh please," he said. "Help yourself. I didn't want those at all."

I picked up another and munched it down before aiming a most contrite expression his way. "You didn't actually expect to sit there eating steak and fries while I eat boiled chicken and kale without sharing, did you?"

Dylan cut a piece of his T-bone and shoveled it between his lips. As he chewed on it he grinned at me, and I was relieved to be back in his good graces.

"Not at all," he said, and then licked his lips. "What's mine is yours."

My cock twitched at his obvious connotation, and since I didn't want our first public kiss—*or groping, for that matter*—to be across a lunch table on set, I settled for stealing another one of his fries and biting down into it before saying, "That, Mr. Prescott, is very good to know."

"I'm glad you think so," he said with a mischievous grin, and if there was anyone else lingering in the lunch tent after that, I couldn't have said, because I only had eyes for the man across from me.

5
LOUD AND
PROUD

"DON'T BE MAD," Ace said, from where he stood in the center of his trailer zipping up his bag. It was the end of the worst day we'd had on set—so far, anyway—and with the tension thick among the other cast members, I'd come over to Ace's trailer to shower and get changed.

I looked up from where I'd been flipping through one of Ace's muscle mags. "Mad? Why would I be mad?"

"Because half of your daily exercise is about to get cut out."

"Half of my… What are you talking about?"

Ace flipped open the blinds and pointed to a sleek black Town Car idling next to his SUV. "I'm afraid you're not going to be able to walk home anymore, so when you're not with me, you'll be in that."

"Why can't I walk home? It's less than a mile."

"Remember the crowd we hit outside this morning?"

"Yeah…"

"Get used to it. They'll probably be outside the studio exits now too, and I can't have you mobbed."

I tossed the magazine on the couch beside me and walked over to Ace, my hands going to his hips. "The only reason I'd be mad is if you were cutting my nightly exercise," I said.

"Not a chance."

"Good. Then I'll behave and not complain about a driver."

Ace grinned and his hands went to my ass, pulling me forward for a kiss. "I hate you won't be in my bed tonight," he murmured against my mouth.

"I'd rather not be there while Roger tears you a new asshole. Plus, I should sleep in my own bed one of these days."

With a groan, he pushed me away. "Not a fan of either of those things, but…"

"Gotta face 'em, though I may have to put on one of your films to keep me company. Call me after? Let me know Roger didn't strangle you with his bare hands?"

Ace let out a laugh as he grabbed his bag and then held open the door for me. "Nah, he's all bark and no bite. But I'll call you anyway."

As we headed out of the trailer and to the cars, I couldn't help the twinge of sadness at having to go our separate ways, even if it was only for a night. It felt like we'd lived a lifetime over the past few days. Those events had cemented Ace's presence in my life in a way that, if I stopped and thought about it too much, could've scared me off at the rate things were moving. But it all just felt...right. We weren't rushing; we were simply getting to know each other, and could I help it that I wanted to spend all my time with the gorgeous man beside me?

I glanced over to where Ace was pulling his keys out of the pocket of his dark jeans, and then, as he moved ahead of me, let my eyes roam over the way he filled out the back of them.

Oh yeah. That's all mine.

"See you bright and early?" he asked, looking over his shoulder, and when he noticed where my eyes were focused, he laughed.

"What's so funny?"

"You. It's a good thing we're not hiding anymore."

"Can I help it if your ass is the kind of thing people would gladly drop to their knees for?"

"I only care about one particular person dropping to their knees for me. See you soon, Daydream," Ace said with a wink, and then slipped inside his Range Rover.

With a sigh, I got into the back of the Town Car, said hey to Ace's security guard, Frank, and let him drive me away from the man I'd be breaking out the lube for later.

And what movie of his should I watch tonight to get myself off to —

"Oh holy shit," I said as the Town Car passed through the studio gate and directly into a horde of people on both sides of the sidewalk shouting out questions, their cameras going off as we passed. I slid down in the seat and shielded my face with my hand like a visor as we drove the short distance to my place.

It wasn't any better when we got there, either.

You've gotta be kidding me, I thought, as the car slowed in front of my apartment building. I couldn't even see the entrance to the stairs that led up to my studio because the entire lawn and sidewalk were covered in a sea of strangers, and as we came to a stop, what had been a quiet assembly seconds ago was now full-on pandemonium.

"Stay right there, Mr. Prescott. I'll take you up to your place. What floor?"

I numbly gave him my apartment number, and then he was out of the car, fighting through the crowd to come open my door.

Oh God... Do I really have to get out of the car, or can I just hide in here? I reached for my sunglasses that I usually left hanging at the top of my shirt, but when they weren't there, I cursed. Then the back door cracked open and Frank was there, his arm stretched out to ward off anyone that came too close. The shouts were deafening as I got out, and after Frank shut the door behind me, he put his large hand on my back and slowly guided us through the crushing mob. I felt pressed in on on all sides, as I heard:

"What can you tell us about your relationship with Ace

Locke?"

"How long have you been keeping your romance quiet?"

"Did Ace get you the part in Insurrection 2*?"*

Keeping my chin tucked to my chest and my eyes down on the ground in front of me so I wouldn't trip, I let Frank lead me for what felt like an eternity. By the time we got to the base of the stairs that led up to my apartment, I was sweating, and it wasn't until Frank dropped me off, and I shut and locked the door after him, that I was able to take my first deep breath.

That was crazy…

I hadn't seen Ace deal with crowds to that extent since I'd known him, and I'd foolishly let myself forget that he wasn't just a normal guy who might have a couple of people follow him every now and again. No, he was a mega freakin' movie star, and people all over the world knew who he was. I let that sink in for a minute. People all over *the world.* So it wasn't just that crowd outside, or the press waiting outside the studio, or the ones that followed him home. No, those people were just the messengers that reported back to those thousands and thousands of people who were hungry for anything and everything about Ace they could get their hands on.

I rubbed my hand over my eyes and went to the kitchen to pour a cold glass of water, downing it in one long gulp. As I leaned back against the counter, I bumped into the vase of flowers Ace had given me before we'd left for Vegas. The mix of bright yellow, purple, and pink blooms were as fresh as ever, untainted by the insanity of the past two days, and after taking in a deep breath of them, I pulled out my phone and hit a button.

"Miss me already?" came Ace's deep voice, though it sounded like I was on speakerphone. A quick glance at the time told me there was no way he'd made it home yet, especially not if he had anyone trailing him.

"Always," I said, and then, "Ace, they've got my apartment surrounded."

"What? The press is there?"

"Frank just had to pull us through...fuck, I don't even know how many people are out there."

"Damn, they work fast. I thought we had a little more time before they found out where you were."

"Not so lucky."

Ace let out a long sigh. "I'm sorry—"

"I said no more apologizing."

"Yeah, but they're staked out at your place. It's not like you have a gate to keep them out. Do you want me to have Frank bring you over here?"

"No, no, of course not. They're not gonna be breaking and entering or anything, I just thought...you should know. Is all."

"I'm serious, if you want to pack your shit and come over here—"

"Then I'll do that. But I'm good. Really. I'm just gonna eat dinner, stalk you on TV, and then pass the hell out. Promise."

"Okay…" Ace still sounded unsure, but I was adamant.

"Have fun with Roger."

"Oh God. I will. Call you after?"

"Looking forward to it."

After hanging up, I ventured into my cramped living room area and flopped on the couch. Then I flicked on the TV, and shot straight up when the image staring back at me was—me.

Wow. Okay, that's new.

The reporter was smiling broadly at her co-anchor as they speculated over Ace's new *hottie in the hotel.*

Oh Lord. I brought the heels of my hands to my eyes and rubbed them as if I could erase the images following the original one, but no, there I was.

Me, standing in the doorway to Ace's suite with a towel wrapped around my waist, my hair slicked back from the shower, and my mouth hanging open. And right there, over my shoulder, was Ace wearing exactly the same thing. *Incriminating much?* We looked like we'd spent the morning together in the shower…which, of course, we had.

The next photo to pop up on the screen was Ace leading me through Syn's hotel lobby. My head was down, but whoever had caught the photo had snapped it at the perfect moment, because Ace had looked directly at them and damn, his eyes were volatile there. A gorgeous, thunderous blue.

The man sure was magnetic, there was no doubt

about it, even when he was pissed as hell.

Then up flashed the photo the reporter proclaimed was her favorite, and I sat up on the couch, scooting to the edge of the seat, almost dreading what I would see.

It was a snapshot of Ace opening the car door for me once we'd passed through the paparazzi at Syn, and his hand was on my lower back as he'd helped me inside the Town Car. They showed the faraway shot encompassing the crowd and the two of us, and then zoomed in on the hand on my back, and the reporter giggled like a high school girl.

"Oh, I don't know about you, Brad, but it makes my heart flutter to finally see Ace out and about with someone he clearly can't keep his hands off."

Brad, her co-anchor, a man who could pass as a Ken doll, shot her a bright white smile and nodded. "Yes, it'll be interesting to find out more about this mysterious stranger who seems to have captured Hollywood's favorite action star. Up until now, Ace has been very private in respect to his recent, and very public, coming out. But with the way this story has exploded over the last forty-eight hours, and with no denial of what we're all seeing, it's obvious this man is someone special that Locke has been keeping under wraps."

I hit the off button on the remote and the TV went black. How weird was it to have people talking about you as if you'd been part of some huge conspiracy or cover-up? And now I understood what Ace meant about everything changing now that the public knew, because it was only a matter of hours before they learned my name. I was actually shocked they didn't know it already, and then everything in my world would be up for scrutiny—not just the way I looked.

Was I ready for that? Fuck, I sure hoped so.

* * *

AFTER WEAVING MY way through the crowd of photographers surrounding the front gate of my subdivision, I drove up my driveway toward the garage and spotted Roger's SUV parked off to the side waiting on me.

Great. He was early. I wasn't even going to get five minutes to get myself together after my shit-tastic day before I had to deal with him. I pressed the button for my garage, and as it slowly rose I saw the door to Roger's car open and he stepped down, his eyes pinned to the tinted window on my driver's side.

Oh yeah, he was good and pissed. Whatever. I'd had it with people having a damn opinion on mine and Dylan's relationship today. Between Ron, and the entire cast of *Insurrection 2,* treating us like lepers, Roger's attitude was the *last* thing I wanted to deal with.

Not five seconds after I pulled the car to a stop and got out, Roger was on me like white on rice.

"Well, I hope you're proud of yourself," he said.

I shut the door and moved past him to open the back one, leaning in to grab my bag. Once it was slung over my shoulder, I rounded back to face my silver-haired, red-faced manager.

"Loud *and* proud, haven't you heard?"

Roger's beady eyes grew shrewd, and he pointed a finger at me. "Oh, you think you're real slick, don't you? Do you know what a clusterfuck you've caused us over these past two days?"

"I've caused an issue? Really? Huh, I hadn't heard a word about it."

I shoved by him and made my way toward the connecting door to my house. He followed so close behind that I was surprised the toes of his shoes weren't hitting the backs of my heels.

"Why are you doing this?"

I didn't bother stopping; I just rolled my eyes and continued down the hall into the seating area off the kitchen.

"I mean, help me understand, Ace. Why now? Why, when your career is off the charts and everything you touch turns to goddamn gold, would you parade around a boy toy?"

I chose to ignore him as I kicked off my shoes, determined to get a beer from the fridge before I engaged, but Roger wasn't letting up.

"Were you lonely? Horny? We could've hooked you up discreetly."

"Oh give it a—"

"Does he have a fifteen-inch cock or something? I mean, tell me what is so special about this kid that you're willing to fuck us all over."

That. Was. It.

I whirled around on the man who'd been in charge of my career for nearly a decade and lost it. "First," I said, and took a step toward Roger that had him backing away. *Good to know he's smart in some aspects.* "You need to shut up for one damn second in your life, and listen to me. Let's get a few things straight. Or maybe we should finally lay this out exactly for what it is, and get things *not* so fucking straight."

Roger's jaw bunched, and I could tell he was physically holding back some sort of comment that was dying to slip free. But that was too bad. I was sick and tired of tiptoeing around my sexuality, and it was high time they knew it, got on board with it, or got the hell out of my life.

For as long as I could remember I had, in some respect, been hiding who I was. Whether it was from my parents, myself, or the public, I was always hiding—and I was done. No one was going to tell me this was wrong. No one was going to talk shit about Dylan in my presence, and as long as he was willing to put up with all the bullshit that came with my baggage, then by God I was going to fight to make him feel as comfortable by my side as humanly possible.

Starting with Roger.

"*You* work for *me.* So I am not screwing you over as far as I am aware. This really has no direct impact on you. I hire you for one specific reason: to keep my career on track. I *pay* you for that reason too. Not to speculate and have an

opinion, like everyone else in the world is doing right now."
I paused to take a calming breath, because I could feel my
anger close to boiling over on the man glaring back at me. A
man whose advice a year ago had been: *Stay in the closet,*
because no one will understand and your career will tank. Who
cares if you're unhappy in your private life for your prime years?
Being gay is not good for your image.

 Yeah? Well, to hell with that shit. "Here's a news flash
for you, Roger. I'm gay. As in, I like dating, hugging,
kissing, and fucking men, and you need to get on board and
accept that. As for the 'kid' I'm seeing. He is a man. His
name is Dylan Prescott. And if I ever hear you refer to him
in such a disrespectful way ever again, privately or publicly,
I'll fire you quicker than you can blink." Roger's mouth
opened, and before he could say anything I interrupted, "*Got*
it?"

 He gave a curt nod. "Got it. Guess you won't care
then that the worldwide Blue Obsession ad just pulled out of
their contract. You know, since we're laying everything out
on the table."

 Roger's words were like a right hook to the jaw as
they penetrated my brain and I comprehended exactly what
he'd just said.

 Blue Obsession dropped me? Really? I'd just signed
those papers last week. My shock must've been evident,
because Roger looked triumphant as he nodded and slipped
his hands into his pockets, delighted that he'd gotten in his
own jab after my tirade.

I raised my hands to my face and rubbed it, weary beyond belief. This was exactly what I'd feared would happen, and then stupidly told myself wouldn't. People were running scared from the gay action star because, *Shit…we've never had one of those before.*

"Shocking, isn't it? How the wants of one person can cause issues for so many around them."

"Get out."

"What—"

"Get. *Out*," I said again.

"We need to—"

"I don't want to talk to another fucking soul until I'm good and ready. That includes you, Martina, the press, everyfuckingone."

"And when will that be?"

"Whenever the hell I call you. Jesus, Roger," I said. "Back off."

Roger held his hands up, palms showing in a sign of surrender as he backed away from me. "You should've had a plan in place before this got out."

I glared over at him. "Because you would've been so helpful about it? Ha, you haven't exactly been receptive on the topic, Roger. So don't start lecturing me on what I should've and shouldn't have done. It's too late. Now we have to deal with the way things are."

"And how's that?"

"I told you, when I feel like talking to you about it, I will. Until then, get out of my house."

After Roger grudgingly walked out, I flipped the lock, set the alarm, and then made myself a stiff drink.

Christ, it'd been a long day. My entire world bursting open in one big bang. The fact that I was still standing after the last forty-eight hours was a miracle.

As I sat at the island and took another long pull of my drink, my eyes ran over the marble counter. Had it only been the night before that Dylan had spread himself out, naked and willing, on this very counter to take my mind off the conversation I'd been having with Roger? It was amazing how just the thought of the man I'd known a few short weeks could calm me down and help to tune the rest of the world out. And it was shocking to realize how much I wished he was there beside me.

6
YOU WIN SOME,
YOU LOSE SOME

"LOOKS LIKE YOU'RE going to be a very busy man over the next few months, Dylan. Demand has gone through the roof, and so has your rate, so we'll get you out on as many shoots as we can," Claudia, my agent at JGE Models, said as she handed me a thick stack of contracts requiring my signature and leaned against her desk. "Since you're still filming, most of these jobs won't require that you travel too far outside of L.A., but once you wrap *Insurrection 2*, expect a few overseas trips. Paris is *dying* for you."

I blinked up at her, not sure I'd heard her correctly. "Paris? Seriously?" When she nodded, I looked down at the brands I'd be shooting ads for over the next few months and couldn't believe my luck. Damn, that Calvin Klein ad had paid off tenfold. "I've never been to Europe," I said softly.

"Trust me, you'll love it there."

"I'm sure I will. Wow. This…this is unreal. Thank you." *Holy shit.* Goodbye, student loans. Hello, financial freedom.

"No need to thank me. You did this all on your own."

I lifted my hand to run it through my hair out of habit, but stopped when my fingers hit the shorter, spiky strands. Guess I'd need to buy some Miracle-Gro to get it long again after filming wrapped.

"Keep that," Claudia said. "The spiky 'do you've got going on."

"Really?"

"It's the look people are starting to know you for. Don't want to change it up just yet."

The look they know me for? "But…it was longer for the Calvin Klein ad. What do you mean it's what people know me for? I haven't shot anything other than the film since I cut it."

Claudia's green eyes gleamed from behind her wire-rimmed glasses. "Other than the hot candids published on the covers of every magazine in the country. My phone has been blowing up for weeks since you guys exploded on the scene."

What? Wait a second…

Holding up my hand, I said, "Um, hang on. Who specifically are the 'people starting to know me' that you're referring to?"

She nodded at the papers in my hands. "The ones that matter."

"And when did they reach out to you about me exactly?"

"Hmm. I'd say about…three weeks ago, maybe? I'd have to look, but it's been nonstop."

Three weeks ago…

It wasn't lost on me that three weeks was also the amount of time that had passed since Ace and I had been outed in Vegas. If our relationship was the reason I was getting all these offers, I needed to find out before I signed any kind of contract.

"Claudia…can I ask why these companies are reaching out all of a sudden? It's not because of anything in my…personal life. Is it?"

She gave a trilling laugh and fingered the pearls at her neck. "Oh, Dylan. Of course it is. Your Calvin Klein ad was already generating a lot of buzz for you, but now you're the guy on the arm of the hottest star in the world. People are falling over themselves to get more of you."

My mouth dropped open. *Guy on the arm of the hottest star in the world…* Was that what it took to get ahead? "Uh…" I said, rubbing the back of my neck. "I'm not so sure I'm okay with that."

"Well, what did you expect would happen when you two got together?"

That it would be kept a secret, was my first thought, but

the next was, *What did I expect?* That it wouldn't be a big deal to anyone if we went public? That had been incredibly naive thinking on my part.

"So these companies want me because of who I'm with?" I asked.

"That's not what I said at all. But before you grow a conscience over there, here's what you need to understand about this world you're in: it's all based on popular demand, and when you get a big wave, you need to ride it out."

"A big wave? Courtesy of my boyfriend?"

"Do you know how lucky you are? Most people don't get Gucci and the cover of *GQ*. It doesn't matter how the break comes about. It matters what you do with it once you get that break, so don't be stubborn. Use what you've got going for you to your advantage."

Use what I've got? So use Ace. Was that what she was saying?

I bit down on my lower lip and read over the list in my lap again. They were dream companies, the kind that got you international recognition and paid off student loans and a mega-mortgage with enough left over to buy a small island. Okay, that could be a bit of an exaggeration, but the figure was more than I'd ever expected to see in my lifetime. But now it all felt…tainted. Like I hadn't done anything to deserve this other than be with a man that I would've chosen no matter what his profession was.

"I'm gonna need some time to think about this," I said.

"Think about it?" Claudia's eyebrows shot up to her hairline. "What's there to think about? This is huge. It'll make your career—"

"Which I wouldn't have if not for a certain someone, wouldn't you say?" When she shut her mouth, I let out a derisive laugh and stood up. "I'll let you know something within the week."

Claudia just stared at me like I'd grown two heads as I rolled up the contracts and then tucked them into the back of my pants. With a curt nod, I left her office and headed down the hallway that opened up to the lobby of the agency. Before heading out the main door, I put my sunglasses on and grabbed the keys of the rental I'd been driving for the past couple of weeks out of my pocket. Then, with a deep breath, I pushed open the door to face the dozens of paparazzi who seemed to follow my every move lately.

* * *

"ACE, HOW DOES it feel to lose out on the Destroyers role to Norman Rockwell?"

"Are you and Dylan Prescott living together?"

"Ace, what do you think about the press calling you two PresLocke?"

As I pulled past my neighborhood's main gate and left the shouts of the press lined up on the sidewalks behind, my cell rang, the ringtone indicating someone who'd been calling on a much more regular basis lately, despite our falling out weeks ago. Gone was the small talk, and in its place were clipped, to-the-point conversations.

"Roger," I said when I answered.

"I'm afraid I have bad news."

"More bad news? This is beginning to become a daily thing."

"Main Line Studios decided to go with someone else for *First Watch*."

My stomach dropped. I hadn't been surprised at losing out on the *Destroyers* role, hadn't blinked—much—when Blue Obsession and Ashland had dropped me as a spokesman. But I'd been a fan of the *First Watch* comics since I was a kid, and it was a major gut punch to lose out on something I'd had on the line for over two years.

With a deep sigh, I pulled past my gate and into the garage. "Can I ask why?"

"You know as well as I do they don't have to give a reason."

"It's a character in tights, for fuck's sake. You think they'd be smart enough to keep me for that."

Roger stayed silent, but I knew there was a smartass dig on the tip of his tongue, just waiting to be unleashed. Didn't need to be said, though, for me to hear it.

"I'm sorry to be the bearer of bad news," he said. "Maybe you can take that vacation to Bora Bora sooner than you'd thought."

Shit, at the rate my schedule was clearing, I'd be able to retire there in a matter of weeks.

"Right. Thanks."

I hit the end call button, and, after turning off the engine, sank back into my seat. The past three weeks had sent my career into a nosedive, companies fleeing left and right before the inevitable crash. I knew back when I'd sat in the presidential suite of Syn that things were about to go bad. But I'd never in my wildest dreams thought how low things could get.

Ace Locke, the sinking ship. Appropriate, considering the premise of the movie I was currently filming. And the worst part about it was that Dylan would probably go down with me.

His rental was already parked next to mine, since he'd had the day off from shooting, and he'd used the key I'd given him the other day to head inside.

It was crazy to think how important he'd become to me in such a short period, but as I climbed out of my car and headed into the house to find him, the sound of him banging around in my kitchen had the first sliver of joy creeping into my day.

How is it that just like that he manages to make everything feel a little less hopeless? What kind of magic did he hold over me that just the sight of him made me forget what a disaster every other part of my life currently was?

As I stepped into the open seating area that connected with the kitchen, I dumped my bag on the floor and waited for that moment… *And there it is.* Dylan looked at me over his shoulder from where he stood in front of the sink with the water running, and a slow smile spread across his lips.

God. It was always a shock to the heart to see him there in my house. To know that he'd chosen to be there with me, even with all of that shit that came with that.

I crossed the tiled floor in his direction, and as I got closer I noticed he was holding a stainless steel colander in the sink as he watched my approach. As I came around the counter and stopped beside him, I noticed his bare feet, well-worn jeans, and casual blue polo, and thought he'd never looked more beautiful—or at home.

"Good evening," he said as I settled in beside him, my hip against the sink.

I peered over his shoulder into the colander to see what was inside, and let out an appreciative groan at the cooked shells of pasta he was rinsing.

"Evening," I said, and leaned in to press my lips to his temple. "The good part is up for debate...but whatever you're cooking smells heavenly."

Dylan frowned, and then reached for the tap to shut the water off before he shook the colander. After he'd placed it over the empty pot on the counter beside him and snagged the dishtowel to wipe his hands, he turned back to mirror my stance. Hip against the sink and arms crossed. "Not so fast, hotshot... We promised we would talk about things, no matter how good or bad they were. Remember? So, do you want to tell me now? Or over dinner?"

"Later...after. We can talk about it *after* dinner. I

don't want to ruin your hard work or a good meal."

Dylan's face twisted into a grimace. "It's that bad?"

I tried for a careless shrug, but I was pretty sure he knew I was full of shit. "The same old, same old. It's just…"

"Yeah?"

I took in a deep breath before I let it out in a shaky sigh. "It's just so much *more* than I expected. To be experiencing this. You know? Rather than just thinking about *what if* it happens. It's…frightening how quickly everything is going downhill. Does that make sense?"

I couldn't bear to look at Dylan then, as the past few weeks started to replay in my mind. How we'd go to work, I'd get bad news, we'd come back to my place and discuss it. Then, depending on what time of the day that was and how many people we'd had to dodge or shove our way through, we'd fall asleep within seconds. Sometimes Dylan would even head home if he was feeling particularly brave, and then race up his stairs like some sort of Olympic fucking stair climber to avoid snapping cameras.

Christ. Who did I think I was putting him through all of this? This was no way to live. This wasn't even any way to date. But what stopped me from letting Dylan go—what stopped me from doing what I knew would be the easiest solution for us both and ending things—was each and every one of the emotions swirling in Dylan's eyes whenever he looked at me the way he was right now. Those extraordinary eyes of his that were full of compassion, desire, understanding, and the one emotion I was beginning to believe was…love?

He dropped his arms down by his sides and took a step forward, where he placed a palm on my chest and said, "It makes sense. Perfect sense. Nobody could know what to feel in your situation. Not only are you dealing with the entire world being interested in your partner, a significant other…you're dealing with coming out of the closet. You aren't just saying it; you're showing it. And that would scare anyone. Even you, Mr. Locke. So the fact that you're finding this difficult to deal with doesn't make you less of a person, man, or, hell, even a celebrity. Because *no one* has had to do what you're doing." Dylan then tilted his face to the side and swept his lips in a soft kiss by the corner of my mouth. "I think that makes you incredibly courageous."

He went to step away, but I was quicker. I unfolded my arms and wrapped them around his waist and held him in place as I lowered my head, resting my forehead against his and shutting my eyes.

"I don't feel brave," I whispered. "I feel like everyone is running away from me."

Dylan touched his fingers to my cheek, and as they stroked down my jaw, he said, "I'm not."

I opened my eyes to see his lips slanting into a grin. "No, you're not. Are you?"

He leaned back in my arms and shook his head. "Nope. In fact, I'm pretty sure you'll soon get sick of me with as much time as I'm spending here."

"Impossible."

"Ha, you say that now," Dylan said, and then moved to loop his arms around my neck and smack his lips to mine. "But that's 'cause you can send me home whenever you like."

This time when he moved to step away I let him go, swatting him on the ass. As he reached the stove and rubbed a hand over his abused posterior, he glanced back with a mock frown and promised I'd pay for that later. And that was the other reason I would put up with whatever I had to in order to keep Dylan in my life. His innate ability to make even the darkest of days a little bit brighter.

* * *

AFTER WE'D CONSUMED enough pasta that we'd be running a few extra miles on the treadmill in Ace's workout room tomorrow morning, we settled side by side on the comfy patio lounge in front of the fire pit on Ace's back deck, and I cuddled into his side. His mood had somewhat thawed from when he'd first arrived home, and I was pleased I was able to do that for him. Comfort him while he was going through all of this bullshit. It was maddening to have to sit back and watch as sponsors, directors, and producers continued to pull away from him, and when he'd finally told me that the *First Watch* role had fallen through, my heart had broken for him. I remember how excited he'd been when he'd told me about that upcoming film and how being cast in it was like a dream come true, so tonight's news had been the biggest blow so far.

As his hand curled around my shoulder and he tugged me into his body, I laid my palm on his chest and wound a leg over the top of his. When I was practically draped over him, Ace took my chin between his fingers and tipped my face up to his and kissed me reverently. *And wow... Who knew that Ace would be one of the sweetest damn men on the planet?*

"I'm sick of talking about me," he said. "I feel like that's all I do lately. How did it go with your agent today?"

Shit. I wasn't sure how Ace would feel about that, so instead of answering, I decided to concentrate on the first half of his sentence.

"Oh, I don't know. I kind of like the topic. I'm a bit of an expert." When a soft rumble had his chest vibrating against me, I started to rattle off his stats. "Your full name is Ace Samuel Locke. You're thirty-three years old. You're six foot two and weigh approximately two hundred and thirty pounds. You have brown hair, piercing blue eyes, and I would say about an eight-inch cock, maybe an inch or so more—"

"Are you serious?" Ace asked as he sat up straight, and I nearly toppled off him. I reached out and clutched at his bicep to keep myself in place. "You can look up my dick size online?"

I kept my lips drawn tight in a very serious expression and feigned shock. "You didn't know?"

He held my stare long enough that I was unable to

fight back my laugh, and when he tackled me down onto my back and pinned me there, he rocked his hips against me and growled.

"You think you're real funny, don't you?"

I craned up to nip at his chin, but Ace moved his head to the side. "Had you worried, didn't I?"

"Well, lately, nothing would surprise me. But if that was on there, then yeah, I'd be shocked." He paused as he hovered over me with my arms restrained by my head. "But you made a very accurate guess, all things considered."

I wrapped my legs around his waist and bucked up under him. "What can I say? I'm somewhat of an expert on it."

He let out a booming laugh, and I grinned at his amusement. It was so few and far between lately it was nice to hear it, and made me hesitant to talk about the rest of my day. I was about to try and convince Ace to let the subject go when he rolled to his side and pulled me with him.

"Tell me about your day, Dylan. How'd it go with your agent?"

I pursed my lips, and when I looked away from him, Ace said my name, drawing my gaze back to him.

"What's wrong? Did something happen? Did you get fired? Dropped—"

"No. No. Nothing like that. Actually...it's just the opposite."

Ace cocked his head to the side as I gnawed on my lower lip. *Fuck. Shit.* Why did this have to be so damn difficult?

"The opposite? That would be...good. Right?"

I nodded, and Ace reached up and smoothed a thumb over the frown I could feel etched between my eyebrows.

"Why do you look so worried? Tell me."

"Well...it's just my agent is all excited because I've been getting offer after offer from big clients. I mean, like...really *big* clients, Ace. Gucci, *GQ*, *Italian Vogue*, and they even want me to go to Paris and...and—"

"And what? That's fantastic," Ace said. "Really terrific news."

"No," I said, and shook my head. "You're not understanding. The only reason I got those offers is because of you. Because of us. They weren't interested in me before and likely wouldn't have—"

"Hang on one damn second—"

"Ace—"

"I said hang on."

I shut my mouth and waited for whatever he was going to say, not having a clue how he was going to react. But when a grin so wide it threatened to slide from his face appeared, I felt—confused.

"You don't see it, do you?" he asked.

I narrowed my eyes as Ace's gaze roved over me. "Don't see what?"

"What everyone else sees when they look at you.

Dylan, you didn't get this because of me—"

"Yes, I—"

"Shhh…" he said, and put a finger to my lips. "I *mean*, maybe it happened a little faster because of what went down in Vegas and everything that's happened since. But they aren't calling you because of that. If you had been just some average Joe, magazines around the world wouldn't be lining up to put you on their cover. No, sir. You were already on your way. You have the face of an angel. It's perfect. I thought so even before I knew you. Hell, I used to drive miles out of my way *just* to see you. You got this all on your own merit, and the fact they noticed you a little sooner is just a bonus."

I wondered if my eyes were as wide as my mouth, which I knew had fallen open. Wow. That was so not what I'd been expecting, at all.

"You said yes to them, right? You signed the contracts?"

"Well, no," I said. "I wanted to think about it. Talk to you about it."

Ace's lips curled as he pressed them to mine. "You're very sweet, Dylan Prescott."

"Hey, don't try and distract me."

"I'm not. There's nothing more that really needs to be talked about. This is an amazing chance, one you need to take full advantage of. That's how it works in this industry. Connections, people who know other people." He paused and kissed me again. "You deserve this."

My heart squeezed at his sincerity, and just how generous a soul he was that even at his lowest point ever in his career he was right there cheering me on, truly proud of me.

7
KNOCKED UP

I PRACTICALLY HELD my breath as Ace limped across the deck of the rescue ship, gazing out at what was left of the ruined expanse of the *U.S.S. Alabama*. From where I sat off camera, I had a view of his strong backside, his Navy uniform looking more like tattered rags than the pristine outfit he'd worn at the beginning of the film.

It was the final day of shooting after a long twelve weeks, and though my last scene had been a few days ago, I wasn't about to miss being here for Ace's big end scene. To say my first experience making a movie was an odd one was an understatement. Things had never quite thawed between us and the cast and crew, and it felt like we'd spent more time in Ace's trailer avoiding the stares than actually shooting.

Well, it wasn't like that time in Ace's trailer hadn't been *very* well spent.

Since I had no plans to continue with acting, I was soaking in the remaining minutes, watching my man from the sidelines. The set was completely still as one of the cameras caught Ace's reaction to the destruction before him and the fact that he made it out alive. I wished I could see his face, but I could feel the mood he'd set, could see the tension in his shoulders and the way he held his body.

"Daddy!"

A little boy, about four, went running toward Ace, who'd jerked his head around at the sound. Even from across the room I could see the tears form in his eyes, and the smile that lit up his face as he hobbled toward the boy had me biting down hard on my lower lip. As he swooped the kid up into his big arms and held him close, his eyes caught on a woman with fair hair walking hesitantly his way. Tears streamed down her face, and as she finally came to a stop before Ace, he pulled her to his chest and kissed the top of her head. The picture the three of them made against the green screen that stood in for a sunset background caused a couple of audible sniffs, and then the cameras panned out slowly, fully exploiting the reunion and happy ending.

"Cut! And that's a wrap on *Insurrection 2!*" Ron called out, and the remaining cast and crew on set burst into cheers and whistles.

I stood up and clapped along as Ace set the boy

down and then rubbed the back of his neck. When he glanced up, his eyes met mine, and the grin he gave me was more heart melting than the scene we'd all just witnessed.

As Ace headed in my direction, Ron continued speaking, but I couldn't tell what he said. My focus was solely on the gorgeous—though slightly worn—man in front of me.

"Congratulations, mister. Great scene," I said.

Ace's smile grew. "Coming from my biggest fan, that means a lot."

"I am *definitely* your biggest fan in bed, and don't you forget it. I kinda like your movies too."

He laughed and gave me a shove. "Ass."

"Mhmm, I like that too."

"Oh yeah? Maybe I'll let you kiss it later."

"Maybe I'll do more than that." Then I winked at him and said, "So how does it feel? You're all done."

"Well, except for any pick-up shots, but yeah. Feels…like a relief, honestly."

"You know I have no idea what a pick-up shot means."

Ace's arm went around my shoulders, and he walked us toward where Ron and the cameras were. "How about I explain it tonight *after* you give me what you promised."

"I could get on board with that…"

He gave me a final squeeze, and then his arm left me, reaching out toward Ron instead.

"I just wanted to say thank you. I think the film's going to be great, and I'm proud to be a part of it," Ace said.

Damn. I had to hand it to the guy for being the bigger man, considering the hard time Ron had given him for weeks on end. No way in hell would I have done the same, especially with the way Ron was eyeing Ace's hand before reluctantly shaking it.

"Always a pleasure, Ace," he said, and I didn't miss the way he wouldn't look in my direction. As Ron let go and shoved his hands in his pockets, he rocked back on his heels. "And, uh...I meant to talk to you before you left."

Was he about to apologize? *He fucking better.* Ace deserved at least that much.

"You mentioned before that you would throw the wrap party, and I just wanted to make sure that was still on. Announce it to everyone before they head out today and all."

Are you fucking serious?

To his credit, Ace didn't blink. Instead, he replied smoothly, "Of course. I'll have my party planner email everyone the details."

Ron clapped Ace on the shoulder and nodded. "Great." Then he turned around and went back to deconstructing his setup.

Without even thinking about it, I reached for Ace's hand, linking our fingers. After months of being so careful not to throw our relationship in anyone's faces, I couldn't give a fuck anymore what these pricks thought. How could anyone in their right mind treat the man beside me with anything other than total respect and admiration? He'd give the shirt off his back for a stranger. He'd throw a stupid wrap party and spend his own money to make sure the people who'd turned against him still had a good time. He'd bite his tongue instead of saying how he truly felt.

Once we were outside of the soundstage, I found it hard to keep from biting my own tongue. "Why did you do that?"

"Sometimes you have to suck it up and be a team player."

"Or you could just tell them all to go fuck themselves."

"I did in my head."

"Not the same thing."

"What good would it do to stoop to his level? It would just make things worse."

"But this guy is going to make a shit ton of money off you when this movie explodes. The least he could've done was say, 'Sorry, I'm a dick, and I should've been more understanding and treated you like a human being when someone stole your private life away from you and aired it out to the world for everyone to talk about.'"

Ace brought our hands up and kissed my knuckles. "Thank you. But it's fine."

"It's not fine."

"We've gotta let it go."

As we stepped inside his trailer, I sighed, but deep

down I knew he was right. Still didn't make it fair, though. Ace continually amazed me with the kind of man he was. Every day he showed me another side to himself. A side I never imagined someone like him would have, and today it was humility.

Here was a man who, by all standards, was a very influential player in this business. Yet he'd spent the past few weeks doing everything within his power to keep the peace on set. He'd done everything possible to make things less awkward for me and the entire flipping cast, when really he could've acted like an egomaniac and demanded things I probably couldn't have even imagined. I also knew he would've been able to have Russ fired in a heartbeat, and yet he hadn't, which made him…well, it made him pretty damn incredible.

I glanced over to where he was unbuttoning the collar of his torn Navy jacket, and watched him dig around inside his bag for his cell. Once he located it, he took a seat at the small kitchen table and scrolled through his phone, looking for his event planner's number, no doubt, and when I shut the door behind me, he looked up and aimed a half-smile in my direction.

"You're looking pretty serious over there, Daydream." There was humor in his tone, but it didn't quite reach his eyes. "You okay?"

I nodded slowly as I made my way over to where he sat. I reached for the phone and put it on the table, and when I cupped the side of his face and lowered my lips to his, I said, "I'm just great."

Ace pulled away slightly and raised an eyebrow. "Great, huh?"

"Mhmm. I was just thinking…"

"Always a dangerous pastime," Ace said, and brought a palm up to lay it directly over my heart, and I wondered if he could feel it thudding.

"No. Not this time," I said.

"No?"

"Nope. I was just thinking how wonderful you are."

"Okay, sweet talker—"

"I'm serious," I said, bringing my other hand up so I was cradling his face between my palms. "I wish for one day you could be me, so you could see what an incredibly brave, sweet, extraordinary human being you are. You have so much, Ace, yet…you're more generous and humble than anyone I know."

"Dylan—"

"Shh," I whispered against his lips. "I just wanted you to know that I…" I caught myself at the last minute as his eyes pierced mine and I was paralyzed by the enormity of emotions flooding me.

God, how is it that in twelve weeks this man has completely turned my world upside down? But he had. Ace had me wanting things…things I'd never even thought about before. Things I always assumed I would *never* want.

"You…?" he said, but my mind had changed course. The emotions had blurred and morphed into something else entirely, and then, quite unexpectedly, I asked, "Do you want kids?"

From the stunned expression on Ace's face, I might as well have asked him if he were a serial killer. His eyes had widened and his mouth fell open, and he looked so bewildered I couldn't stop the chuckle that bubbled out of me.

"Uhh…" he said.

He appeared so shell-shocked it made me laugh even harder. "I'm sorry…but you should see your face right now… I promise, I'm not pregnant." When I began laughing again, Ace's mouth snapped shut and he brought both his hands up to my wrists to encircle them and tug me down into the booth with him. He scooted across the seat until he was lounging back against the wall and I was awkwardly sprawled across him.

"Excuse me if you took me a little bit off guard," he said.

"A little bit?"

"Okay, a whole fucking lot. But that wasn't where I thought you were going with that at all."

I aimed a grin his way, trying to play down the fact that I'd been about three seconds away from handing over more of me than I knew I could ever get back should Ace decide he didn't—

"Hey?" he said. "Where'd you go?"

"Huh?"

It was Ace's turn to chuckle. "What is *up* with you?

You're all over the place."

I sighed, knowing that he was right. Maybe it was like a postproduction crash or something. But I felt oddly sentimental. Like all of my feelings were right there on the surface.

I stroked my fingers down his cheek. "I just think you would be an amazing father, is all. And I was curious."

He narrowed his eyes on me. "I don't think that's it at all, *but* to answer your question. Yes, I think one day and"—his eyes were so intent on holding mine then that there was no way I could look anywhere but at him, and his meaning was crystal clear before he even said it—"with the right person, I would definitely consider having kids. What about you?"

"I never really thought I would, considering where I came from and all. But…" I chewed on my lower lip, suddenly wishing I'd kept my damn mouth shut.

"But?"

My eyes locked with his and I decided it was now or never to really just lay it out there. "But watching you today on set made me think about what-ifs."

The grin that curved Ace's mouth then was cheeky, and for the first time since we'd entered the trailer, his eyes lit with the same amusement his smile was conveying.

"Are you trying to say you want me to knock you up? Because, Dylan, I have to tell you, I have some pretty powerful boys at work, but no amount of horny goat weed is gonna make *that* happen."

It was my turn for my jaw to drop then, and when Ace started laughing his ass off I punched him in the arm. "Dick."

"Aww, but you just said I was wonderful."

"A wonderful dick."

"But not magical enough to get you pregnant."

"Would you *stop* saying that. You're freaking me out."

Ace's rumble of laughter vibrated through him as he wrapped his arms around my waist, and finally, after a minute or two, when his mirth had subsided, he stroked a hand down my back to my ass and pulled me as close as was possible while wearing clothes.

"It's okay to look at the future and think about what might be, Daydream."

I laid my head against his shoulder and shut my eyes. "I know. This is all just happening so fast. Sometimes I have to pinch myself to believe it's real."

I felt his lips at my temple and then he whispered, "It's real. So believe it. Plan it. Trust it."

I nodded and then angled my face to see him look up at me. He had a soft smile on his face, and for the first time all day he looked relaxed, and I knew that as long as we were together the future looked brighter than ever.

8
I LIKE BIG BUOYS AND I CANNOT LIE

"YOU KNOW, AS much as I love looking at you without any clothes, there's something about you in a suit that just has me…" Dylan leaned back into the leather seat of the Town Car and gave me a slow perusal. His teeth tugged on his lower lip as his gaze drifted back up the length of my body, and then he said, "Mmm. Wanting to tell the driver to turn this car around and head back to your place."

"And miss your first wrap party? Why, Mr. Prescott, you wouldn't dare deny me the opportunity to have you on my arm at our first public event."

"Wouldn't I?" The wolfish grin he gave me made me laugh. There was no way I was letting him off the hook that easy.

"Yeah, okay, you would. And as much as I'd like

nothing more than to strip you naked and fuck you on every surface of my house, I promised the girls I'd introduce you."

Dylan pretended to pout, but his eyes were sparkling. "Looking forward to later, but I'm excited to meet your friends."

"*And* taste the best boozy shakes you've ever had in your life."

"What the hell are boozy shakes?"

"My weakness. They're basically gourmet alcoholic milkshakes. Just wait."

"Do they come with pink umbrellas and shit?"

"Sometimes."

He laughed. "And you're going to carry that around the party proudly, aren't you?"

"Damn right I am."

As the car pulled up to the curb of Licked and the After Dark, where the wrap party for *Insurrection 2* was being held, the gaggle of paparazzi on the sidewalk turned in our direction, the flashes from their cameras immediate and nonstop.

"You ready?" I asked, meaning more than just *are you ready to get out of the car?* I needed to know that he was not only ready to face the onslaught we were about to step into, but ready for every little move we made to be dissected in the tabloids. But Dylan's handsome face was calm and sure, so when he nodded, I smiled in return. "Then let's do it."

Our driver opened the back door and I stepped out first, keeping that smile in place as I gave the cameras a wave, and the shouts that filled my ears were immediate.

"Ace, did you bring your boyfriend?"

"Is it true you and Dylan are moving in together?"

I wasn't about to answer or even acknowledge any questions tonight, or any time in the foreseeable future, so I ignored the shouts and moved to the side so Dylan could exit the car.

And what a fucking exit it was. As he stepped out, the paparazzi crowded in closer, wanting those money shots of the gorgeous man standing next to me, reaching for my hand.

"Dylan, look this way!"

"Can we get a shot of you two kissing?"

When Dylan threaded his fingers through mine, I gave them a gentle squeeze. Then I pushed us through the horde, keeping my eyes forward and my mouth shut, even as I heard:

"What do you have to say about sources who claim there was tension on the set because of your relationship?"

"Ace, did you get Dylan the part in Insurrection 2*?"*

"Dylan, how does Ace measure up in bed?"

At that last comment, I halted and Dylan came to a stop behind me. Then I turned on my heel in the direction of the photographer who'd shouted the out-of-line question, and when he saw that my gaze had landed on him, he lowered his camera a fraction.

But as much as I wanted to give the invasive asshole a piece of my mind, years of experience outweighed what was on the tip of my tongue, so I merely raised an eyebrow as he snapped away at me, and then we were gone. Moving quickly past the flashes that felt as though someone had put a strobe light spotlight on us, we were soon ushered inside Licked, and I could hear Dylan let out an exhale of relief that matched my own.

"Ace Locke," Ryleigh, decked out in a swing-style dress straight out of the fifties, said as she sauntered toward us.

"Ryleigh," I said as I let go of Dylan's hand to embrace my friend and the woman who owned Licked and the After Dark. "I can't thank you enough for letting us hold the party here. *And* for putting up with the chaos that came along with that."

She laughed as she kissed my cheek and then took a step back. "Are you kidding me? That's free press, baby."

"Damn right it is," a familiar voice piped up, and when I looked past Ryleigh's shoulder I saw Paige, my event planner/giver of keycards to Syn, who was bent over slightly at the window to peer out the curtains. "They're going nuts out there," the brassy blonde said as she straightened and rounded on us, and then she started across the black and white floors in her tailored cigarette pants and crop top. When she stopped beside Ryleigh, she gave Dylan and me a thorough once-over, and then held her hand out to him. "And I can see why. Hi, we haven't been formally introduced. I'm Paige Iris Traynor-Ashcroft."

Dylan chuckled, and my heart pounded when his

dimples appeared.

"That's quite a mouthful," he said, taking Paige's hand to shake, and, bold as ever, she looked my way and pursed her lips.

"He say that with those dimples the first time you dropped trou?" she asked me. "If so, I can see why you're willing to brave the hordes of paparazzi out there." When she returned her attention to Dylan, she stated matter-of-factly, "You're sexy."

"Uhh…" Dylan tried to speak, and failed.

"This is Dylan, and how 'bout you be on your best behavior tonight and let go of his hand?" I said.

"How 'bout you try and make me," Paige said with a *good luck with that* grin.

"You do remember he's gay, right, Paige?" Ryleigh reminded her friend, and my soon-to-be *ex*-employee.

Paige acted as though she were thinking that over, and then nodded. "I *do* seem to remember that, but you never know—"

"I don't mean to insult you because you seem really…well, intimidating," Dylan finally said as he drew back his hand and cast his attention my way. "But trust me when I say that I like men. In particular, this man. I have since the first time I saw him, and that was years before we met."

"Ouch. Shot down, P.I.T.A.," Hunter Morgan, Ryleigh's boyfriend, said as he arrived behind his woman. He wrapped an arm around her waist and kissed her

LOCKED 93

temple, and then he grinned at the two of us. "Hey, guys,
don't mind Paige. She's a pain in everyone's ass."

"I never do," I said, throwing a good-natured smile
her way.

"Huge turnout tonight," Hunter said, indicating the
open doors that led through to the After Dark area where
the party was taking place. There was no denying that
Hunter was a good-looking guy, and as his dark hair fell
away from his eyes I could see the appeal he held for
Ryleigh—as could Dylan, apparently, who'd turned his head
to smile at the man who'd just greeted us.

"Yeah, I have a feeling that's going to be the norm for
us for some time," I said, placing a hand on Dylan's back
just to connect myself with him.

"I don't know how you do it," Ryleigh said. "It was
crazy enough last year after you and Shay—" She squeaked
off her final word as Hunter hugged her gently, and aimed a
what look at her guy.

Dylan was the one to speak up. "It's okay. I know all
about Shayne and Ace." He looked around. "Is she going to
be here? I never did get to thank her for sending me upstairs
the night of your birthday."

As that hot memory hit, and transported me back to
my bedroom and Dylan on his knees with—*huh, his mouth
full*—I kissed his ear and said, "I never got to thank her
either."

"She'll be here," Ryleigh said, stepping away from
Hunter and heading over behind a long counter with a glass

case that housed tubs of colorful, and unusually named, ice creams. "She called to tell me that her and Nate were running a little late, which usually means…"

"She was banging her *young* man before they had to make an appearance and behave themselves," Paige interjected as we all made our way to the counter.

"Yes, something like that," Ryleigh said. "I swear, that girl needs better time management."

"Hmm, yes. She should plan to leave at least an extra forty minutes before she has to go anywhere. Isn't that right, Miss Phillips?" Hunter asked, as he passed behind his lady and kissed her on the side of her neck. When Ryleigh's cheeks turned a sweet pink color, he looked at the three of us, grinned like a devil, and then turned to the back to get some glassware.

"So what's it gonna be tonight, Ace? A Master Baiter shake or a Boatload of Seamen shake?"

Dylan sputtered next to me, and then burst out laughing. "*That's* the name of the drinks?"

"I told you," I said, and wrapped an arm around his shoulder. "These are adult alcoholic milkshakes."

"You didn't tell me they had filthy names," Dylan said, leaning in to kiss my lips lightly. "No wonder you like them so much."

"Mhmm," I agreed against his mouth, until Paige began an elaborate coughing fit off to the side.

"Get a room, you two." She paused and picked up a maraschino cherry from a small bowl in front of Ryleigh, and then chomped down on it. "Oh, that's right, you already did. It's all over the news."

I rolled my eyes and flipped her off as she twirled the stem of the eaten cherry between her fingers. "I'll have a Boatload of Seamen, and I think Dylan would like the Master Baiter tonight."

"Is that a hint?" Dylan asked.

I flirted my lips across the shell of his ear and whispered, "Or an invitation."

"Okay, okay, you two. You're even worse than the practically married couple over there," Paige said, nodding to Ryleigh and Hunter as she walked around to insinuate herself in between the two of us. She looped her arms through the crooks of our elbows and looked up at Dylan first, and then me. "So…tell me the truth. You two doing okay with all of that? The press? I know they can be nuts, and that night I dropped off some clothes when you got back from Vegas they were camped out in front of Ace's gates like a pack of hungry hyenas."

"It's been intense," Dylan admitted, but then his eyes found mine and softened. "But totally worth it."

"Oh God," Paige said. "Don't you even start, Locke. All this sappy shit is seriously starting to kill any residual horniness that may, or may not, have been aroused when you two were kissing."

And that was Paige. Blunt and offering no apologies for her lack of filter.

"Well, all I'm saying is if you need someone to kick

some ass, to distract, run interference, play beard to either of you hot, *hot* men—"

"Paige," Ryleigh said as she slid two drinks across the counter to us decorated with, *what do you know*, pink umbrellas and all.

"I'm *just* offering my services."

"Sure you are. Let them head into the party. That *is* what they're here for, remember?"

"Fine, fine. But remember. If you two need anything, call me."

I smiled at her, knowing she truly meant what she'd just said as she moved out of the way, allowing me to put my hand on Dylan's lower back where I'd had it earlier. "Thanks, Paige. We appreciate it, really."

"You better," she said, snatching up the drink Ryleigh had put in place for her. "I don't offer myself to just anyone."

"Now that's way too easy," Hunter quipped, and took a chug of the beer he'd just taken the cap off. "Where's Dawson when you need him?"

And as I steered Dylan away from the three of them with a wave, I thought I heard Paige say, "No doubt off somewhere being a dirty dick."

I shuddered at the thought of her and Richard Dawson's volatile run-ins the handful of times I'd seen them, and didn't envy that guy what he would have to go through to soften her up.

"So…you ready?" I asked, and watched as Dylan's

smile faded and he nodded like a man fated to an unwanted destiny. Right now, I knew exactly how he felt. But this wasn't going to be over until it began. So it was time to face the music.

* * *

AS ACE'S HAND smoothed down to rest at the curve of my lower back, we headed in the direction of the open doors Hunter had indicated earlier. I couldn't remember the last time I'd felt this nervous, but the idea of stepping through those doors and into a party full of people who no doubt would be waiting for Ace's arrival had my pulse racing.

But that's stupid, I told myself. All of these people had worked on set with us for weeks. It wasn't like this relationship was new to them, so we had nothing to worry about...*right?*

I swallowed back my nerves, trying to hang on to the relaxed feeling that Ryleigh and her friends had managed to instill in me, and just when I was starting to feel a modicum of calm, Ron walked out in front of us.

"Ace," he said, stopping to look up at my date.

Ace came to a halt beside me and his shoulders stiffened much like mine had. *Damn it,* oh well, at least we could say we'd had fun for the first five minutes of the night with his friends.

"Ron," Ace said in a clipped tone.

"Look… I… Uhh…" Ron glanced in my direction, probably waiting for me to excuse myself, but that wasn't going to happen—not tonight. I wasn't on set anymore, and this guy didn't own my actions when I wasn't working for him, so if Ace was happy to keep his arm around me while they talked, then I was more than happy to stay.

When it became clear he would need to keep speaking or leave without saying anything at all, Ron faced Ace once more and started again. "I owe you an apology."

Well, how do you like that? I tried to keep my mouth from falling open, but it was hard because never in a million years had I expected *that* to come out of Ron King's mouth.

"I shouldn't have taken my frustration over certain situations out on you. And I apologize for that."

As far as apologies went it was fairly half-assed, but considering it was a shock to be hearing one at all, I wasn't surprised when Ace held his hand out to the older man.

"I appreciate that, Ron. I've always enjoyed working with you."

"And I you, Ace," Ron said, and then his eyes drifted to mine. "You aren't bad either, when you're not busy ogling the lead."

Ace's laugh made my eyes fly to his, and the slight nod he gave had me turning a smile of my own toward Ron. "Well, it's a compliment to you, really. Just means you have a magnetic leading man."

"Yeah, he sure is a draw at the box office. People love him. Make sure he remembers that, okay, kid?" When Ron held his hand out to me, I felt a deep swell of pride in my chest, because Ron was right: Ace was a *huge* draw all over the world, and the fact that he wanted to be with me was still somewhat shocking. "For your first movie you did pretty good, all things considered."

"Ha," I said, shaking his hand. "I don't think movies is the life for me, but I thank you for that slight boost in my fragile confidence."

As the pressure of Ace's hand increased slightly, I looked his way and saw a healthy dose of the same emotion I'd been feeling, pride, shining back at me.

"Okay, then. I won't hold you two up any longer. I just wanted to clear the air."

"It's much appreciated, Ron," Ace said as the director headed off inside the club, leaving Ace and me still several steps from the main entrance.

"Wow," I said with a disbelieving shake of my head. "I did not see that coming."

"I kinda did. Ron's not a bad guy. He's just a hothead, and our relationship brought up a lot of questions in the press about the movie he didn't want to deal with in the last few weeks."

I guess I could understand that. "Yeah, when you put it like that."

"You ready to face the rest of them?"

I scrunched my nose up. "Sure we can't slip out the front door of Licked?"

"I wish. But we should make an appearance."

"Okay, you're right. I'm sure it won't be that bad anyway. It's not like we're news to them."

"I guess we'll soon find out," Ace said, and we took the several steps needed to put us through the open doors and into the After Dark, and as if time stood still, all music, dancing, and conversation ceased.

9
BUG UNDER
A MICROSCOPE

JESUS, AND HERE I thought Ace and I could just slip in unnoticed.

I scanned the sea of people standing around high-top tables in small groups laughing and chatting with drinks in their hands, and tilted my head up to take in the exquisite pink and purple fabric that lined the ceiling. It was stunning in the way that it swept out to each corner of the room, and then flowed to the floor, giving the place an intimate and elegant feel. I recognized several actresses from the golden era hanging on the walls, and thought what a perfect location this was for a movie industry wrap party. The lighting was low, the center chandelier giving off a muted glow, and there were booths lining the walls that were U-shaped and looked comfortable enough to sleep in should one want to, though currently they were all claimed and filled to capacity.

Although the space was vast and I could see a cleared area a little ways away from us and through the crowd, it seemed like the walls were closing in on us. I moved a little closer to Ace's side and didn't miss the way his fingers tightened around mine. My heart thumped at all the eyes on us, and I could feel my cheeks heating as though we were under a fucking spotlight. I swallowed around the lump in my throat, and just as I was about to try and say something witty to Ace, who was frozen beside me, he took a step forward and began walking through the familiar faces of the cast and crew and the not-so-familiar but *curious* onlookers in their partners.

It was like being a bug under a microscope. Ace's warm palm was pressed intimately against mine as he strode ahead of me, and with each group of people we passed, it didn't escape my notice how they smiled at Ace, but then their eyes would travel down to the hand he had wrapped around mine. *Nosy fucks.*

There was no way Ace had missed the scrutiny we were under as he continued through the crowd, but he greeted each and every person who managed to say hi instead of merely gawk at us. He was heading toward the shadowed corner I had seen when we'd entered the After Dark, and the direct beeline he was making was an indication he was in need of a moment, or perhaps five, to get himself together.

When we reached the empty space, he maneuvered me so I was standing with my back to the wall and he was caging me in, giving all those in attendance a fantastic view of his broad back, and not a whole lot more.

"Christ," he said.

"Yeah," I said. "Intense, huh?"

Ace shook his head. "I figured this would be okay, you know? We worked with these people daily. They saw us and knew we were together, but..."

He didn't have to say it. I knew exactly how he felt. We'd both thought tonight would be a good time for our first somewhat public outing as a couple because it would be around Ace's friends and our peers. But we hadn't counted on the instant gossip and murmurs from their partners and spouses that had begun the second we'd left Ryleigh and her friends.

Yeah, the second we'd left their side and stepped into the party we'd become the "entertainment," and if it was making me nervous, someone who'd been out and proud most of their life, I had no idea how Ace must be feeling.

Trying to be the calm one here, the one to reassure him, I squeezed my fingers around his and shot him my most winning smile. "Hey, they're just curious."

"They're fucking nosy is what they are," he said, expressing my exact thought from earlier. "You'd think they'd never seen a gay couple before. And living in L.A., I find that difficult to believe."

I gave a small shrug, understanding his frustration,

but also had to break it to him: "They've never seen *you* as part of a gay couple. Do you really think they'd be looking if I walked in here holding some other guy's hand?"

A frown furrowed Ace's brow. "How about we *don't* test that theory."

I chuckled, and Ace took a step closer.

"I wasn't meaning we should. All I'm saying is, it's the fact that it's you that has everyone gawking at us."

Ace sighed, and I reached out to run a soothing hand down his cheek, but at the last second stopped myself. When his eyes fired and shifted to the hand I'd just lowered, he said, "Don't for one second feel like you can't do what you want to me in public. If you want to touch me, you fucking touch me. That's the reason we came out, remember?"

Ohh, I like that. The pissy attitude because I hadn't touched him. So I raised my hand and trailed my fingers along his jaw. "I believe you might be right. But I don't think I should do *everything* I want to…"

That made Ace's lips tug into a grin. "No?"

"Unfortunately, no. I don't think this is the time or the *place* for that. But if you're ever interested in performing in public, I know somewhere we could go." I made sure to add a sexy wink as I thought back to that forbidden night at Syn. Ace's eyes lowered to my lips and I ran my tongue along them, keeping his mind off being the object of so many, and instead letting him know he was the sole focus of one—*me.*

"Are you trying to distract me?" he asked.

I cocked my head to the side. "Why? Is it working?"

When Ace closed the remaining gap between us and lowered his head by my cheek, I almost hyperventilated. It wasn't that he was so close, but the fact he was so close out in public. It was doing serious things to my heart *and* my dick.

"The reminder of you naked with my cock inside you? Yep, pretty much one hundred percent distracted over here," he said.

I was about to turn my head and tell Ace that not only was I distracted, I was now really fucking hard, but before I could, a couple moved into my line of sight. I recognized the woman in an instant—Mallory Jacobs. She'd played Ace's wife in *Insurrection 2* and was one of Hollywood's sweethearts. Her long blonde hair had been swept to the side and cascaded over her left shoulder in beautiful, soft waves. However, the siren-red dress she wore with a plunging neckline made it quite clear that while she may have been dubbed a "sweetheart," Mallory was more than capable of pulling off seductive bombshell too, and standing by her side...*oh my God*, was that really Alejandro Mendez? *Shit, it really is.* If Mallory was America's sweetheart then her longtime boyfriend had been dubbed her prince. True Hollywood royalty, that is, with his parents both being bigwigs in the industry. He had an arm wrapped around her waist and was nuzzling into her neck as she giggled, and when her eyes met mine she grinned as if we were both sharing the same predicament. Ace's lips then pressed to the side of my neck and I chuckled at the accuracy of the assessment, and gave him a gentle shove.

"Problem?" Ace asked, his eyes twinkling, and I shook my head because *God* he was gorgeous when he was aroused, and the flush on his cheeks hinted he was becoming more so the longer we stood there in our dark corner.

"No, but we have company. So behave yourself, hotshot."

He straightened, his shoulders tensing, but when he turned and spotted Mallory, I noted the way his entire frame seemed to relax.

"Ace." She beamed and disengaged her arm from Alejandro and stepped forward. She took Ace's arms between her hands and leaned up on tiptoes to press a kiss to his cheek. Ace returned the affectionate gesture, and I knew from the conversations I'd had with him over the past few weeks that the friendship these two shared was genuine. He'd expressed many times how he'd wished Mallory had had a more integral part, because then at least there would've been a friendly face on set. As it was, she had fewer lines than I did, so really she'd only been there a handful of days.

"Mallory, man am I glad to see you here tonight," Ace said.

"Needing some moral support?" she asked as her eyes found mine again and she smiled.

"You could say that. Or maybe I just want someone

else here to take the spotlight off us."

She flashed her famous smile and ran her hand down Ace's arm to give his fingers a squeeze. "Hate to break it to you, but I could walk in here naked and no one would look away from the two of you."

"I find that difficult to believe, Mallory," Alejandro said as he moved up by her side, and she slipped her arm through the crook of his.

"Oh please, these two are the talk of the town...hell, the world right now."

"Thanks for the reminder," Ace said, and when I moved up to stand by his side, he automatically reached for my hand, and that small gesture had my heart thudding.

"It's nice to finally meet you," Alejandro said as he held his hand out to Ace. "I've been wanting to work with you for some time, and when Mallory said she was going to be in one of your movies I knew this would be the perfect place to make a shameless pitch. I'm a huge fan."

Wow, I thought as I watched the two extraordinarily handsome men shake hands. *Now that's one hell of a compliment.* I barely stopped my mouth from falling open, but if Alejandro had just told me he was a fan of *mine,* I might've passed out. As it was, I was finding it increasingly difficult not to act like a total fanboy in front of this couple. But Ace, as always, was cool under pressure. Calm in the face of the unbelievable. Because these were his peers, Mallory was his friend, something I always seemed to forget until moments like this where I felt star-struck and he was…well, Ace was himself. This was all part of his world.

"Are you kidding?" Ace chuckled. "I'm pretty sure you wouldn't have to twist my arm. If we can find the right project, that would be fantastic."

Mallory snuggled into her man's side and aimed her megawatt smile at him. "See, what'd I tell you? No need to be nervous."

I glanced at Ace's strong profile as he smiled at the two of them, and in that instant I was in complete and utter awe. These two had three Academy Awards between the two of them, and here they were practically giddy over the prospect of working with my man. *And damn if that doesn't make me proud to be the one on his arm.*

As if Ace had read my mind, he turned to face me and then frowned a little. "I'm sorry. I'm being so rude," he said, and then looked back to the two of them. "I've been so hellbent on keeping things to myself I forgot to introduce—"

"Dylan Prescott," Alejandro said just as Mallory said, "Oh please, Ace. As if everyone in this room doesn't know your lovely young man's name."

See. I knew I liked her. "Lovely…" I said, holding out my hand in her direction. "I'll take that."

As she shook my hand, she laughed, and it was so charming I couldn't help but reply in kind. "Well, you should, you're gorgeous. Ace here's lucky to have caught you before anyone else did."

I was about to respond when she released my hand

and I took her boyfriend's to shake. But when I glanced up at him and met his gaze head-on for the first time, I tripped over my words. "I uh...um..."

Ace chuckled beside me, and I wanted to turn around and whack him in the arm. So sue me, Alejandro was a very attractive man. A very *famous*, attractive man, and it was odd to be the sole focus of someone that felt so familiar because you'd seen him on the big screen. There was no way any normal person, a.k.a. myself, wouldn't get tongue-tied.

"It's nice to meet you, Dylan," Alejandro said.

Locating my tongue, I managed to somehow agree that it was nice to meet him too, and then the moment passed and Ace was talking again. The three of them discussed their upcoming movies and how they thought they would do, and then they both inquired after what I did until Mallory declared she was ready for another Gilligan's Bitch boozy shake and Alejandro excused the two of them and they headed off toward the bar.

As I watched them go, I kept my eyes on them as they wove their way through the crowd.

"So, what do you think of Hollywood's golden couple?" Ace asked, his lips by my ear.

My eyes followed the two of them until they reached the counter, and once they were there and Mallory had leaned over to talk to the bartender, Alejandro glanced over his shoulder, and this time when his eyes met mine and his lips curved in an immoral smile, my breath caught and I coughed.

No way.

There's no fucking way…

But as Alejandro ran his eyes down over me and then they flicked between Ace and myself, I knew I was spot-on.

It appeared that Hollywood's golden couple had a secret even bigger than ours, because I was one hundred percent positive in that moment that I was staring at…Zorro.

* * *

AS MALLORY AND Alejandro left to head over to the bar, I was trying to come up with an excuse Dylan would agree to so we could leave as his fingers tightened around mine. I turned to step in front of him and looked into his wide eyes, and then noticed the way his mouth had fallen open and he seemed to be searching for words.

Star-struck. I knew how intimidating it could be to meet people as famous as those two. I'd been a wreck at my first wrap party too, but that just made Dylan more endearing. That innocence and… *Hang on a second.* Dylan's cheeks had turned bright pink and he kept darting his eyes over my shoulder, which in turn had me looking back. But all I saw was Mallory and—

Oh. My. Fucking. God. My eyes locked with Alejandro's dark ones, and as he swiped his lower lip with his tongue, I had a very immediate reaction to him watching us, just as I had that night at Syn.

No... I had to be imagining this, right? But one look at Dylan's flushed face told me I wasn't. He had recognized him too. Recognized the stranger who had stood across from us, much like Alejandro was now, in the shadows and light as I'd fucked Dylan like I never had before.

"Ace," Dylan whispered, and shook my wrist gently. But it was no use; it was like I was in some kind of trance. Hypnotized by the man still watching us.

How had I missed that? How was it that up close and smiling at us I hadn't put it together, but from a distance one glimpse of that arrogant smirk full of sex and I was right back at the club deep inside Dylan, coming in time with the man I'd just shaken hands with?

I tore my eyes away from the one who'd just rocked my entire world in a matter of seconds and looked at Dylan. I wasn't sure what I expected to find there, but the fevered arousal was not it. His expression was tense, on edge, but not because he was worried or annoyed. Oh no, Dylan had a look he'd once told me meant one thing in particular. He had the look of a man who wanted to be fucked. And I was just the man for that job.

I aimed a look to the exit of the After Dark and said in a tone that was so raspy I was surprised he could hear me, "Let's get out of here."

And Dylan's answering nod was all the permission I required.

10
BLOW
(MY MIND)

IT WAS EVIDENT as we dashed past Ace's friends with just a wave that he didn't seem to mind that we'd spent less than an hour at the party he'd sponsored. But I didn't think he'd fully thought through what the press would think when we emerged onto the sidewalk and the questions started.

"Were you asked to leave the party early?"

"Is it true you're feuding with the cast?"

Jesus, I hadn't even thought about what it would look like if we left early, and Ace hesitated for the briefest of moments. Two seconds later, though, we were moving again, and thankfully our driver had parked directly in front of Licked, so we were through the crowd and in the back of the Town Car in record time.

As we pulled away, I kept my head down, not

wanting to give them a clear shot, but when Ace's palm landed on my thigh, my eyes shot to his. There was a smile playing on his lips as he ran his fingers lightly across the material.

"What?" he asked. "I can't...*soothe* my boyfriend after walking through a group of hungry paparazzi?" The fevered look in his eyes from minutes ago hadn't been tempered; it was even more intense now in the dark, confined space.

"Right here? In the car?" I whispered.

He bit into his bottom lip and his fingers inched toward my cock, which was stiffening at a rapid pace at the arousal I felt radiating off Ace. I managed to tear my gaze away from his to look out the windows, checking to make sure there wasn't anyone staring inside, but I could only see the lights of buildings we passed whiz by.

I tried to keep my voice down so the driver couldn't hear me, but nodded in his direction when I said, "What if someone sees?"

"Guess we'll have to be careful."

Well, shit. "You like taking risks, don't you, Locke?"

When he leaned across the seat and pressed his lips to my cheek, I swallowed back the groan that wanted to slip free.

"I never use to..." Ace said, and then chose that moment to graze his flattened palm over the zipper of my pants. "But lately it's become *harder* to curb my impulses."

I turned my head, and with his face so close I could

see the way his pupils were blown and it had my breathing coming faster.

"Let me touch you," Ace said, and I automatically looked toward the driver, but Ace wasn't having any of that. His hand left its place between my legs to come up and grip my chin, turning my head back so I was facing him, and his eyes fell to my mouth. "Don't worry about him. He's paid well."

Yeah, hell, who was I trying to kid? As if I wasn't going to let him do what he'd just asked. I slid a little farther into the leather of the seat and spread my legs. Ace dropped his gaze down to my movements, and when a rumble of approval left his throat, I close to whimpered.

"See, this won't be hard to achieve at all, will it?"

"Would you stop saying that word right now?" I knew I sounded particularly put out, but good God, I knew my limits and sitting in the back of a Town Car with Ace palming my—*Fuck*—

"*Hard?* Is that what you want me to stop saying? Because, Dylan," Ace said, his warm breath ghosting over my parted lips as he continued to hold me captive with his powerful stare, "my cock's been hard ever since I worked out that Alejandro was the one who watched me fuck you until you couldn't walk that night at Syn."

Damn… The reminder of why we were now in the back of this car speeding across town to Ace's house was enough to have me bucking my hips up against the pressure of Ace's hand.

"Do you remember how it felt?" he asked, as his fingers curled around the erection I now had no hope of controlling. "When I stripped you down to nothing, and had you kneel in front of me? In front of *him*?"

I gasped and reached down with one hand to press *his* more firmly against me. It wasn't enough, though. I didn't think anything could be enough to ease the ache he'd built with his words, the imagery, and the fierce way he was holding my gaze like some kind of sexual magician.

"Do you remember?" he asked again, this time in a voice that said he expected an answer.

I lifted my hand from where it was covering the top of his and gripped his bicep so hard I was surprised he didn't tell me to let up. But if he was going to drive me out of my ever-loving mind with his filthy fucking recap of one of the hottest nights of my life, then I needed something to keep me grounded.

"Yes," I said in a breathy voice I didn't recognize. Ace nodded slowly, and then he reached up to untuck my button-down shirt from my pants, letting the length of it fall over where his hand had grazed only seconds earlier.

When my eyes flitted to the window to see if anyone was pulled up alongside or trailing behind us, Ace's voice snapped me back to him.

"Close your eyes," he said, and I gave him an incredulous look. "Pretend we're back there...back at Syn...everyone's eyes on us as I touch you."

His hand moved under my shirt, and he unbuttoned

my pants and then drew the zipper down. With a devilish smile on his face, his fingers dipped beneath my boxer briefs, and though my shirt somewhat concealed what his fingers were—*fuck*—wrapping around, I still found myself looking at the rearview mirror ahead to make sure the driver wasn't paying attention.

"I won't ask you again," Ace said, his grip firm around my cock, but he wasn't moving it farther, wasn't giving me the friction I needed, so when my hips jerked up, he shook his head. Then his hand began to withdraw, and I quickly grabbed his wrist to stop him.

As he waited to see what I would do, I tried to clear my mind of anything other than the man beside me, daring to make me feel good. Closing my eyes, I let my head fall back against the seat and pushed his hand back down under my briefs. When his finger circled the head of my cock and then slicked the pre-cum down my length, I swallowed the groan that wanted to break free. He curled his hand around me again, gripping the base of my dick, and slowly—torturously—began to move up.

When his fist stroked back down and tightened at the root of my cock, my eyes flew open and I gritted my teeth. Ace's lips curled into a smug smile of someone who knew he held all the power in the exchange going on, and while he was making me crazy, the fact that he felt this kind of freedom around me made me really fucking excited.

Was it really only weeks ago that I wasn't even allowed to be seen *in* a car with him? And now here we were— *Oh God…*

"Problem, Daydream?"

The raspy sound of my name had me reaching for his face, and when I held his cheek in my hand, I searched his eyes for any kind of resistance, any kind of message that I shouldn't do what I knew would be clearly written all over my expression. When I got nothing but another firm pull of my dick, that was it: this teasing fucker was mine.

I ran my hand to the back of his neck and tugged him forward so I could crush our lips together. The pressure around my shaft increased as I speared my tongue between Ace's lips and tangled it with his, and as he began to really work me, I couldn't have kept my hips still if my life depended on it.

I slid my fingers up the back of his neck and over his short hair until I was cradling the back of his head, holding him where I wanted him. *Hot damn.* I wanted to turn to Ace, crawl on his lap, and fuck the fist pumping me. But no matter how much money Ace paid the driver of this car, there was a difference between him seeing us kissing in his rearview mirror and seeing me sitting astride Ace.

I tore my lips from Ace's and snaked a hand down to halt his fingers. As my breathing came in heaving pants, I rested my forehead to his and shut my eyes. If I didn't calm down, I was going to shoot all over his palm in the back of this damn car, and when we neared Ace's gated community I was coherent enough to know that wasn't how I wanted this to end.

"Ace, you need to…" I tried to push him back from me as I saw several flashes going off, but he was nuzzling in against my temple with his arm across my hips and I wasn't about to shove him off me if he didn't want to go.

"Relax," he said, and I caught my breath and moved my head so I could rub my temple to his. The move was both affectionate and incredibly intimate considering where his hand was, and with a quick glance out the window I noticed several random flashes going off as the car drove past and knew they'd get nothing in the darkness of night as we sat behind tinted windows.

"But there are cameras just outside," I said. "And I really would rather come with your cock inside me. Think you can wait the two minutes it's gonna take to pull into your driveway and get inside your front door, hotshot?"

Ace released my aching flesh and drew his hand out of my pants, and when he brushed his sticky, wet thumb over my lip in a dirty caress, I sucked and he growled.

"Two minutes," he warned. "I'm holding you to that." And as the car came to a halt in front of his house, he said, "Zip up, but don't button up. It'll just be a waste of fucking time."

Oh yeah, who in their right mind would ever disobey that command? Certainly not I.

11
STAIRWAY TO HEAVEN

AFTER THE DRIVER left, I turned to see Dylan standing on the front porch leaning against the wall waiting on me. His shirt was untucked and hanging out over his pants and he had a look on his face that screamed one thing—sex.

I reached down to adjust my erection before I headed in his direction, and tried to calm the arousal that was clawing at me. Ever since Alejandro had looked over at the two of us, and the car ride back here, I'd been battling the urge to strip Dylan of his clothes and get my mouth around him or my cock inside him, and it was going to be a miracle if I got him up the stairs to my bedroom before I attacked.

As I walked over to where he stood, his eyes traveled down my shirt and pants, which only made it harder for me to walk, because when he finally brought his gaze back to mine and our eyes clashed, I knew he was feeling it. The tension, the electricity crackling between us, was so tangible it was a wonder the air didn't spark and sizzle when we were within touching distance.

"You could've let yourself in. You have a key and the code," I reminded him as I brought my own key out and inserted it in the lock.

Dylan ran his tongue over his top teeth as his eyelids lowered to half-mast, and the light overhead showed the red tinge on his cheeks as he pushed off the door and took a step up beside me so the entire front of his body was grazing against my arm, hand, and leg.

"But then I would've missed out on this," he said, and leaned in to press a kiss to my jaw.

"If you don't fucking stop—"

"Then what?" he whispered, and then sank his teeth into my jaw as I twisted the key, shoved the door open, and disarmed the alarm. I turned and grabbed a fistful of his shirt, hauling him in close as I walked him backward over the threshold.

"You're really asking for it," I said, and Dylan aimed a smile at me that let me know he knew exactly what he was doing. I kicked the front door shut as my eyes scanned the foyer, searching for the best place to— "*Dylan...*" I said as he slipped a hand down to palm me through my pants.

"I thought you said two minutes. You better hurry if you plan to hold true to *that* promise, Locke..."

As he let go of me and started to move away, I

released his shirt. He winked at me and turned to head toward the stairs. I followed but then had a better idea, and snagged his wrist between my fingers, hauling the smartass back to me.

"Two minutes, you say?" I asked.

As Dylan's eyes narrowed on me, I muscled him backward past the sweeping staircase and around the side. When we reached exactly where I wanted him, I let loose a savage smile, spun him around, and placed my lips by his ear. Then I whispered, "I believe if we do this right here, I'll have seconds to spare. Hands on the banister, Dylan, I'm about to make your knees give the fuck out."

* * *

FUCK, THERE WAS nothing hotter than Ace Locke making sexual demands. The fantasy I'd always had of him was nothing compared to the reality of the man behind me, and I marveled in that moment at how my life had changed. As much as I wanted to turn back around to face Ace so I could watch every dirty thing he planned to do to me, I wanted to please him even more, so I reached up and took a hold of the banister that lined the stairs.

"You planning to strip-search me now, Locke?" I said, and widened my stance.

"Not even close."

Ace pressed himself up against my backside, his

hands unzipping my pants again, and then he stroked his palm along my rock-hard length. As I moaned, his thick erection ground against my ass cheeks, and I cursed that I hadn't shoved one of those lubed condoms in my pocket before we'd left. Now that we'd started, there was no way I wanted to stop. *Fuck.*

"Something wrong?" Ace asked, as he dipped his hand below the elastic of my boxer briefs for the second time tonight. But when he didn't reach for my cock, waiting instead for my answer, I gritted my teeth.

"Swear to God, if you don't let me come in the next minute and a half…"

Without warning, Ace shoved my pants and briefs down my hips in one smooth move, leaving them just under my ass, and then I heard a zipper and the rip of a foil packet.

"You'll what?"

Yeah, genius, whatcha gonna do? Hell if I knew, but the threat had sounded good at the time. I was racking my brain trying to think of something to dish out to the arrogant man behind me, but before I could formulate anything, Ace's large palms were on my bare hips, his fingers spread, as he positioned me exactly where he wanted me.

Ace hummed, and the guttural sound vibrated along my spine to my balls, drawing them up to my body, taut and tense, as he smoothed one of his hands over my ass cheek.

"That's what I thought," he said as his thumb flirted with the top of my crack. "You want this just as badly as I do, and if I want you to wait for thirty minutes…" Ace whispered as his lips caressed over the shell of my ear. "Then you'll stand here and wait for thirty fucking minutes."

Okay...shit. I'm gonna lose it. I'm gonna goddamn lose it if he doesn't stop talking like— "Oh hell, Ace." I moaned when he licked a path up my neck and then placed his left hand over mine where I was white knuckling the banister. I could feel his covered cock grinding against my ass as he kissed and sucked the sensitive skin beneath my ear.

"Luckily for you," he said, "thirty minutes is about thirty too long. God, Dylan, I need to get inside you."

"Yesss..." I said, and Ace brought the hand he had resting on my hip up to my mouth and touched a finger to my lower lip. "Suck."

Sweet fuck. I wasn't sure how he expected me to survive much more of this, but I knew the only way I was going to get what I wanted was if I did what I was told. I'd barely parted my lips when Ace slipped his pointer finger inside along my tongue. A rumbly groan emerged from the man tormenting me as I swirled my tongue around his long digit, and the hand he had curled around mine on the rail above tightened and his hips jutted forward against me.

As I continued to suck on him, he pushed it in and out of my mouth as though fucking it, and then added his middle finger to the mix.

"There you go, Dylan. Get 'em good and wet. Need you ready and stretched before I..." He paused to drag his dick along my crack, and I heard a whimper slip free of me as I shoved back against him, craving the feel of his hot flesh against mine. "Before I unleash on you."

Shit, is he kidding right now? How was I supposed to think or control myself when he was hellbent on destroying any semblance of composure I possessed? I was beyond anything rational at this stage; all I could do was hope to survive because when Ace got like this...when he really let go and was running on raw desire, he was a force to behold. All of that strength, and all of that pent-up emotion, made for a combustible coupling that never failed to leave me close to paralytic, and I *loved* being the one he let loose on.

Ace removed his fingers from between my lips, and when I felt the wet tips of them down between the cheeks of my ass, slicking a path to my pucker, I clamped my teeth into my lower lip.

"No, don't do that," Ace said as he massaged the pads of his fingers over my tight hole. "Don't deny me the pleasure of hearing how much you enjoy what I'm doing to you."

As the word *you* left his lips, he pushed the tip of his finger inside me and I groaned.

"Yeah, Dylan...fuck yes, just like that," he said as he tunneled his finger in deeper, and then he brought his lips to my ear and whispered, "I want to hear the catch in your breath when I sink inside you. And I want to hear you shout the roof off my fucking house when I take you so hard you collapse and I have to carry you up these goddamn stairs."

"*Ahh*, Ace..." I managed as he thrust two fingers

inside me, and bit down on my earlobe.

"Tonight, you're mine. Your frustration," he said, dragging his fingers free so I cried out, begging for him to fill me again—and he did. "Your orgasm. Your pleasure. And your shouts of need," he told me, punctuating each desire with a jab of his fingers before he removed them to grip my hip and the wide head of his covered cock pressed against my hole. "Tonight, all of it is *mine*, Dylan."

Hell if he wasn't spot-on with that, because in that second I would've given my last breath to have him inside me. Luckily, my last breath wasn't needed, just one word. *"Yesss."*

* * *

SOMEWHERE BETWEEN STEPPING inside my house and getting Dylan up against my staircase, I'd lost my mind. Because something about seeing him standing there with his arms raised, his fingers around the wrought iron swirls of my banister, and his black pants shoved down under his ass had brought to the surface a side of myself I was still becoming acquainted with. The side that Dylan had given me permission to let loose on him but I was still learning to accept. Most of the time I was able to temper it somewhat, rein it in a little. But there were other times, like that night at Syn and right now, when I felt as though I was looking through a red haze of lust.

My cock throbbed as it sat poised at Dylan's tight entrance, and the moans that escaped him each time I pushed against that delicious pucker made me tease him more and more. I couldn't explain why hearing his frustration ramped this up, but fuck did it ever. I could see his tense shoulders under his shirt and the way his fingers were flexing every time I rocked gently back and forth, and finally when it appeared he'd had enough, Dylan's head whipped around and his fiery eyes caught mine and I knew he was right there with me.

Red haze.

Lust.

That was what I'd been waiting for. I secured my grip over his on the iron above him and dug my fingers into his hip, and without a word I thrust forward and sank my cock inside the most perfect place it had ever been. Dylan's gorgeous ass.

The shout that ripped free of him was monumentally satisfying as he used the banister to haul himself upright and bow back into me, and I staggered forward, my front slamming into his back as my dick filled him. I was lodged so deep that I couldn't see between our bodies. As we each stood there, our loud panting breaths were the only sounds that could be heard echoing in the cavernous space. The fact that we were as close as two people could possibly be, intimately connected, and yet still both fully clothed, was so unbelievably arousing that I had to shut my eyes for a second and compose myself. I felt like a beast was clawing at me, trying to escape and go wild on the one that was under him, and when Dylan demanded, "Fucking do it," and let go of one of the rails to grab a hold of his cock, I was done for.

I withdrew from his body and then plunged back inside, making him stumble, but he soon got himself stable and shoved back on me with just as much force, his ass swallowing my shaft to the root—*and hell*—my eyes blurred with how phenomenal it felt.

"Dylan…" I said. A warning of sorts as he slid himself off me and then, once again, propelled his hips back, impaling himself.

"Do it," he said, and aimed frenzied eyes my way. "Stop being so damn polite when we both know you're dying to be anything but."

And with those words, something inside me snapped. The hand I had covering Dylan's on the rail moved to the back of his shirt, which was hanging over the two of us, obstructing my view, and now I wanted to see, wanted to watch my shaft disappear in his hole.

I gathered the black material of his shirt and balled it into my fist, and then slid it up his spine to hold it at the back of his neck in a firm grip. As I held it there, I forced Dylan forward until he was so close to the staircase I knew I would be cleaning up the mess he was about to make, as opposed to having to explain it to someone. But for now, watching both of his hands come up and twine around the banister for a better hold, as I began to piston into him with as much power and force as I was capable of, was a rush.

The words escaping Dylan were demanding and uninhibited as he asked for exactly what he wanted from me.

Bite me.

Harder.

More.

Deeper.

Give it to me.

And I did every single thing he asked of me, as he hung on for dear life, and I took him in a way I'd only ever imagined taking someone.

With my hand still gripping his neck, I brought my other one up to cover his on the banister and crushed him to the solid surface of the base of the stairs. I wedged my feet between his as I pounded into him, completely out of my mind with my need and lust for him, and when he turned his head, I caught his lips in an aggressive and bruising kiss.

The taste of him and the moan that drifted past his lips had my orgasm slamming into me, and Dylan jerked his head away and shut his eyes as his arms tensed and his fingers turned white where he had a killer grasp on the rails. Then, without any physical stimulation to his engorged cock, Dylan came with so much passion and force that my breath rushed out of me as my name left his throat on a thunderous shout.

Fuck. That was so damn sexy, and I couldn't help but wonder if he'd be able to talk tomorrow as I slumped against him, curious as to how quickly I could strip him from his clothes and convince him to start round two.

12
PG-13

"ACE," I MUMBLED the next morning through the haze of sleep. His bare chest was currently serving as my pillow, and I snuggled into him deeper, unwilling and unable to open my eyes yet. But the persistent ring of Ace's phone had other ideas.

"Ace." I gave him a gentle shake. "Gonna get that?"

All that greeted me was a grumble, and then Ace's strong arms wrapped around my back, holding me in place against him. His voice was thick with sleep as he said, "They can leave a message."

And just as the words came out of his mouth, the ringing stopped, and with a yawn, I settled back into him. For about five seconds.

As the rings reverberated again off the walls of Ace's

mammoth bedroom, my eyes finally cracked open. Pushing myself up, I said, "Okay, you have to answer that or turn the phone off."

"Too early."

A quick glance at the clock told me otherwise. "Actually, it's after ten."

"What?" Ace said, shooting up in the bed. "How is it after ten?"

Stretching my arms over my head, I gave him a grin. "That's what happens when you fuck me all night." When Ace's brow shot up as if to ask, *Is that a problem?* I added, "Not that I'll ever complain about that."

"That's just cause for more punishment right there," he said, with a sinful smile on his lips, and when he went to move on top of me, I pushed him back.

"Ace, I'm gonna drown your phone in the hot tub if you don't answer it."

His hand went over his heart, and then he laughed and rolled over to grab his phone. He hit the speakerphone button and said, "Hello?"

"Mr. Locke, we've got unannounced visitors at the gate for you."

"I'm sure you do, Pete. All with cameras in their hands, no doubt."

The neighborhood security guard cleared his throat. "Actually, sir, they claim to be your parents."

"My parents?" Ace frowned. "Are you sure?"

"Yes, sir. Dan and Patricia Locke, of twenty-three

Cliff Acre Court in Chicago—"

"Ace Samuel Locke, you tell this young man we didn't fly across the country to see our son through a fence. Now, be a doll and open up."

"Yeah, yeah, that's… Shit. Send them through." Ace rubbed his forehead as Pete acknowledged his request and hung up. Then he looked at me, his face full of apology.

"So…" I said. "Your parents are here."

"And I'm sorry in advance," he said, jumping out of the bed and then throwing on his pants from the night before.

"I think I said those same words to you before you Skyped with mine."

"And the difference there is that your family is chill as hell."

"Chill is definitely the right word."

"Mine are…" Ace hit a button on his phone to open the gate in front of his house. Then he looked at me and shrugged. "Not."

As a silver Mercedes-Benz pulled into Ace's driveway, he leaned over the bed and gave me a quick kiss.

"Just come down when you're ready," he said, and then left the room to head downstairs.

I watched from the window as the car pulled to a stop in front of the house, and a silver-haired man in a pristine suit got out from the driver's seat and went around to the passenger's side to open the door. The woman that stepped out had a shock of short white-blonde hair, and she wore a below-the-knee dress. As Ace's mom took her husband's arm and walked up to the front door, my first thought was that they looked like they were heading to a church service. Ace hadn't spoken much about his parents, but I did know he'd been raised Catholic and was an only child, and, merely from a first impression, I could tell they were the complete opposite to Ziggy and Sunshine.

My second thought was that my pants were still on the floor of the foyer from where I'd kicked them off before Ace and I had gone for round two last night. *Shit. Double shit.* Hopefully Ace had gotten rid of them before they walked in, or that'd be a helluva way to make a first impression. But considering I couldn't just go bare-assed downstairs, I was now officially pantsless. That's what I got for never being presumptuous and bringing an overnight bag.

Rifling through Ace's drawers, I pulled out a pair of jeans that I knew would be way too big on me—his quads were huge—and a plain t-shirt. Best I could do under the circumstances, but then, it wasn't like they were seeing me for the first time either. They were well aware of who their son was dating, and I could only hope this visit was a positive one. Ace had enough people giving him a hard time right now, so the last thing he needed was to have his parents jumping on him.

Voices echoed up from the foyer as I headed to the master bathroom to freshen up, and I felt a slight flutter of nerves in the pit of my stomach.

Time to meet the parents.

* * *

"MOM, DAD," I said, after opening the front door to greet them before they could knock. "This is a nice surprise. What brings you out this way?"

"Look at you, not even dressed yet," my mom said, her sharp eyes giving me a once-over before she stepped inside and greeted me with an air kiss on each side of my face.

"I had a late night."

"Mhmm, so I read." She took out a rolled newspaper from her purse and held it up. On the front page was a picture of me and Dylan with our heads close together in an intimate embrace.

At least they only caught us from the waist up.

"Hey, Dad," I said when he walked inside and gave me the firm, take-no-bullshit handshake I'd learned from him.

Giving me a curt nod, he said, "Good to see you, son."

"Why didn't you tell me you were in town?" I asked.

"It wasn't to ambush you, dear. No need to act so defensive," my mom said as the two of them walked farther into the foyer.

"Of course not," I muttered, closing the door behind

them. And when I turned around to see my mother staring over at the pants that were—*yeah, shit, exactly where I'd stripped them off Dylan the night before*—I jumped into action, stepping around in front of them and ushering them off toward the large sitting room at the front of the house. "It's just you usually call and let me know when you're coming. And it's been, what? Seven…no, eight months since you last visited?"

My mother's heels click-clacked over the tile as she followed behind my father, who'd strolled through the archway entry and headed over to the recliner he favored when he came over. "Ace, let's not play stupid. We raised you better than that," she said.

I slid my hands into the pockets of my crumpled pants, and when I caught my mother's disapproving gaze, I bit my tongue. "So, you're here because of…?"

"Why don't you get dressed and we'll discuss it over brunch?"

"I'm not really up for a big scene today, so why don't we just hang out here and I'll make some tea and coffee—"

"And deprive us of the fabulous restaurants just down the street?" My mom tsked. "We don't get to enjoy the sunshine and fresh air with our meals, so how about you be a dear and run up and get a shower. We'll wait."

I let out a sigh. "Look, I've actually got company, so it's not a great time right now. And you've seen the papers. It's not exactly going to be a fun, quiet outing."

When my mom couldn't hide the sparkle of

excitement that lit her eyes at that comment, I felt a stab of resentment. That was why they were here. For the attention. For their friends at the elite Cliff Acre Country Club to see them in the papers and on TV dining in Beverly Hills, surrounded by a frenzy of people shouting questions at them like they were superstars. I cringed at the thought of anyone enjoying what I tried so hard to avoid, but it wasn't like I hadn't known the kind of people my parents were. They weren't bad people by any means, but they definitely…*enjoyed* the lifestyle my success had afforded them.

"Oh, pish posh," Mom said with a wave of her hand. "You know we don't care about a little ruckus."

Yeah, but I do.

"Why don't you go and get yourself put together and we'll head out on the hour?"

I glanced at the clock to see it was ten fifteen, and wanted to groan. The last thing I wanted to do today was head out for brunch where we would be inundated by every single photographer within a twenty-mile radius. But what was the alternative? Start an argument?

I was about to turn on my heel and head back upstairs to see if Dylan had climbed out one of the windows and shimmied down a drainpipe, when I heard a throat clear from behind me. I pivoted around to see him standing just inside the archway in one of my Nike workout shirts, which swam all over him, and a pair of my jeans that made him look like a wannabe rap artist because they were barely hanging on to his hips.

The chagrined expression on his face was full of apology as he walked over to me, and when the denim slipped a notch and he had to tug them back up his legs, I couldn't help the laugh that escaped me. His eyes darted over my shoulder, and I knew Dylan well enough to know that he wished he looked more put together than he currently was, but hell, he looked kind of adorable. Plus, he wasn't the only one who'd been taken by surprise; I was in last night's dress slacks, which had definitely seen better days, and a faded t-shirt that read *Morning Wood Lumber Company*, and had pine trees across the chest.

Yeah, clearly we hadn't been expecting to receive visitors this morning.

"Hi," Dylan said, giving my parents a smile that was bigger than anything I'd had yet to muster. Then he stepped forward to shake my father's hand. "Dylan Prescott. It's nice to finally meet you both."

My father nodded. "Dan Locke, and this is Patricia."

When Dylan went to greet my mother, she gave him her standard double air kisses—where she'd learned that in the past few years, I had no idea—and then moved back to give him another assessing look.

"You're taller than I thought you'd be," she said, tapping her lips with her pointer finger. "Oh, I don't mean any offense by that, of course. It's just I've seen these actors that work with Ace, and he always towers above them in person. So tiny, these men. They make them much bigger in

Chicago."

Dylan gave her a megawatt smile, the one he'd be famous for sooner than later. "I live in Florida."

"Ah, well then, there you go," she said, nodding, her eyes dropping down to the hand he had holding his—well, *my*—jeans up.

"Sorry," he said, looking down at his outfit. "It's laundry day."

My parents chuckled, and then turned toward each other, a look I couldn't decipher passing between them. When my mother turned back to us, she gave Dylan a pleasant, but stiff, smile.

"Well, dear, it's nice to meet you," she said, and then her eyes shifted to me. "We came by because we were hoping we could take Ace out for brunch to…catch up on things. It's so impersonal to have these conversations over the phone, you know."

But in front of eavesdropping patrons and a fuck ton of paparazzi is much more personal.

Understanding crossed Dylan's face, and he nodded. "Yeah, that sounds great. You should do that." Then he glanced at me. "I've actually got to get going."

"No, you're coming with—" I started, but then my mother chimed in.

"I think it's gracious of Dylan to want to give us family time, don't you?"

No, I don't, I wanted to say, but I could tell by the look on Dylan's face and the way he was slowly backing out of the room to escape that he was more than happy with this arrangement. In all honesty, I would've been okay with the *same* arrangement, but—"Chop chop, Ace. We want to get there and get a good table before all the ones outside are taken"—I had no choice.

With a put-upon sigh, I rubbed a hand over the top of my head and nodded. "Okay. Give me twenty."

My mother finally sat down on one of the couches and crossed her legs as she angled her body toward my father. Then she glanced over her shoulder at the two of us. "Of course, we'll just wait here, dear."

This time when she looked away, I couldn't stop the eye roll, and turned to see Dylan heading toward the stairs. When he got to the bottom of them he stopped in his tracks, and I noticed him looking down at the pants I'd kicked away from us in our haste to get each other naked last night. Then his head whipped around and his eyes found mine and practically drilled a hole in me.

Shit... I gave a "sorry" shrug, because what else could I really do at this stage? I hadn't had time to grab them out of the foyer, and when his cheeks flamed and his jaw ticked, I knew that little fact both annoyed and embarrassed him.

Okay, yeah, I wasn't winning any points with that. So I headed over to grab his pants off the floor, and when I reached him at the bottom of the stairs, he shook his head.

"No wonder they don't want to eat lunch with me."

As Dylan started up the stairs, I followed closely

behind. "Trust me when I tell you, you aren't missing out on anything. But if you want to—"

"Are you kidding me?" he said as we hit the landing and headed down to my bedroom. "I might've wanted to a minute ago, but that was before I knew your mother and father had seen my pants in your hallway, Ace. Jesus."

"Oh please, like they don't know with the way we're dressed what's been happening here. They're fine." Shutting the door behind us, I said, "And trust me when I tell you, the only reason they're here is to see and be seen, and to remind me how badly my career's going down the toilet."

"Don't say that."

"Why not? It's the truth." I peeled off my shirt as I headed into the master bathroom and then started the shower. When I turned around, Dylan was standing in front of me, and I gave him a mischievous grin. "Care to join me?"

"I don't think that's a good idea."

"Why not? Because my parents are downstairs?"

"No, because you only have twenty minutes, and I'm a greedy bastard."

I laughed, and when I grabbed his shirt and pulled him forward, the loose jeans hanging off his hips fell to the ground. Laughing harder, I dropped my hand and said, "Looks like your clothes are throwing themselves at me."

Dylan pulled them back up and held onto them as he grumbled his way out of the bathroom. "Damn muscly giant," he said under his breath.

"Hey, maybe think about bringing some extra clothes

over here next time. And a toothbrush. Maybe the thirteen-inch dildo—"

When Dylan slammed the door shut, I chuckled and kicked off my pants. I'd been half joking, but I couldn't deny the thought of having Dylan's clothes hanging next to mine did amazing things to my heart. And the thought of that thirteen-incher did fucking wondrous things to my cock.

Twenty minutes? I only need five with that wicked-hot visual, regardless of who's downstairs, I thought as I stepped under the spray.

13
TANGLED VINES

"ACE, WHERE'S YOUR boy toy?"

    "Did Dylan already meet the parents?"

    "Is it true you two broke up this morning?"

    As I handed the valet the keys to my Range Rover, I had to stop myself from rolling my eyes at the shouts coming from the photographers lining the sidewalk of The Vine, the popular lunch spot my parents had chosen. *Yeah, popular as in every goddamn celebrity whored themselves out to paparazzi here to get in the news.* Which was exactly what it would look like. You didn't go to places like The Vine if you wanted to stay under the radar, so the fact that I was there, with my parents but without Dylan, would likely set off another shitstorm of gossip.

    My mom took the crook of my arm as I directed her

up the brick walkway that led inside, and as we passed the full-to-capacity patio area, I could feel the stares of the patrons boring holes like bullets into my body.

Smile, asshole, I thought. It was like I'd forgotten how to play the game. How to keep the press and any onlookers charmed by giving a smile, a wave, a friendly quip. Swallowing thickly, I forced a smile on my face and nodded at a few of the people looking in my direction, and then I held open the door for my parents to walk through and stepped inside the arctic interior.

"My, my, all those people there for my boy," my mom said, looking up at me under her long false lashes.

I managed to hold my tongue as the hostess eventually found hers and asked whether we preferred indoor or outdoor dining.

"Indoor—" I started.

"Oh, Ace, it's so chilly in here and I forgot my sweater." Mom rubbed her arms to warm herself and craned her neck to look outside. "We should probably sit under one of those lovely umbrellas and get some fresh air. Don't you think?"

My teeth gritted together so hard at that moment, it was a wonder I didn't spit them out. "Actually, it's a little chaotic out there."

"Oh, I'm sure this lovely young lady can find us something that isn't in amongst all the chaos. Can't you, dear?"

As my mother turned back to the hostess, the girl's

wide eyes flicked to mine, and I could tell she was thinking—*ain't nowhere out there that's not gonna be chaotic when it comes to you*—and I gave her a brief nod, letting her know I was more than aware that what my mother was asking was next to impossible.

"If you could give me one second, Mr. Locke, I'll have a table cleared."

In other words, she was about to go out to the cramped patio and boot someone *less* important from one of the more visible tables. *This is the last thing I wanted to do today.* I had a feeling that not only was I about to get the whole *are you thinking with your head* speech from my parents, it was also about to take place in the middle of a goddamn circus.

"Okay," the hostess said when she came back, rubbing her hands together. She beamed at the three of us, probably extremely proud of the fact she'd snagged herself a celebrity that was going to attract a ton of press for her boss, and then she said, "If you'll follow me."

Without a care in the world, my mother and father began walking after the woman, and I noted the way my mom smiled down at all the eyes watching us weave our way through the tables. She then glanced out at the gaggle of paparazzi pressed up against the white picket fence that surrounded the tiny restaurant, and tucked a piece of her hair behind her ear in a coy move designed to make her look shy and unsuspecting of the attention, when really she was anything but. Me…I was sure I looked like a man being led to his execution.

* * *

"CAN I SAY it? You know I've been dying to."

I could practically see Derek's self-satisfied face through the phone, and I rolled my eyes.

"If you must," I said.

"Oh, I must, you withholding motherfucker. Or should I say Ace Locke fucker?"

"Me, withholding? You didn't tell me Jordan's name for years, dick."

Derek's laugh was loud and obnoxious. "See? You didn't deny that you're an Ace Locke fucker. Now we're getting somewhere. Speaking of, where are you this time? His house? His bed? His Ferrari? Fiji?"

"He doesn't have a Ferrari."

"Aaand he deflects again, ladies and gents."

"Not deflecting," I said, leaning back against the couch and mindlessly flipping through the limited channels.

"Bullshit. He's there, isn't he?"

"No."

"Why's it so quiet, hmm? You got his mouth otherwise occupied?"

"Fuck off." I stopped flipping the channels when a shaky image of a man's profile came across the screen, as if the cameraman was running toward the object of his attention. When they came to a stop and refocused on the man and the older couple sitting opposite him, it became more than clear where Ace's parents had decided they'd go for lunch today. *Ah hell.*

"He on his knees?" Derek asked.

As the camera zoomed in on Ace's chiseled profile, I could see the way his jaw was clenched shut, a thunderous expression on his face, and when he spoke, his lips moved so fast you couldn't get a read on what he was saying. But whatever it was, it didn't look like it was good.

"Oh god*dammit.*" I gripped the back of my neck and watched as Ace's mom responded to whatever he said with a smile, and when she was done, she casually looked at the camera and gave a little nod.

"Dude, it was a joke," Derek said, reminding me he was still on the phone.

"Yeah, shit...sorry, man. I know that, it's just—" I cut myself off and wondered if I was crossing any lines by telling Derek to switch on the TV. But deciding I needed someone other than myself to freak out about this with, I said, "Turn on channel"—I racked my brain, trying to remember the Florida channels—"two."

"Huh?"

"Just turn on channel fucking two, Derek."

"Jeez, Prescott. Cool your jets. One sec." There was some rustling in the background as I continued to sit on the edge of my couch with a death grip on the back of my neck, and then Derek was back. "*Holy.* Shit."

"Yeah," I said as the image on the screen switched to some other cameraman's feed, and he was clearly not as fortunate as the paparazzo who'd bolted across the street for a prime view, because this was a panoramic shot of the street, and to say Ace had attracted a crowd was a mighty big understatement.

"Christ," Derek said as I got to my feet, unable to sit still. "Check out that headline scrolling across the bottom."

As if I could miss it. Bold print in the box down at the bottom of the screen read, DYLAN BREAKS ACE'S HEART; REFUSES TO MEET HIS PARENTS.

"You're really dating him, aren't you?"

At Derek's question, I began to pace back and forth in my tiny apartment. "I didn't realize that was still a question. Unless you believe that trash."

"Dylan...you're dating Ace fucking Locke. Until you call and say, hey, Derek, everything you've read is true and I really am seeing Hollywood's biggest action star, I ain't gonna jump on the bandwagon of speculation."

It was that right there that made Derek Pearson someone I knew I would always be able to trust. Someone I knew I could have a moment of *oh shit* with, and it was also right then that I realized...I hadn't had a moment to even *have* that yet.

"So...?" he said, and I let out a breath.

"Yes. I'm dating Ace Locke."

Derek's booming laugh crashed through the phone and into my ear, and even with everything I was seeing on the TV, I felt a grin tug at my lips.

"Dude...he's a goddamn superstar. I mean, I know I said you would go off one day and marry some rich fucker. But really, Ace Locke?"

"Trust me, I'm as surprised as you."

"Come on, give me details. What's he like, all tough and shit?"

Deciding to have a bit of fun with Derek, I said, "Yeah, real tough. Whenever he steps in a room, explosions go off, and every now and then he'll throw in a commando roll."

"Hey, fuck you, man."

"Nah, I think you'd like him. He's...very..." I couldn't think of one damn thing to say that would encompass all that Ace was. He was kind, generous, humble, and, yeah, sexy, but I wasn't about to tell Derek all that and get accused of turning into a sappy bastard.

"At a loss for words? Wow. How about you bring him down here for a visit and let us see for ourselves, yeah? Introduce him to the family and shit?"

"Uh..." I thought about Ace in the same room with Sunshine, Ziggy, and Lennon, and chuckled. "I hadn't thought much about it until now, but maybe one of these days. I do need to head down there soon."

"You do that, Prescott. We'll throw a killer welcome party for your man."

I laughed. *Yeah, no doubt.* "Appreciate that. Talk later."

"Yeah, later."

When I ended the call, my eyes flicked back up to the screen to where half of the TV focused on Ace. His face had gone red as he sat there stabbing at something on his plate, while the other side of the screen was a reporter giving a play-by-play of what she assumed was happening.

Maybe I should've gone to lunch with them after all. At least then he wouldn't have to take the brunt of what his parents were discussing alone.

* * *

I AM IN hell. This was the thought that was playing on a friggin' loop in my mind as I sat center stage in my worst nightmare.

To my left, it felt as though the entire population of L.A. had gathered on the sidewalk of The Vine with a camera in their hand, and across from me sat my mother, preening for the vultures as they snapped shot after shot of the most uncomfortable lunch I'd ever had the displeasure of sitting through. On my *mother's* left sat my father, and to his credit he wasn't hamming it up as much for the spectators, but he wasn't doing much to stop my mother's sole focus of this meal beyond the fame this little outing was garnering. And that was to tell me what a colossal mistake I was making in openly acknowledging my relationship with Dylan. Her last statement, actually giving me the need to cut something, beyond the steak in front of me.

"Well, dear. What do you say?" my mother started up again, relentless in her quest now that she'd posed the most insulting of questions to me. I knew my face had to relay to everyone who was looking—and I was convinced that was well over a hundred people at this stage—just how disgusted I was. But at least the sunglasses I'd jammed up my nose to cover my eyes could hide some of the...what? *Shock, hurt, and anger...*that my parents were doing this here—in public.

"What do I say?" I said between clenched teeth. I leaned across the table until I could lower my voice to a whisper and know I would still be heard, and asked, "Are you serious? Do you really for one second think I would do what you just suggested?"

My mother's eyes widened a fraction at the tone of my voice, but I'd just about had all I could take. And considering that was probably more than the average person being drilled about their love life, I thought she was lucky I hadn't gotten up from the table and walked the fuck out.

Trying to continue the ruse of a happy family outing, my mom reached for her water and took a sip before replying. "I think you should consider it carefully, Ace. We are only thinking of your career and all your hard work."

"I'm not going back in the fucking closet, no matter how many jobs I lose."

"Ace—" my dad started, but I shook my head.

"No, you two don't get to have an opinion anymore

about how I live my life. I did what you said for years, too many years, and I was miserable. I'm not putting a woman on my arm and calling it a day. No one would believe it now anyway."

"Just think about what you're doing," my mom said in a hushed whisper, cracks of frustration beginning to show through her sweet tone. "Look at the roles you've already been fired from. And your spokesman responsibilities? We're talking millions of dollars here, Ace. You might not recover from this."

"If I don't, I've got more money than I know what to do with."

"You think that now, but what will you *do* with your life?" she said.

My lips went tight. "I guess I'll take up a pottery class. Try my hand at bartending. Or *maybe* I should just find something a little gayer—"

"That's enough," my father said, and my mom put her hand over his in a move that had him shutting his mouth.

Then she gave a quick side-glance at the camera and when she looked back at me, she smiled. "Look, sweetie, we aren't saying you can't be"—her eyes darted around us and she leaned forward—"*gay*. That's your choice and your private life, but this is about so much more than that. I mean, Dylan seems like a nice enough man, but is he really worth throwing away everything you've worked so hard for—"

"Yes!" I exploded, and the chatter going on around

us ceased. All eyes—well, the ones that weren't already on us—turned in our direction, and I had to physically put my hand over my jaw to keep it shut. It wasn't like I didn't know this conversation was coming. Hell, my parents had been helping arrange my "girlfriends" for years, but I didn't think they'd want to put me on blast in public, not when any of these people could, and would, go running to those cameras after we left with the scoop.

I pushed the plate away, too sick to my stomach to even try to shove anything into it. When I looked up again, my mom had a heartbroken expression, and I knew what that meant—the tears were next. They usually worked on me, too, but not this time. Whatever was coming was getting shut down real fast.

"But…what about us?" she said in a small voice. "Haven't you thought about what people will think of us—"

"No," I said.

"And what if we end up destitute? We're retired now, and your father has bad knees, so how can you ask us to go back to work—"

"Okay, just stop right there. You know damn well you both are set for life. If what I've put aside for you isn't enough, take it all. I don't want it. I'm happy for the first time in my life. Do you understand? Can't you just let me have that?" Not even caring about the answer, I stood, and wasn't oblivious to the way everyone watching angled their cameras to get the shot of me on my feet.

Ugh, this fishbowl routine was making me want to

fucking scream. The pressure from every facet of my life was closing in on me, and the longer I stayed there, the more claustrophobic I felt. This was the problem with this level of fame. Oh, it came with a lot of glitz, glam, and money. But every little thing you did was monitored. It was judged, scrutinized, and analyzed until you wanted to rip your damn hair out. And the longer I sat there without Dylan by my side and an angry expression on my face, the more I knew the stories circulating were gonna be so jacked up I would want to kick everyone's ass.

I tossed my napkin onto the table and glared down at my parents. "I'm leaving," I announced, just in case that wasn't clear. "I'll let the hostess know to bill me once you're done, and I'll have Frank come and pick you up."

"What? *Ace*," my mom said, her eyes as round as the bread plate in front of her, scandalized now. "You are not walking out of here and leaving us. Sit down."

"No. I'm done. This conversation is over." As I bit out the last word, a young woman chose that unfortunate moment to interrupt me.

"Excuse me, Mr. Locke?"

"What?" I snapped in a caustic tone as I whirled around to see a petite brunette with a pen and notepad in her hand. *Is she for fucking real?*

It confounded me, the presumptiveness of the public. I understood my role, I loved my fans, but at some point I had to wonder if they forgot that we were human beings too. Because I couldn't believe that anyone who saw me in this moment would believe it was a good time to come and ask for an autograph. Yet here she was, looking up at me as if I should just expect this kind of shit—and really, I should, right?

Jesus, the throbbing in my head was relentless, and I knew if I didn't get out of there soon I was about to go postal.

"I'm sorry, it's just…you're my favorite actor, and it's my birthday, and oh my God, I can't believe I'm actually meeting you." The girl's eyes glistened in excitement, a bright pink flush stained her cheeks, and I immediately felt the stab of guilt.

I rubbed my hand over my head and tried for a smile. "Well, happy birthday…?"

"Oh! It's Amanda," she said, and then bit down on her lip. "I mean, I'm Amanda."

"Happy birthday, Amanda," I said, nodding, and then I took the pen and paper from her. I scribbled out a quick message and signed my name, and when I handed the pad back to her, she put her hand on my arm.

"Can I have a hug too?"

"Uh…sure."

"Ah, thank you," she said, throwing her arms around me. "*Thief of Joy* is my favorite movie ever. I think I've seen it a hundred times."

"Thanks, it's one of my favorites too."

"And, um, I just wanted to say…" She lowered her voice and I bent my head down to hear her. "I think you and

Dylan are really cute. Like, together."

When she pulled away, I swallowed hard. That was the first time anyone outside of Shayne and the girls had said anything even halfway accepting of Dylan and me, and I was struck by the emotion triggered by that one sentence spoken by a stranger.

I couldn't find any words for the longest time, and then I finally managed to say, "I appreciate that," before she headed back to her table and proudly showed off the message to the group she was dining with.

As I headed out to the valet, however, any sentimental feeling that'd been stirred got stomped to the ground. Once I stepped onto the sidewalk, at least a dozen or more different cameras were in my face, so many questions being shouted at me that I could barely decipher them individually.

"Ace, are you ditching your parents to fend for themselves because they disapprove of your relationship?"

It was like I was in the middle of a hurricane, photographers swirling around me on all sides, blocking my path as I struggled to shove myself through. My patience was wearing thin, as I said, "Please move."

"Ace, aren't you worried that Dylan could be using you for money after growing up in foster care?"

I stopped and scanned the sea of faces for the asshole that had said that. *Are they fucking serious with this shit?*

"Can we just ask you —"

"Get out of my face," I growled, holding up my hand

to block the lens of the camera directly in my eye line. The flashes were blinding, and on top of that, I couldn't see past the people crowding in on me to even take a step. "You need to move or someone's going to get hurt."

I pushed my way toward the driver's side of my SUV, and I didn't give two fucks that it sent people stumbling backward.

As I slammed the door shut and put the car in drive, I could only inch forward because of the mob surrounding the vehicle. All I could do was lay my fist down on the horn and pray I had enough patience to not run anyone over today.

* * *

I WAS STANDING at the counter in my miniscule kitchen with my cell phone secured between my ear and neck as I scribbled down the final date my agent Claudia had just relayed through the phone. The TV was on across from me, but the entertainment program that had been running round-the-clock surveillance on Ace's lunch outing had gone to commercial after telling its viewers to stay tuned because they wouldn't want to miss what was coming up next. Personally I wished their signal would fail so no one would find out what was up next, but so far...willing that to happen had yet to make it so.

"Dylan?" Claudia said, recapturing my attention. "Did you get all of that?"

I scanned the offers, and the companies *doing* the offering, and had to remind myself again that this was my life. It was ludicrous.

These were dream jobs. *My* dream jobs. But they had all been on my radar for years from now. Goals to work toward when I'd come out here to L.A. Now, all of a sudden, after being connected to Ace, I had a deluge of work coming my way from all corners of the world and it was…it was… *Well, it's overwhelming, and damn exciting.*

Ace had been adamant that I enjoy the perks of what was coming my way, telling me it might be the one positive, work-wise, to eventuate from it. But I was still hesitant to actually believe any of it was real.

"Yeah, I got it. So I have the next couple of weeks free and then shit's gonna get insane?"

"Insane in the best possible way ever. Dylan, you're about to become one of the world's most sought-after models."

And it's words like that which make this all seem unbelievable. I was about to ask her if tomorrow morning was okay for me to come down and sign these contracts and get a proper schedule of my upcoming shoots when there was a loud banging on my front door.

"Hang on a sec, would you, Claudia?"

"Sure thing, hon."

I tossed the pen down on the notepad and headed to the door when the pounding started up again, and I had a feeling I knew exactly who was on the other side of the—

"Hey," I said by way of greeting as I opened the front door.

"Hey," was Ace's gruff reply as he brushed by me and marched inside. I saw the familiar swarm of photogs down on the lawn clicking away, and it took everything inside of me not to give them the finger.

Lifting the phone back to my ear, I said, "Claudia, I'll have to call you back," and then shoved my cell in my pocket. Ace's eyes were on the television screen, and I reached for the remote and quickly shut it off.

"I'd ask how you are, but..." I said, tossing the remote on the couch.

"Yeah. Not fucking good."

"I can see that. Saw that."

"I can't do this anymore."

My heart dropped to the pit of my stomach, and the blood in my veins turned to ice. As Ace's gaze lifted to mine, there was a defeated expression there that I hadn't seen from him before, but it was also mixed with a spark of rage, and that look had me terrified to hear his next words. He was going to say it was too much. That I wasn't worth the harassment he endured every time he stepped out of the house. That our relationship couldn't sustain the blow his career had taken. That it had been fun, a nice dip in the relationship waters, but it wasn't the right time, and I wasn't the right guy.

"I'm sorry," he said, and then he turned away, his

hand squeezing the back of his neck. "I thought I was stronger than this, but I can't..."

Unable to stand still, I took the steps needed to reach him, and even though I knew what he was going to say, I still needed to touch him.

"Ace. It's okay," I said, wanting to reassure him that I wanted what was best for him even if it meant breaking my heart.

He whirled around so fast it knocked my hand off. "Can we just go? Somewhere? Anywhere?"

"What?"

"They're everywhere, following us constantly, saying the most horrible shit, and I can't even escape my goddamn parents. Let's just go away."

My brain was trying to keep up with what he was saying, but all I could feel was relief that the words I'd been expecting hadn't come out of his mouth. Instead, he wanted to— "You want us to go away somewhere...together? Am I hearing you right?"

"Well, I'm not leaving without you."

I knew the smile that spread across my face then had to be super out of place, but damn if what he'd just said didn't melt the ice from seconds ago.

"What on earth could you possibly have to smile about right now?"

"I'm sorry," I said, sounding anything but as I took a step to him and wrapped my arms around his waist. When I leaned back a little I continued to beam up at him, and Ace's frown merely deepened between his brows.

"Okay, you're starting to appear a little deranged now," he said.

"I *thought* you were here to break up with me, you big…"

"Be nice…" he warned, his frown finally beginning to relax.

"I was going to be," I said, and kissed my way up his jaw line to his ear. "You just about gave me a heart attack because I thought you were here to end things, you big, sappy bastard." His chest rumbled against me and I nipped at his earlobe, happy that I'd gotten him to relax into me. "So where do you want to go?"

"Koh Samui? Hawaii? Vanuatu?"

"Where the fuck is Vanuatu?"

"It's a little island off the coast of Australia, about as far away from here as I can think to go."

I smoothed a hand down his chest and rested it over his heart. I could feel it pounding out a steady rhythm as he stood there waiting for my answer, and I twisted my lips.

"Actually…I have somewhere better in mind."

"You do, huh?"

I nodded, then patted his chest as I stepped away to grab my cell phone. "Now, how quickly can we leave?"

14
BETTER THAN
THE MOVIE

"YOU'RE KINDA CUTE when you're nervous," Dylan said, his lips quirking up as he looked over at me.

"I'm not nervous."

"You're fidgeting."

"I'm not—" Glancing down at where I'd been twisting the watch on my wrist, I quickly let go, and Dylan reached over to grab my hand.

"Mhmm. Hard to believe Ace Locke gets nervous about anything, but here you are, nervous about—"

"Meeting your friends. Your family. Yeah, no pressure."

"Exactly. *No pressure.* That's why we're here. To relax and fucking breathe, and I promise you that no one here will be on your ass."

"Except for you, I hope." I grinned at him, and his answering dimples made me wish we'd gone off to somewhere a little more private. The world at our fingertips, and my guy wanted to be here, in sunny, humid Florida. But Dylan hadn't seen his friends and family in months, and as apprehensive as I was about meeting the people he cared about most, I was also a little excited—not that I'd tell him. I'd never met the family of anyone I'd dated before, because they'd all been such insignificant relationships that it hadn't much mattered. But I knew my future lay with the man beside me, and that meant this was an important first visit.

"It's just going to be Derek, and trust me, he's going to be more nervous than you when you step through the door."

I narrowed my eyes on the wicked gleam of mischief on Dylan's face. "He doesn't know we're coming?"

Dylan grinned. "Now where would the fun be in that?"

"Why do I get the feeling you are up to no good?"

"Because you're a smart man."

"Dylan…maybe you should call him. He might not want-—" When Dylan busted up laughing, cutting my words short, I frowned.

"I'm sorry," he said, trying to compose himself. "You just don't know how wrong you are. He's going to die when he sees you. Plus, this is my house too. I can bring whoever I want over."

I knew that was supposed to reassure me, but I still wasn't convinced that anyone would enjoy being surprised with a guest in their house. Especially one that could potentially come with a trail of photographers. The one saving grace so far for having left on the spur of the moment was that no one knew where we were...yet.

I took in a deep breath and looked out the window as the car drew to a stop at the curb of a modest one-story home. There was a black Jeep parked in the drive, but beyond that no activity outside. It was a welcome relief. The quiet and stillness of it all.

"You good?" Dylan asked, and I turned to face him knowing it was my turn to reassure him. I squeezed his fingers and nodded, and when he rewarded me with a blinding smile, I couldn't stop myself from leaning in, cupping his cheek in my hand, and pressing a soft kiss to his lips. When I pulled away, I skimmed the pad of my thumb over his cheek and his gorgeous green eyes opened.

"Thank you for bringing me here," I said, and Dylan gently bit his lower lip in a way that made me want to kiss him forever.

God, how was it that I was sitting here with him? How was it possible that I was this damn lucky?

"Thank you for being here," he said when he pulled away and then reached for the door handle just as the driver opened it wide. "Ready?"

I let out a feigned groan, and then followed him to the trunk to grab our suitcases. Directly across the street from their house was a long stretch of white, sandy beach, interspersed with fewer people than I'd expected during this time of year. The clear aquamarine water beckoned, and I knew it would be a warmer welcome than the frigid Pacific waves I was used to. As I took a deep lungful of the salty air, my body began to relax for the first time in weeks. Dylan was right. This was exactly what I needed—what *we* needed.

As we headed up the sidewalk, Dylan reached for the keys he'd tucked away in his pocket, and it struck me as strange that *this* was his home. Not the cramped studio in L.A., but this house I'd never seen before, almost three thousand miles away from where I lived, and not only that, but he shared this place with another man. I didn't know anything firsthand about his life here, and that realization had the nerves dissolving and a burning curiosity roaring to life instead.

Dylan unlocked the front door and pushed it open, giving it a few loud raps before walking on through.

"Honey, I'm home," he called out, rolling his suitcase into a small, but nicely furnished living room and dropping the keys on a side table.

"What the shit," I heard a guy—presumably Derek— say from somewhere in the back of the house, and then his heavy footsteps were heading toward us. I'd never actually seen a picture of Dylan's friend and roommate before, but when a tattooed man in a black tank, camo shorts, and black combat boots stepped into view, toweling off a head full of wet brown hair, I knew who he was immediately. Dylan's description of the guy had nailed him to a T—including the brash greeting he gave as he caught sight of his friend.

"Dude, how the hell are you just gonna slide into town the day after you told me you weren't coming anytime soon? I could've picked your ass up from the airport." Dylan met Derek halfway across the room, and clapped hands with the guy before giving him a hug.

"No need. I actually brought—"

"Holy fucking shit." Derek's eyes landed on me from over Dylan's shoulder, and Dylan turned around and gestured in my direction.

"Ace," he finished.

* * *

AS I STOOD there beside Derek staring at the man lingering in our foyer, I had to agree with Derek's assessment, because if someone had told me before I left for L.A. that the next time I came home Ace Locke would be with me, I would've called them a big fucking liar.

But…there he was. A suitcase by his side, his hands shoved in the pockets of his shorts, and a half-smile on his face. And though he looked a little anxious, to me he'd never looked handsomer.

"Derek—" I started, but Derek waved me off and took a step forward.

"You're…" he said, and then stopped and looked at

me over his shoulder, and I couldn't help the smirk on my face as he then looked back to Ace, whose lips tugged into a smug line of their own. *Oh yeah, this is sweet.* It wasn't often Derek Pearson was rendered mute, but hell if this wasn't a satisfying moment. It was an awesome sight to see two of the cockiest men I knew tiptoeing around the other.

"You're Ace Locke," Derek informed Ace, just in case he'd forgotten. Then he whipped his head back to look at me, and his eyes were massive. "You brought Ace fucking Locke to our house without telling me?"

I couldn't help the *yes I did* smile that was now spread across my entire face. Then I caught Ace move, and my eyes flicked up to see him step forward to stop just in front of Derek, who'd now turned back to face him. Ace held his hand out, and when Derek raised his to take it like a robot, Ace flashed his thirty-million-dollar smile and shook it.

"You would be right. I am Ace Locke. And you must be Derek, the guy I have to thank for not being able to get it up."

Oh no he didn't.

Derek's eyes bugged out of his head as he continued to shake Ace's hand, and his mouth opened and shut several times, like he was trying to work out a response and physically couldn't.

I couldn't help the laugh that escaped me then. "Okay, I need to record this moment, because a speechless Derek is not one we'll ever see again."

"What… I can't believe… Shit," Derek said, and Ace pulled him forward to clap him on the back.

"Sorry, man, I couldn't resist," Ace said with a chuckle. "But seriously, I've heard a lot of great things about you."

"Unless it was about my ten-inch dick, don't believe a word that asshole says." When we laughed harder, Derek turned back to me and pointed. "I can't believe you did that, man. You better keep one eye open when you sleep."

"You forget I'll have Ace Locke sleeping with me. I'm pretty sure he could take you."

Derek scoffed, but when he eyed the size of Ace's biceps in person, he twisted his lips. "The fuck do you bench-press? A cow?"

"About three eighty-five on a good day."

Derek's eyes popped wide, and he nodded slowly. "Right…uh…well, come on in." He motioned toward the leather couch and chairs, and then plopped himself in one as Ace took a spot on the couch. I grabbed a couple of bottled waters out of the fridge and then took the empty place next to Ace. When I settled in beside him and rested a hand on his thigh, I caught a brief tensing in Ace's body, and then, as if he realized this was a safe place, he relaxed into himself.

"So is it okay for me to ask how in the world you ended up with Prescott here? Tell me to butt out if I'm being too nosy—"

"Butt out," I joked, and Derek flipped me off, making Ace chuckle.

"Nah, you're fine," Ace said, and then shifted on the couch to lay his arm across the back of it. *Look at him getting all cozy,* I thought, as I snuggled into his side, knowing Derek wouldn't bat an eye at the move. "I actually nearly hit him with my car."

"Get the fuck out of here."

"It's true," I said, then uncapped my water and took a swig. "Then he proceeded to be a jerk about it."

"I guess that's about right. I was ready to give the new guy a piece of my mind once I found out we were working together but then I realized…" When Ace trailed off, Derek looked to me then back to Ace.

"You realized…?"

"He realized I was the guy on the billboard he'd been drooling all over for weeks," I said.

As Derek let out a rumbling laugh, I angled my head back so my eyes found Ace's, and I waggled my eyebrows.

"You're a troublemaker," he said with a grin. "How did I not know this?"

"Because you were too busy trying to get in my pants."

Ace's cheeks flushed bright red, and when his eyes darted over to Derek, I leaned up and kissed him just by his ear. "Relax, he's cool."

"Plus," Derek said, "you forget I know this guy. He's been watching you on his private DVD collection for years."

"Derek, shut the fuck up," I said.

"What? It's true."

"You were right there watching them with me," I pointed out.

Derek's eyes shifted between the two of us and then landed on Ace's. "For very different reasons, I would like to note."

"Yeah, whatever, Pearson. You were just as—"

"Right, Ace," Derek interrupted, glaring at me like he was going to throw his water in my face. "Want a tour? I believe Dylan has a nice little setup you would be very interested in just down the hall."

"He already knows I'm a fan—"

"An *obsessive* fan?"

"Not the word I'd use."

"Dude, if you were in high school, you'd have posters of his ass all over your room, don't lie."

"Jesus," I said, and chanced a look at Ace's face to see how freaked out this conversation had him. But he was grinning, clearly enjoying hearing Derek's take on my...err, fandom.

"Well, if it's any consolation," Ace said, his eyes locking on mine, "I'd still put up a poster of this guy. That's a great idea, actually… Let me see if I can call in a favor to Calvin Klein for a copy of that hot shot."

I groaned and shook my head. "Absofuckinglutely not. No way."

"Hey, speaking of, pretty boy," Derek said, "don't you have some Gucci shit to shoot or something? I thought we wouldn't see you for a few more months."

"You complaining about me being here?" I teased.

"Hell no. You know better. But you didn't give me time to plan that killer party."

Ace's forehead lifted. "Killer party?"

"Derek wanted to get the crew together to give you a welcome party when I brought you down here. But that's too mu—"

"Awesome," Ace said.

"Awesome?" I asked. "I thought you wanted some downtime and peace and quiet."

"I wouldn't mind meeting your friends while we're here."

"Really?"

"Really."

Derek slapped a hand on his knee and got to his feet. "Looks like I'd better get started, then. How long you in town for?"

"I've got to be back for a shoot in a couple weeks."

"Perfect." Derek grabbed his wallet and keys from the coffee table, shoved them in his pocket, and then held out a hand to Ace. "I've gotta get to work and make some phone calls for the party, but it was great to meet you, man."

"Yeah, likewise," Ace said, and then Derek pointed at me.

"Don't think I'm gonna forget. One eye open, fucker."

Laughing, I nodded, and watched Derek head out. As the sound of his boots on the pavement faded, I shifted and then climbed onto the couch to straddle Ace's lap. I looped my arms around his neck, and when his hands moved down to my hips and pulled me in closer, he grinned, and I smacked a quick kiss to his lips and said, "So, wanna see my bedroom?"

* * *

THERE WERE SO many things I liked about the man clambering off my lap, but when he held out a hand to me with a bright smile, this side of him was fast becoming my favorite. It was clear that here, Dylan was completely at home, and that ease and simple acceptance was something I'd longed for my entire life. It was funny that in a little more than twenty minutes I felt more myself than I ever had before, and it was all to do with the man whose fingers were now wrapping around mine as I pushed off the couch and got to my feet.

"Do I look stupid to you?" I asked as I took a step closer to Dylan only to have him back away from me and tug on my hand.

"No. You look...really, *really* sexy sitting in my living room. But," he said, raising a hand, "I will not be distracted by all that Locke charm."

"Oh you won't, huh?"

Dylan continued backward pulling me along with him. His eyes were sparkling as he ran them over me.

"Nope. You see, there's something I want more than anything else in the world right now."

Playing along, I followed him down the hall and past two doors. Then he stopped at the final one on the left, which was shut, and I couldn't help myself from putting my hands on either side of his head and ghosting my lips over the top of his. "And what's that?" I whispered.

Dylan sucked in a shaky breath, and as his eyelids lowered to half-mast, he wasn't the only one left breathless. *Christ.* "Pretty boy" was what Derek had called him, and I remembered Russ using the term once also, and as we stood there in his hall, which had slivers of sunlight slipping through the windows, I was taken away by just how striking Dylan was.

Before I could comment, or crush his mouth under mine, though, the tease slipped away and into the room behind him. As I took a step inside, he continued to back up and nod. "Yes...see. This right here," he said, shaking his head as if in disbelief. "This is what I wanted. Ace Locke standing in *my* bedroom."

I glanced at my surroundings, a neatly made queen-size pushed up against the far wall, a window cracked enough to let in the breezy beach air, and on the far side opposite the bed was a dresser with a large TV. But that wasn't what caught and held my attention. No, that honor went to the tall bookcase beside it, which housed an extensive DVD collection.

Okay, Daydream, let's see just how big a fan you are.

The first thing I noticed when I walked closer to the bookcase was that they were all in alphabetical order, same as my collection back home. I wanted to make a joke about us being anal, but then I figured that punch line was a little too easy, so I scanned through the titles instead, and the farther I went, the bigger my eyes got. *Fuck me*, he wasn't kidding.

When I looked up at Dylan, he just shrugged as if to say *told you*, and his expression was so unapologetic it sent a sharp spike of lust straight to my dick. Glancing back at the collection, I swept over the titles until I found the one I was looking for, and then I pulled out the DVD case and held it up.

"Mmm, *Original Bourbon*, one of my favorites." Dylan nodded in approval as I sauntered toward him.

"I bet I can guess your favorite scene," I told him.

"Oh, you think so, huh?"

I pushed Dylan back onto the bed, and as he laughed in surprise, I crawled up between his thighs and hovered over him, placing my hands on either side of his head.

"This position does seem vaguely familiar," he said, smiling broadly as my hips grazed against his. "There was just one major difference—it wasn't you on top."

"Ah, that's right." Rolling us over so Dylan was now on top, I said, "What else?"

"Well, I'm pretty sure she wasn't facing you."

"No?"

Dylan shook his head and stood up, then he turned

around and straddled my hips again. Looking over his shoulder, he said, "Now all we're missing is that bottle of High Horse bourbon."

"Okay, now you're starting to freak me out."

"Liar."

"You're right," I said, running my hands up his legs. "I must be a sick fuck that this is hot right now. But the thought of you lying in bed, memorizing every detail...damn."

"It's no different than you fucking yourself to the thought of my pictures, right?" He pulled the zipper of my jeans down, and when his palm ran over the erection straining against my briefs, I arched my hips up into his touch.

"Right?" he asked again, and aimed a look over his shoulder, waiting for my response.

"God yes."

When he turned his attention back to what he was doing, I couldn't have kept my hands to myself if I tried. I ran them over his hips and then up his sides as he slipped his fingers beneath the elastic of my briefs, and when they grazed over the swollen head of my cock, I groaned.

"Oh fuck. Do that again," I said, and Dylan was quick to comply, but this time he trailed his wet fingers down the underside of my shaft, shoving my briefs aside. As my dick sprang free, he wrapped his hand around my length and gave a firm tug. I dug my fingers into his thighs as Dylan continued to tease and torment the ache throbbing between my legs, and I widened them to give him better access. My breathing was labored as he slid his fist up and down my length from root to tip, and it was all I could do not to flip him back over, rip his pants off, and shove inside of him.

"Dylan," I said, when he slipped a hand down between my legs to cup my balls.

"*Ace...*" the flirt astride me moaned, and then canted his hips toward what his hands were doing, giving me a perfect view of his upturned ass as he began to rock over the top of me.

I gripped him around the waist and shut my eyes as I halted his wayward hips and said in a gruff voice, "Get undressed."

Dylan glanced back at me, and the arousal was stamped all over his features. Flushed cheeks, dilated eyes, and wet, plump lips that had been sucked between his teeth as he'd teased me, and the look of him just made me even more turned on. He climbed off me and stood by the bed, and as I went to sit up and do the same, he shook his head and placed a palm on my chest, shoving me to my back.

"You stay like that, hotshot," he said, and whipped his shirt over his head and then went for the button of his shorts. "Flat on your back, pants undone, cock waiting for me to suck...in *my* bed."

"I do like this bed. Nice and firm..." My words trailed off when Dylan's clothes came off and something *else* nice and firm caught my attention. As he put one knee on the bed, I reached down to grip the base of my cock and said, "Stop."

"Stop?"

"I know you're all about accuracy in these films, but I think this particular scene needs…a different position."

One of Dylan's eyebrows shot up. "And what position is that?"

"I want you to sit on my fucking face."

A sensual grin crossed those pouty lips, and he took his knee off the mattress. Walking up to the head of the bed, he leaned down and gave me an earth-shattering kiss that told me exactly what he thought of my idea. Then he climbed up and over me, positioning himself so that not only did his mouth have easy access to my cock, but I had a perfect view of everything I wanted to lick and suck.

As Dylan's hot mouth came down over my dick, I craned my head up and swiped my tongue over his sac. He reared back on me and I took hold of his hips, keeping him in place as I sucked the hot skin between my lips and Dylan continued to suck on my cock like it was a Popsicle.

"Oh, Dylan," I growled, and tore my lips from him. My head flopped back on the bed when his hands smoothed down my thighs, and then he lowered his body slightly to rub his erection against my shirt. He moaned around my thick length at the friction and then did it again, getting off on the feel of the material brushing against his sensitive flesh before he shoved back, and I took in the firm ass cheeks hovering above my face. I drew in a ragged breath, trying to get myself under control, and then brought my hands up to plump and spread him apart so I could look at everything he was offering. *Hell*, this wasn't gonna last long, and I could only hope the warm moisture now seeping through my shirt was an indication that he was as close to completion as I was.

With a soothing stroke of my hand over his bare ass, I raised my fingers to my lips and sucked them inside, getting them nice and wet before I drew a slippery path down his crack. When Dylan tensed, and the fingers on my thighs tightened, I bucked up, shoving between his lips at the same time I pushed the tip of my finger against his pucker.

Dylan raised his head then and demanded, "More." But I was right there sliding my finger deep inside him as he took me between his lips once again. It didn't take long after that. The heat of his mouth surrounding me, the visual of my finger, first one, and then two, disappearing into his tight hole, and the deliciously depraved sounds of him sucking and whimpering around my dick had my orgasm shooting out of me and into the warmth of Dylan's mouth. As he swallowed greedily, my fingers bumped against his prostate and his hips jerked once, twice, and then he was coming all over my shirt in a hot, sticky rush. Our breaths were labored as Dylan turned himself around and lay on top of me, licking his lips.

"Fucking delicious," he said. "Better than the movie."

I chuckled as he dipped his head down for a soft kiss that I felt all the way to my toes, and I loved that I could taste myself on his tongue. Loved that he wanted any and every part of me he could have inside him. I reached up to push a strand of hair off his forehead, and he leaned into my touch.

"Dylan," I said softly, running my fingers through his hair.

"Hmm?"

"There's something important I think we need to discuss."

Dylan's eyes went alert as they shot to mine, and I wondered what he thought it was I was going to say.

I caught his lower lip between my teeth and sucked it into my mouth, and then I gave him a playful grin and said, "I think you owe me a new shirt."

15
PEACE, LOVE...
AND PUMPKINS

THE NEXT DAY, we'd dusted off Dylan's Honda Accord from where it'd been sitting in the garage for the past few months and made our way to the outskirts of Sunset Cove to have lunch with his family. He'd called them last night to surprise them with the news we were in town, and they immediately suggested we pop over for a late round of campfire corn, whatever that was, but we'd begged off and gone for a walk along the beach instead.

The warm, salty air already had me feeling rejuvenated, and I wondered when had been the last time I'd felt so free. It wouldn't last, of course, since word was bound to get out as to where we were, but for at least last night, with Dylan's hand in mine as we watched the crashing waves, my world had found steady footing. Peace.

"You don't look nearly as nervous to meet the parents as you did walking into my apartment yesterday," Dylan said, aiming a quick look my way as he turned onto a long strip of dirt road. "Why is that?"

"Technically, I've already met your parents. And yesterday I was just preparing to hold myself back in case Derek ended up being a little too friendly."

Dylan laughed at that and made a left, passing a mailbox in the shape of a two-story wood house that had me doing a double take. The trees were thick on our sides as we rode along a bumpy dirt and gravel driveway, and then Dylan said, "But, as you saw, our relationship is purely platonic."

"I approve."

"And if you hadn't? Would there have been a wrestling match? Tearing each other apart for my affections?"

"You'd like that, wouldn't you?"

"I'd like to watch," he said.

"And here I thought you just wanted to be watched. Learning more about you every day, Prescott."

He laughed, and as the trees thinned out, a two-story wood house, an exact match to the mailbox, rose up in front of us, accented by a jagged staircase that went down from the top floor and a two-person rainbow hammock out in front. It looked exactly like the kind of place I expected the Prescotts to live. In the green wilderness without neighbors, and in a larger version of a shack-style house. The exact opposite to my mother and father's pristine multimillion-dollar estate in their gated community just outside of Chicago.

After Dylan parked the car and we got out, Sunshine opened the front door and gave a big wave.

"Hey, boys!" she said, and then went to the railing of the porch and leaned out over it to yell toward the backyard. "Ziggy, put the hoe down and come and greet your son and his new boyfriend."

I glanced over the top of the car at Dylan, who was grinning but shaking his head.

"Don't worry." I chuckled. "My mother is always telling my father the same thing. Hos can be such a problem."

Dylan let out a bark of laughter, and then raised a hand to shield his eyes as he gazed up at Sunshine. I followed his line of sight to see her running toward the stairs, and as she went her flowy, tie-dyed purple dress billowed out from where it was cinched around her breastbone and swished down around her legs and ankles. When her feet hit the stairs, I noticed she was without shoes as she raced down, excited to see her boy, and I was blown away by how that made me feel.

How comforting it must be to have such unconditional love. To know that no matter what you did, or who you were, all you had to do was come home and you would be accepted. No matter who you were.

Dylan was so lucky, and it explained so much about

the man I was coming to know with each passing day. The reason he was so open, so free with himself, and so unbelievably kind and loving. It was all right here. The heart of Dylan was now standing in front of us with warmth in her eyes and what I knew to be pure happiness for the two of us in her heart.

"Ahh! I'm so pleased you're here," Sunshine said when she got to the bottom of the stairs. She looked between the two of us, and her smile was so full of love that I swore I could feel it pouring off her as she came toward us with her arms outstretched. Her long blonde hair was left free, save for two braids on either side of her head that were secured at the nape of her neck, and her tanned skin made her look positively radiant.

Sunshine Prescott was everything I'd thought she would be, and after she'd finished hugging her son and stepped in front of me, I couldn't help but return her warm smile.

"Hercules," she said, before wrapping her arms around my waist and giving me a welcoming hug. As I returned the gesture, I looked over the top of her head to Dylan, who winked at me. Just as she released her hold and took a step back, a tall man dressed in a dirt-smeared tank and faded denim shorts with frayed ends came walking toward us, wiping his hands on his legs. He was wearing a pair of flip-flops and a wide-brimmed hat that showed his long, dark hair to match the Frank Zappa mustache that declared this man Ziggy Prescott.

"There's my boy," he said as he came forward and reached for Dylan, pulling him into a bear hug. As he clapped him on the back, I saw the way Dylan tightened his hold around the man and knew he'd needed this just as much as it seemed they did. This family was a close one, which was something…new for me, and though Dylan was a grown man, this injection of family love was already having a calming effect, if the way he settled into his father's embrace was any indication.

When Ziggy released him and cupped the sides of Dylan's neck, he asked, "Are you okay? You know Sunshine and I don't watch TV and all that junk, but we have the laptop you got us, and after you called we looked at a few things."

My stomach knotted at those words, as I wondered if they would hold some kind of resentment toward me for putting their son through all of this. But when Dylan nodded and looked my way to say, "I don't care about all of that. Ace is totally worth it," my heart pounded. And when both Ziggy and Sunshine followed suit, I felt my cheeks flush.

"Well, aren't you a looker," Ziggy said as his eyes fell on me, and with the hand he still held on Dylan's shoulder, he gave his son a shake. "And here I thought you said you weren't into pretty boys."

"Pretty boys?" I repeated. "I don't think I've ever heard that one."

Ziggy pulled me into a hug and laughed as he patted

me on the back. As he leaned back, his hands went to my shoulders, and he said, "Whoa. Pretty boy has pretty big arms. You garden?"

My lips twitched at the rapid change in conversation. "Garden? Uh, I don't, but I did take an agriculture class in high school."

"Shoulda kept at it," Ziggy said, his arm going around my shoulder, and then he began walking us toward the backyard. "You should see my garden. You could have a garden like this. I got rhubarb and zucchini, 'shrooms—"

"You grow 'shrooms?" I asked, my eyes going wide.

"Course I do. Can't have a garden without 'shrooms." Then he leaned in like he was going to tell me a secret and whispered, "We'd have the real Mary Jane out here if the government didn't have a big ole stick up its ass. I always was good at trimming trees."

I coughed and then looked over my shoulder to see where Dylan had gone off to, but he and Sunshine were trailing behind us, and there was a grin on his face. Made me wonder how much "gardening" he'd had to do when he lived with his parents.

* * *

ACE WAS GIVING me a *don't you dare leave me* look as Ziggy steered him away, and I gave him an answering smile. I had a feeling I was going to enjoy seeing Ace outside of his element way too much today.

Ziggy gestured toward a square of four equal-sized patches filled with plants. "This here's the pepper pin, or as I like to call it, 'fruits that burn the hair off my ass.'"

"Oh, Ziggy," Sunshine said, covering a giggle.

He answered her with a wink and then nudged Ace. "Betcha didn't know chili peppers were a fruit, did ya?"

"No, sir, I didn't," Ace said.

"Mhmm, most people don't. And don't call me sir. I'll be forced to spike your food with the chilies."

"Yes, sir," Ace said, and when Ziggy's eyes narrowed, he backtracked. "I mean Ziggy."

"That's better. Now, here," Ziggy said, handing Ace a shovel and indicating a small section he looked to be making holes in. "I'm getting ready to plant some pumpkins and I could use a hand. You up for a bit of good ole manly bonding, Ace?"

Sunshine looped her arm through the crook of my elbow and bumped into my side. I looked down at her to see a smile on her face, and I knew it was her way of conveying how happy she was that Ziggy had taken such a liking to Ace.

I'd always been very private about my family life, even with Derek and my friends. It wasn't because I was ashamed of them, more because they meant the world to me and I wouldn't allow anyone to have an opinion one way or another on how I was raised. But seeing Ace laughing alongside Ziggy solidified that this had been the right decision.

"Daydream…" Sunshine said in a wistful tone as she patted her hand over my chest. "It's so good to have you home, my son."

The lines around her eyes creased as she continued to grin up at me, and I leaned down to press a kiss to her forehead. "It's good to be home."

"Yes, I can see you needed it. I understand it's good to go away, but it's always important to come home to your roots. To refuel with what's truly important."

There's my Sunshine. Peace and love. Never was this a more welcome speech. Until recently, I didn't think I'd truly appreciated how lucky I was when it came to both those things. But until witnessing Ace's life, and the small amount of time I'd been living it, I had never realized how important peace was. As for love and understanding, I almost wished Ziggy and Sunshine could sit down with Ace's parents and give them a lesson in the basics.

"How about you take a walk with me?" she said.

When I didn't make a move to follow, she rubbed her hand over my chest. "Oh, don't go getting all paranoid. I just want to ask you a couple of things and show you the gazebo Ziggy finally finished building for me. The grapevines have thrived this year. You know what that means?"

"Plenty of wine this summer?" I guessed.

"Mhmm, plenty of wine."

I glanced over to where Ace was now crouched down beside Ziggy, listening intently to the instructions being given, and then turned back to Sunshine. "Okay, let's go. I'd love to see it."

As we wandered down the dirt path that wound through Ziggy's boxed gardens, Sunshine stayed suspiciously pensive, and I could tell by the way she was gripping my arm that whatever she wanted to talk to me about was weighing heavily on her. And that meant one thing only—Brenda.

I knew what this was about. I'd been actively avoiding it since that morning at Syn when mine and Ace's lives had been turned on its ass. It had been an easy out. A convenient way to push aside a subject I wasn't comfortable discussing, but at the same time I knew it wasn't going to go away. I also knew that I needed to sit down with Ace one of these days, sooner rather than later, and lay my miserable childhood tale out for him before he heard it from someone else. And with the way the press was relentlessly digging through every aspect of my life, there was no doubt in my mind that the conversation needed to happen soon.

When we got to the end of the path, Sunshine stopped me and looked down at my loafers. I followed her gaze, and when I raised my eyes, she cocked her head to the side. "You know he'll take it as an insult if you don't take those off and feel the grass between your toes."

I chuckled, knowing she was right. Ziggy took great pride in his garden and the extensive spread of grass that spanned the length of the property down to the back of their yard, where Lennon lived.

I toed off my shoes and then stepped with her onto

the cool carpet of grass. God, I'd missed this place. It was so easy to get caught up in the rush of the city, the busy mainstream of life where everyone was consumed with their phones, computers, social media, and who was doing what. But none of that was here. Peace was here.

Sunshine led us across the grass, toward the cluster of trees on the right side of the property, and as she went she stroked a hand down my arm. "We're very pleased you brought Ace home to meet us."

"I am too," I said, looking her way. "He needed it." And then I corrected myself: "We both needed it."

Sunshine nodded. "I can't even imagine what his life is like. All that scrutiny. Twenty-four seven."

"It's pretty wild. He can't even walk to his car without some photographer jamming a camera and microphone in his face."

Sunshine stopped and looked at me, and I instantly knew what she was worried about. It was written in her troubled expression. That was one of the best things about Ziggy and Sunshine—they never hid things from their children. They were open and honest with everything they were thinking and feeling, and that was a welcome relief, considering most people spent their lives tiptoeing around the hard shit.

"Are you…sure you're okay with that? With being in someone's life who's under so much of a spotlight?"

"Yes, I told—"

"I know what you told me, Daydream," she said, a

frown marring her forehead. "But have you really thought it through? Ace is lovely, dear; we aren't saying he isn't. Ziggy and I just want to make sure you've thought about...everything."

"Everything as in Brenda?"

Sunshine lowered her eyes to the ground. "Well, yes. That's..." She paused and then let out a sigh before peering back at me. "That's information that hungry vultures will feast on. Vultures who are already digging around in your past."

I knew she was right. When Ace had been leaving lunch with his parents that day at The Vine, the first question had surfaced regarding my foster care days, and I knew it would only be a matter of time before they looked deeper.

"I know. I want to talk to him about it while we're down here. It's one of the reasons I thought this would be a good place to come. So he can see where I truly grew up. That way when I tell him all the stuff that came before it, it won't seem so bad."

Hell, who was I kidding? No matter what I did or what I showed Ace, nothing would take away the shock of hearing what I would have to tell him.

"Oh, honey," Sunshine said, squeezing my arm to her side. "You're not worried about his reaction, are you? That man looks at you like you hung the moon."

"Of course I'm worried. Not because I don't trust him, but because I don't want him to look at me differently. I don't want that 'hung the moon' expression to go away."

"There's nothing you can do about your past, Daydream. He accepts you as you are or he's not worthy of you."

"I know that. I do. I'll tell him."

"Good boy."

"And what about Brenda? Any more calls? Surprise visits?"

"Not a peep, and if she knows what's good for her, she'll stay away."

"Or Ziggy'll bury her in the backyard?"

Sunshine grimaced. "That was one option. But don't you worry about her."

"I'll try." I ran a hand through my hair and blew out a breath, gazing around at the newly erected gazebo, decorated by the lush green grape vines punctuated with plump purple muscadine grapes that wound their way up the trellis. "This looks great, Sunshine. I like that he put the rosebushes around it."

"All of our favorites, see?" She went over and pointed to the one to the right of the entrance and went down the line. "Gypsy Sue for Ziggy, April Moon for me, Earth Song for Lennon, and New Dawn for my Daydream."

Walking over to the bushes, I grinned at her and then bent down to smell each one. It reminded me of the first time I'd met Sunshine. When the lady from child protective services had pulled up in their driveway, she'd been out front, busying herself planting a bush of New Dawns for my arrival, and when she hugged me, she smelled sweet and earthy, same as she did now. I'd never been hugged before that moment, and I'd had no idea what I was missing. How important and necessary another person's touch could be. I'd felt that way with Sunshine and Ziggy from day one, and the only other person who'd had that effect on me was currently planting pumpkins in my parents' backyard.

"I love you, Mom."

Sunshine's head shot up, and when she straightened, her eyes glistened a little. "I love you too, baby."

I wrapped my arms around her shoulders then, hers going around my waist, and I stayed there, content to be comforted by the woman who'd raised me—the only woman that mattered.

As a loud whoop let out from behind the house, Sunshine looked up at me. "We'd better get back. Sounds like Lennon's found your boy."

16
CAMPFIRE
CONFESSIONS

"ALL RIGHT, HERCULES, you're up. Two lies and a truth. Let's see how good of an actor you really are."

I grinned at Ziggy from across the campfire and rubbed my hands over my shorts. "No pressure or anything."

"No, not at all. We'll only make you chug that glass beside you."

Lifting the plastic cup filled to the brim with what they'd told me was Ziggy's special homemade muscadine wine, I took a big whiff of the sweet liquid. "Doesn't seem too potent to me. It's just wine, right?"

"Yeeeeah," Lennon said from next to me, leaning back in his folded chair so I could barely make out his eyes under all that hair. The guy had definitely been a Beatle in his past life. "If it's just wine it shouldn't mess with you, big guy."

I narrowed my eyes on him, and then looked around the circle to Ziggy, Sunshine, and Dylan's innocent expressions. "Why do I get the feeling you're playing with me?"

"It's just a game, hotshot," Dylan said, his lips quirking to the side. "Want me to go first?"

"No, no, I got this. Two lies and a truth...okay, let me think." Knowing this family, they'd have some wild shit up their sleeves, so I needed to bring it. My acting career depended on it, apparently. "Okay, here we go: number one, I got arrested for pranking our rival high school. Number two: I've visited all seven continents. Number three: I'm actually allergic to muscadines."

Laughs broke out around the campfire, and Lennon said, "Oh shit, bro, I hope that last one isn't true, but if it is, we'll make you chug Benadryl after."

"I'm gonna guess—" Dylan started, but Sunshine clamped a hand over his mouth.

"You can't go first. You probably already know the answer."

"I don't, I swear," Dylan said.

Sunshine shook her head. "No, sir. Now, I'm gonna say number two is true and the others are false."

Ziggy raised an eyebrow at her. "You think he's been to Antarctica?"

"He does have a private jet," Dylan chimed in.

"So? No one in their right mind wants to go there," Ziggy said.

Lennon sat up and pointed at me. "Hang on, man. Where'd you shoot that ice movie? You know, the one with the avalanche, what's it called…"

"Uh, *Avalanche*?" Dylan said.

"Oh yeah. Yeah, that one. Where'd you shoot it, Hercules?"

I held up my hands. "Can't tell you that."

Lennon leaned over the arm of his chair and squinted at me, studying my face. "Hmm. I say…number one is the truth."

Dylan snorted. "Yeah, right. If Ace had been arrested, I'd know about it."

"Course you would, stalker bro," Lennon replied. "So what's the truth, then?"

"Easy. Number two," Dylan said.

"Yeah, I agree." Ziggy nodded. "Number two's the truth."

As I looked around the circle, I twisted my lips. "Seems like you all agree except for Lennon here. I can't believe you think I'd do something so foolish. Breaking into another school and getting arrested for vandalizing their mascot? Yeah, that's stupid. Too bad it's true." My gaze went over to Dylan, Ziggy, and Sunshine, and I smirked. "Looks like you three better drink up."

"What! No way in hell," Dylan protested, moving to the edge of his seat.

"Way, bro." Lennon pointed at Dylan's cup and mimicked throwing it back. "Cheers."

Dylan eyed me over the flickering flames, and I dropped my eyes to the cup he held before pointing to his drink. "Hope you have a high tolerance, Daydream."

Ziggy let out a bark of laughter. "Now there's a good joke."

"Ohhh," I said, watching Dylan bring the cup to his lips. "This is something new. Are you saying he *can't* handle his liquor?"

"Well, let's just say Dylan's been known to—"

"Hey, Zig. How about you don't give away all my secrets so I have some left to dish out when it's my turn?" Dylan said.

Ziggy made a show of zipping his lips shut, and then the three Prescotts sitting opposite myself and Lennon brought the cups to their lips and chugged back the first round of wine. Ziggy smacked his lips together and threw his cup to the ground, letting out a whoop, and then looked toward his wife.

"Ready over there, 'Shine?"

The mischievous grin that tugged at her lips made me chuckle as I settled back into my chair. I couldn't remember a time where I'd felt so relaxed, and staring at the family across from me made me realize what an integral part of Dylan these people were. His easy laugh, his generous nature, it stemmed from these people who'd opened their arms to a complete stranger and were now sitting around a campfire shooting the shit with him.

"I'm ready," Sunshine declared, and pushed a strand of her blonde hair behind her ear. "Number one: the tree that you and Lennon are sitting under over there..." She paused, as I turned my head to look up at the thick trunk of the tree behind us and then returned my attention to her. "That's where Lennon was conceived and born. Number two: I was arrested after a peace protest in 1978 along with around sixty others, including Ziggy here. It's how we met. And number three: my real name is Barbara."

I scanned the grinning faces all aimed in my direction as I fingered the lip of the cup. Dylan was sitting back in his seat with his cup resting on his knee with a sly smile on his gorgeous face as he shook his head at me. He had to know I would remember our conversation of him having moved here when he was in college...*so yeah*, I was pretty confident I had this one.

"Okay," I said, sitting up a little straighter in my seat. "Nice try with number one, Sunshine. And not that I don't doubt you and Ziggy getting in touch with nature...I just have it on good authority that you moved here when Dylan was in college."

Sunshine's mouth fell open and she whipped her head around to pin Dylan with an accusatory glare. Dylan gave an *I'm sorry* shrug. "What? How was I supposed to know not to tell him stuff you could use against him later?"

I laughed at that, and Dylan's eyes found mine. "Oh, don't laugh too hard over there, Locke. You're a dirty player. And dirty players *always* get what's coming to them."

I wasn't sure Dylan realized the way his words sounded, or how the look he was aiming my way would affect me, but both went directly south and had me squirming in my chair.

"See?" the tease said, and added a wink. *Okay, yeah.* He knew exactly what he'd done.

"Oh, leave the poor man alone, Dylan. He's trying to think about the answer, not what you want to do to him later," Ziggy said, reminding me of just how open this family was about, well…everything. "So, okay. That still doesn't mean you're off the hook. So give us your best shot."

I thought about the other two options. I could definitely see Ziggy and Sunshine meeting after being arrested, but I also had to wonder if Sunshine had been legally named *Sunshine* from birth. Dylan had been given the name Daydream when adopted into the family, so… "Okay. I think the *truth* is that your real name is Barbara."

When my eyes landed on Sunshine's, she pretended to ponder it for a second and then shook her head, laughing. "Sorry, Hercules…my parents were the original flower children. I've been Sunshine since the day my mother and father knew I was on the way."

I caught Dylan's cocky laugh, and when I looked at him he raised his glass in mock salute. "Bottoms up, big guy."

Christ. He was only one drink in and it was becoming

more and more obvious that Dylan liquored up was going to be a handful. His flirtatious vibe—and the memory of my words to him at my birthday months ago—was not lost on me as I raised the cup and chugged down the wine. *Mmm, not bad. Pretty damn good, actually.* I'd never had muscadine before. The drink was sweet and tasted like grapes, but it had a kick to it for sure.

"You make this yourself?" I asked Ziggy, and he inclined his head before getting up to grab the container of wine.

"The stuff you get in the store may as well be called grape juice for babes. This stuff," he said, going around to refill our cups, "will put some hair on your chest. Well, not you, 'Shine."

Sunshine smiled at her husband, and then threw a marshmallow across the fire at Lennon, who caught it with his mouth.

"Guess I'm up, huh?" he said with his mouth full, and then he swallowed and kicked out his legs before crossing them at the ankles. Holding up three fingers, he proceeded to tick them off. "One: I once rode a cow naked on a dare and made it a good ten seconds before his ass bucked me off. Two: I poured detergent in every fountain downtown to make that shit bubble over, also on a dare. Three: I once climbed the water tower and pissed off the side when I saw my ex coming. Not a dare. Just for fun."

We all stared at him with our mouths agape until Dylan busted out laughing.

"How have you never been arrested?" he said.

A Cheshire grin took over Lennon's face. "Skills, man. Mad stealth skills."

Ziggy held up his cup. "Cow is true."

"Bubble fountains," Sunshine said.

I mimicked Lennon's pose from earlier and leaned over to squint at him. "Gotta be water tower pissing. Whaddya think over there, pretty boy?"

Dylan rubbed his hands over his face and leaned forward on his elbows. "Sweet Jesus, I almost don't wanna know. But I'm gonna go with...naked cow ridin'."

"And the winner is..." Lennon beat on his thighs like a drum before pointing at me.

"What! You gotta be kidding me," Dylan said.

"You did not piss all over that nice girl from Elmhurst. No, you did not." Sunshine tried to school her face into disapproval, but she couldn't stop the laugh that emerged.

Lennon shrugged. "Dude, she always said she wanted a golden shower."

"Way to give a girl what she wants *after* the fact," Ziggy said. He held up his cup and then downed it in one long gulp.

Dylan stared into his drink and murmured, "I'm gonna be sooo drunk."

"Now that's something I can't wait to see," I said as he held up his middle finger and downed the fruity liquid.

* * *

THIS PLAN HAD monumentally backfired. Don't ask me how it happened, but somewhere around the second round of two lies and a truth, I'd had to down three more cups of Ziggy's wine while Ace sat across from me cradling his second *un*touched glass.

Who knew the lucky bastard would turn out to be so adept at reading people? So good at it that he'd gotten more answers right about my own family than I had.

My head was buzzing, and my lips were finding it difficult to form full words with how numb they felt, and when Ziggy stood beside me to reach for Sunshine's hand, I glanced across the fire to the man watching me with hooded eyes.

We'd decided around two glasses ago that we would spend the night here in the small wooden guest hut that Ziggy had built off the house a few years back. It was a bare-minimum-only cabin, which I'd been quick to point out to Ace, but he'd told me he was more than happy to stay. So there we were, and as the questions came to a close and Ziggy pulled Sunshine into a gentle sway around the campfire, Lennon downed what had to be his fourth or fifth glass and got to his feet.

"I'm totaled, guys," he said, and hiccupped before he staggered slightly, which had me laughing uproariously. I was happy I wasn't the only one impaired. "I'm just gonna...ya know..." he slurred, indicating with a wave of his hand to the Silver Streak Clipper that sat on the back of Ziggy and Sunshine's property, "go and crash."

Sunshine pulled out of Ziggy's arms and moved over to kiss his cheek, and I was amazed, as always, by her tolerance to Ziggy's house blend. The two of them blurred slightly in the haze of the flame and smoke, and then out of the corner of my eye I caught Ace getting to his feet. I blinked, trying to focus clearly on him, and as he got closer I trailed my gaze over his long legs and up to the sensual smile curving his luscious lips. That expression had me raising the half-empty cup up to my lips to finish the sweet summer wine in a final gulp as Ace stopped in front of me and extended his hand.

As I got to my feet, I was surprised I could stand, and the low chuckle that came from Ace's throat had me edging closer to the solid wall of man opposite me.

"You okay there, Daydream?"

I raised my head and nipped at his chin. "I'm just fiiine..." I drawled, and raised a hand to stroke it down his chest. "And so are you."

Ace planted a kiss on my forehead, and his warm lips had me humming and nestling into his broad chest.

"I think it's time this one lies down before he falls down," I heard Ace say over my head. I'm not sure what was said after that, but before I knew how, I was being led through my parents' garden with my hand secure in the large one wrapped around it.

Lightheaded and more at ease than I had been in

weeks, I practically skipped several steps ahead of Ace before I turned to face him, drawing him along with me.

"Ever had sex under the stars?" I asked him, gazing up at the glittering diamonds in the sky.

"You're drunk, Mr. Prescott."

"Am not." I hiccuped and the rumbly laugh that left him again skated over my hypersensitive skin, making it break out in gooseflesh as he tugged me in so I was crushed up against him. He lowered his head and pressed a kiss to my temple.

"Mhmm. You are. Drunk, flirty, and really fucking cute."

I pulled out of his arms and shook my head, and then grinned when one of Ace's eyebrows winged up. "No? You don't think you're any of those things? Because as far as I can tell you're trying your hardest to lure me into stripping you naked with your parents right over there."

As I backed up, Ace followed my lead, his eyes never wavering from mine. "I would never do that."

That had Ace nodding and contemplating me in a way that screamed one thing: bullshit.

"If I recall, it was your turn back there before it was declared your ass couldn't handle another loss, Daydream. So how about it? One more round of questions for the night, but instead of loser drinks a glass of wine, the loser can—"

"Lie down naked and let the winner do whatever he wants with him?"

Ace tracked my steps until I stumbled, and clapped a

hand over my mouth as I laughed, finding it difficult to locate my feet—and balance. Luckily for me, my back hit the solid surface of the guest cabin and Ace crowded in—you know, just to hold me upright.

"That sounds perfect," he whispered, and swept his lips across mine. "Hmm, you taste like sweet, *sweet* wine."

When he raised his head, his eyes collided with mine, and the intent in them was clear. As soon as we got inside this cabin… It. Was. On.

"One, I gave my partner multiple orgasms with *only* my mouth," Ace said.

Was he kidding right now? Ace's words in my ear were enough to make my knees shake, but imagining him with someone else was not high on my—

"*Two*, I spent the entire night trying every position I'd always been curious about until we both passed out, exhausted."

Okay, that was it. I brought my hands up to Ace's chest, about to shove him back, when he sucked on my earlobe and my traitorous dick went from interested to rock hard.

"And three, I made my partner shout so loud his family was well aware we were in no need of horny goat weed."

As Ace raised his head, he twisted the doorknob and we stumbled into the small space. The arrogant look on his face let me know he was screwing with me, and my heart pounded as he said, "By morning, not one of those are going to be a fucking lie." Then he kicked the door shut behind him.

17
COME SAIL AWAY

"UM. WHEN YOU said you rented a boat for the day, I thought you meant a speedboat, Ace," I said as we came to a stop at the edge of the pier.

It was a couple of days after the day we'd spent at my parents' house—which had been followed by a night that, even as drunk as I'd gotten, I could still remember vividly. It was a damn good thing I could, too, because Ace had been a relentless taskmaster, refusing to stop until his mouth had wrung so many orgasms from my body that I'd lost count. A shiver rolled through me just from thinking about it, but before my cock decided to get any ideas, I tried to focus on the sparkling white yacht before us. There wasn't a cloud in the sky today, and the sun was so blinding, especially reflected off the monstrosity in front of us, that

Ace had to hold up a hand to shield his eyes when he looked over at me.

"What?" he asked. "You said you could drive a boat. You didn't say size mattered."

"Oh, that sentence is just asking for it."

"Maybe *I'm* asking for it."

I arched a brow. "By letting me steer this big, long vessel deep into the ocean?"

"Fuck me." Ace groaned.

"Hey, you started it."

"I'd like to fucking finish it too."

"Then why don't you?"

"Dylan."

"Hmm?"

"Can you drive this thing or not?"

Just as the words left his mouth, a teenage boy— around thirteen or fourteen, I would guess—headed our way out of the mix of tourists and locals lining the boardwalk and pier. He was tanned and wearing a white Rip Curl cap, white board shorts, and the same Sunset Cove shirt I owned—*a proud local.*

"Uhh...excuse me...Mr. Locke?" he said, from behind Ace. The boy caught my eyes and gave a timid smile as he waited expectantly for the man I was with to turn and face him.

As Ace pivoted, the boy took a step back as he looked up at him with a mixture of shock and awe stamped all over his face. It was such a wonderful expression of unbiased adoration that it made my heart swell for Ace.

"Hi there," Ace said as he looked down at the boy.

"Hi...uhh...umm—"

"You can call me Ace," he said, and the excited smile that crossed the boy's features made me chuckle. Ace Locke, bringing joy to the entire damn world.

"I don't mean to interrupt, but I was wondering if you could sign my hat?" the boy said as he reached for it and dragged it off his head. Ace held his hand out for the cap and pen, and when the boy gladly gave them to him, Ace asked, "What's your name?"

"Luke."

"I would love to sign your hat, Luke."

"Thanks. My mom's just over there," he said, gesturing behind him with his thumb, and Ace looked over where I did just in time to see a petite brunette woman give us both a smile and quick wave. Ace waved back, as did I, and then returned his attention to the child and what he was doing.

"So, are you out here to surf today?" he asked, casual as ever, clearly used to making small talk with anyone and everyone in his line of business.

"Nah." The boy laughed. "We're going out on our boat today. Gonna fish, we are."

"Oh well, what do you know. We happen to be going out on a boat too."

Ace signed the cap and then handed it back to the boy as he straightened.

"Is that your boat?" he asked, pointing to the sleek yacht with his mouth dropped open, much like mine had been when Ace had stopped me in front of it.

"Yeah, that's the one we're going on. Dylan here's going to drive it."

"Oh wow," Luke said, and then his eyes found mine. "That's so neat."

I nodded and beamed back at him. "I'm pretty excited about it myself."

Ace chuckled and then the boy started to walk away. "Well, thank you Mr.—uhh…Ace. It was real nice meeting you. I'm a huge fan."

"It was awesome meeting you too, Luke. I hope you and your mom have a good day."

"I hope you do too," he said with a friendly wave before turning to run back to where his mother stood. Ace and I watched him go, and when he reached her he showed her the hat and then gave an excited fist pump in the air.

What a gift Ace had to make others so incredibly happy. It seemed unfair that he would ever be judged for wanting a tiny bit of that happiness for himself.

"So," Ace said, turning back to face me with a grin, "can you drive this thing or not?"

"Didn't that kid teach you anything? You don't spend your life in Florida and not know how to drive a boat of any size, hotshot."

A smirk crossed his lips and he slapped me on the ass. "Then how about you climb aboard before I throw you over my shoulder and make you?"

"Oh yeah? You'd do that in front of all these people?"

Ace crossed his arms, and from the set of his jaw I could tell the look behind his sunglasses was a *dare you to call bullshit* one. I took in the huge muscles of his chest, his arms, his shoulders, and the way the casual white shirt he wore stretched across them, and then my legs were moving up the boat ladder in a hot second. Not because I was scared he'd follow through on his threat—but because I didn't trust myself not to rip his shirt off with my teeth.

Yeah, this guy turns me into a fucking savage.

Once my feet hit the deck, I turned to see Ace climbing aboard behind me. "I have to say, I'm liking that I can do *this*," I said, sidling closer to him and trailing my fingers along his brawny forearm, "without one hundred cameras going off around us."

Ace leaned in to brush a kiss across my lips, and when he pulled back and looked at me over the top of his glasses, there was a wicked gleam in his eyes. "And I like that I can do that. Now get up there to the wheel, Dylan, before I'm tempted to see how much I can get away with."

"Aye, aye, Commander Locke." I took the keys Ace was now dangling in front of me, and then made my way up to the bridge of the boat. Ace then went to untie the ropes from the pilings, so we could head out.

It was a beautiful summer day in Sunset Cove, and I couldn't believe I was behind the controls of this badass boat. Growing up first in San Francisco, then later here in Florida, taking a boat out to deep-sea fish, or even just to spend the day or weekend with friends in a hidden cove, was nothing new. But the size and luxury of this vessel had even me slightly nervous.

We were out of the inlet and heading into open waters in no time, with the wind whipping around us, and the sheer beauty of the pristine waters as far as the eye could see. Standing there at the bridge of this beauty was a little overwhelming. *Then again,* I thought, as I looked to the man standing beside me, *everything Ace does is always with some amount of flair and is generally enough to take my breath away*— including the way he'd casually stripped out of his shirt around ten minutes ago. He was standing beside me at the controls, dressed only in his khaki cargo shorts, flip-flops, and Aviators, and he looked phenomenal. Like he could be in the middle of shooting a scene in one of his movies. Tanned all over, and his muscles were sculpted and so well defined you could follow their path with your tongue should one be so inclined…*which I just so happened to be.*

Ace must've caught my stare out of the corner of his eye, because he turned in my direction and leaned his shoulder up against the railing. "You know, as much as I enjoy being your sole focus, Daydream, don't you think you should pay attention to what you're doing?"

I reached for my glasses and pulled them down my nose a little so I could make a show of checking him out. Then I clucked my tongue and pushed the glasses back in place. "Trust me, I know *exactly* what I'm doing."

"And what's that?"

"Why, I'm kidnapping you, Mr. Locke," I said, in my best impression of a Bond villain.

Ace chuckled, and then pushed off the railing to walk over to me. I kept my eyes forward as he stepped behind me and wrapped his arms around my waist. As I settled back against his chest, I felt him nestle his groin in against my backside and put his lips to my temple.

"Is it really a kidnapping, though, if *I* provided the transportation?"

"Hey," I said. "Don't try and ruin my fantasy here."

"Oh, I'm sorry," he said, nipping at the shell of my ear. "Please continue. Where are you taking me, you scary, *scary* man?"

"That's better... I'm taking you somewhere secluded—"

"I'm liking this."

"Where I can tie you up—"

"I'm *still* liking this."

I whipped my head around. "Really? You like that idea?"

One of Ace's eyebrows winged up in response, and the side of his lips tilted. "Shocked?"

"I shouldn't be, but I think you like surprising the shit out of me."

"I do," he said, nodding.

"Good thing I like surprises."

Ace lifted his sunglasses and put them on his head so I could see his eyes. The look he gave was so full of sensual promise it nearly knocked the breath right out of me, and I had to tighten my grip on the wheel and refocus on trying not to steer us off course.

Today, I wanted to talk with Ace. To finally tell him about my past. But for now, as we stood there at the wheel of the yacht, I was content to relax into him and enjoy the promise of the smooth waters—before they potentially turned turbulent.

* * *

A HALF-HOUR LATER, Dylan had dropped anchor in a secluded little inlet just offshore, and I'd gone down into the cabin to grab the lunch basket I'd ordered for us. When I came back up to the deck, he'd removed his shirt and spread out a couple of large beach towels on the bow. He had a bottle of suntan lotion in one hand, and as he turned and caught sight of me and the basket I carried, he shook his head.

"I was planning to catch a few fish with my bare hands for lunch, but I guess that'll have to do," he said, grinning.

Setting the basket down, I took the bottle out of Dylan's hands and gave it a quick shake. Then I flipped open the cap and poured some of the lotion into my hand. "I'd love to see that. Maybe next time."

"Maybe— Oh, that feels good." He moaned as I took my time rubbing the lotion into his neck and shoulders before massaging my way down his back. I loved the feel of his body beneath my hands, all those lean muscles and smooth skin. When I kissed the spot beneath his ear, he said, "You just want to feel me up."

"I do. I also want to feed you."

Dylan's eyes met mine. "Is that right?"

Nodding, I dropped to my knees and reached for the basket.

"Oh," he said, disappointment in his voice. "I thought you meant...something different."

"I meant that too. But first..." Reaching inside, I took out the contents of the basket—five different containers of sliced cheese and crackers, fruit, wraps, and mini cheesecakes. Then I patted the spot next to me.

Dylan sat down, scooted in closer, and plucked a grape from one of the containers before popping it into his mouth. "Oh, very fancy. Do you have wine to go with?"

I reached back into the basket and pulled out the chilled bottle of white I'd had stashed in the fridge downstairs, and Dylan lounged back on an elbow.

"I sure could get used to this. Lying out on the deck of some luxury yacht and sunning myself while some buff guy pours me wine and feeds me."

I halted mid-pour. "*Some* buff guy?"

Dylan gave a casual shrug, but the curl of his lips belied his indifference. "Sure. As long as he's naked from the waist up and handing me a glass of wine, what do I care about pesky details like his name?"

I finished pouring the alcohol, recorked the bottle, and then leaned across the spread of food to hand Dylan the glass. As he took it from me, our fingers skimmed and I said, "Exactly. What's in a name, right?"

Dylan sat up until his lips were inches from mine, and he licked them. "Right. Unless, of course, that name is Ace Locke, because that's a name I like saying, moaning, and shouting at any given time of the day."

I hummed my agreement before taking Dylan's mouth in a hot, quick kiss. It was a stamp of approval for his words, and if I were honest, a stamp of ownership over the way those same words affected me. I loved hearing my name fall from his lips, no matter which way he was saying it, and right now, as I moved away from him, it was a whisper-soft sigh.

"I'm rather fond of Dylan Prescott, not gonna lie." As I sat back on my side of the towel, Dylan slowly raised the glass to his lips and took a sip, keeping his eyes focused on me the whole while, and when he lowered the glass he swallowed and a frown furrowed his brow.

I wasn't exactly sure what was going through Dylan's head right then, because he'd gone from carefree and relaxed to pensive and what I could've sworn was nervous, and it had me reaching for him. But Dylan shook his head.

"Hey, what's going on over there?" I asked, aiming a

small smile in his direction, but something had definitely shifted here. "Dylan?"

Dylan sat up and placed the glass of wine down by his side. Then he bent his legs and drew them up to his chest, where he wrapped his arms around them. And in an instant he'd gone from open and inviting to closed off.

"Dylan? Did I do something—"

"No," he interrupted, again shaking his head. Eyes downcast. "You're perfect."

Okay... The way he said the word had my concern growing tenfold, because it certainly wasn't said in the same complimentary tone from minutes ago.

"*This* is perfect. All of it...and I joke about it, but Ace," he said, raising his eyes to meet mine across the vast space that now seemed to gape between us, "my life is not perfect. Far from it. Hell, my name isn't even Dylan *Prescott*. I don't even say it out loud anymore. I choose not to acknowledge it. But those reporters, the people digging into every aspect of your life...they're going to work that out, sooner rather than later. And there's things you need to know. About me. About my past."

"And I want to know those things," I said. "I haven't forgotten about what you started to tell me in Vegas. But I'd never push you to open up. If you're ready to tell me, I'm ready to hear you."

"Thank you."

Trying to ease the anxiety I could see building in the tense cords of his neck and shoulders, I held up the wine and said, "Need a bit more?"

"Wouldn't be a bad idea."

As I refilled Dylan's glass, he looked over my shoulder, staring out across the calm, quiet ocean. I'd wondered for a while what he'd wanted to tell me that day we'd lounged on the bed at Syn, but I knew whatever it was, it wasn't something that would be easy for him to talk about. But I wanted to know this man, know every part of him and all the secrets he kept hidden from the rest of the world. I wanted to be the one he shared himself with.

"It's easy…" Dylan said, fingering the lip of the glass. "It's easy to forget myself when I'm off doing things I only ever dreamed of when I was younger. Back then, I started with smaller dreams. I wanted a mom *and* a dad. Ones who cared enough to make sure I did my homework and tucked me in every night. I wanted to live in the same house for more than a week at a time. I wanted to eat something other than stale cereal and fast food scraps my mom's 'boyfriends' left behind." He bit down on his lip before continuing. "But most of all, I wanted to feel safe. I never felt safe until I met Sunshine and Ziggy. And even when they came into my life, I spent a long time waiting for the ball to drop, waiting for them to give me back, or turn into the kind of people my mom had associated with for years."

I stayed silent, not daring to breathe a word that would have him clamming up. I wanted to know what his mom had done, and why he'd never known his father.

As though he'd read my mind, he said, "My mom was…very well known in San Francisco. Not in the political or entertainment circles; not because of any amazing contributions to charity. She was an underground gutter rat, a prostitute turned madam that hustled men, women, sex, and drugs."

My eyes must've widened to saucers, because Dylan let out a humorless chuckle.

"Yeah, I guess you wouldn't have guessed that, huh?" he said.

I shook my head. "No. No, I can't say the thought would've crossed my mind."

"Good."

As I watched him down the rest of his wine, I wondered how long it had taken him to shed the layers of his past, what had led to him being placed in foster care, and how he'd emerged not only alive, but seemingly thriving. There was also something else he'd hinted at that I was curious about.

"Before…you said you never knew your father," I said, and Dylan nodded. "But did you know who he was?"

"I'm sure good ole Mom could've narrowed down the list to about twenty-five potential sperm donors, but finding out who knocked her up was never high on her priority list. Hell, I'm surprised she had me at all, but my guess is she wanted someone to join the family business."

My gut tightened as his last words lingered. "Join?"

The grim line of Dylan's lips made it abundantly

clear how uncomfortable he was talking about this, and though I didn't want to push him, I had this inexplicable need to know what had happened to him, no matter how hard it was to hear.

Dylan's eyes had taken on a faraway look, as if he was no longer even sitting there with me, and before I knew I was going to do it, I leaned over and took his hand in mine. When he looked in my direction, I squeezed his fingers and, without words, invited him to lean on me.

As Dylan silently got to his feet, I made sure to keep his fingers locked in mine. He stepped over the food that had been separating us, and when he stopped in front of my crossed legs, I tilted my head up to see the sun shining around him, and felt breathless at the picture he made.

"Come here," I whispered, and gently tugged on his hand, urging him down to my lap. He lowered himself until he was seated and facing me, his legs on either side of my waist, and his ass nestled on my crossed legs with our hands still entwined between us. "Nothing you tell me is going to change the way I feel about you."

"That's easy to say—"

I tipped his face up so he was looking me directly in the eye then, and told him with more sincerity than I ever remembered feeling, "It's easy to mean when it's you who I'm talking about."

"Ace..." he said, and leaned his forehead to mine, closing his eyes.

I wrapped an arm around his waist and pulled him

as close to me as I could get him. Hoping to make him feel that sense of safety he'd spoken about only moments ago. "Tell me, Dylan. I want to know you. The good, the bad, and the—"

"Ugly?" he said. "If only that had been the case. You know what's crazy?"

Trying to keep up, I just went with it, letting Dylan lead this conversation where he needed it to go. Letting him tell me however he wanted to tell me.

"No. What's crazy?"

"That I use my looks to get paid. In a way, I'm no different—"

"Hey," I said, leaning back a little to get his attention. "Don't you dare compare what you do to what you just told me she did."

"Right, but you don't understand. This face, the face that's getting me contracts with more zeroes than I could ever imagine seeing on a paycheck, is the exact same face she was trying to cash in on."

As a shuddering breath racked Dylan's body, he lowered his eyes from mine, and as much as I'd urged him to tell me about his past, I was terrified of what he was about to reveal. Not because of others knowing, but because I wasn't sure I could stand to hear how someone had hurt this man.

"For years my mother—Brenda—would use me as—" Dylan bit off his words and cringed, and I ran a soothing hand up his back, needing the contact with him to calm my shaking hands.

So Brenda was his mom, and that had been who Sunshine was referring to that day in the desert. "She'd use me as bait, I guess, is what police ended up calling it. She worked out I was a somewhat…powerful lure to certain men, and that they would be willing to pay big bucks to be able to stroke a pretty boy's face. To touch his hair. To have him in the room while they—" Dylan coughed, and it sounded as though he was close to choking on the words he was forcing out of his mouth. His jaw bunched and ticked as he ground his molars together, and when he finally had himself under control, he started to talk again. "She never let them go further than that. Her one act of kindness to me, I suppose, until the final night…"

"Dylan, you don't have to—" I started, guessing where this was going. Hating that he had to tell this story at all. But he shook his head, determined now, it seemed, to get this the fuck out and over with.

"No, let me finish. You need to know. To hear it from me, instead of reading it in some magazine."

I brought my hand up to stroke it over his cheek, and when he shut his eyes and nuzzled into it, my heart ached for the boy he once was. But that wasn't all I felt there on the bow of the boat under the afternoon sun. At that exact, heartbreaking moment, my chest swelled with pride for the demons this man had battled, and I knew without a shred of doubt that I loved Dylan Prescott more than anyone else on this earth.

18
THE GOOD,
THE BAD,
& THE UGLY

I KEPT MY eyes closed as I leaned into Ace's hand and said the words I'd been dreading for months.

"I'd come home from school early that day," I said. "It was the day before Thanksgiving and we only had to attend a half-day, so I planned to drop off my book bag at home—or at least the place we'd been staying for a few weeks at that point—and then go to my friend Bobby's house for the night. I hated being around when my mom had visitors, so I snuck off as much as I could. She was usually wasted, high off whatever drug she'd been paid with the night before. I expected her to be asleep, but that day she was awake and sitting in the living room on the ratty orange couch I knew better than to get near. I'll never forget it...she had a cigarette in one hand, and a face full of thick makeup, but her red lipstick was smeared a little on one side, like she'd already been up to her tricks that afternoon. And when she patted the seat next to her, I didn't move, but then she narrowed her eyes, and I knew what that meant. I'd gone through a growth spurt, but I was still only thirteen, and not only did she have a few inches on me, she had nails that could break through skin. So I sat on that ratty, dirty couch and kept my hands in my lap. She didn't ask me how my day was, which was nothing new, but she did give me the biggest smile I'd ever seen from her and told me she had a surprise for me. 'A good surprise?' I asked. 'Oh, Dylan,' she said, 'a wonderful surprise. That face of yours is going to break hearts. And wallets.'"

My throat had gone dry, like I was still breathing in the fumes from her cheap cigarette, so I paused to take a long swig from one of the water bottles Ace had pulled out of the basket. He was still watching me with careful eyes, but there was something strong behind them, some emotion I couldn't quite place, but I didn't have time to think about what it could be. I needed to just get this out already.

"Well, like any kid, I heard the words 'wonderful surprise' and thought maybe my luck was changing. And it was changing, all right. But *wonderful* in my language didn't mean quite the same thing in my mother's world. She told me then that I'd been freeloading my way through life and it was time to earn my keep. That I could fetch more money in an hour than she could in a night. So it was time for me to get to work, and I'd be starting now." I swallowed hard and said, "I remember that sinking feeling in my stomach when I realized what she meant. I can still feel the way her nails dug into my leg when the man that'd been waiting in the bedroom walked out into the living room. I tried to bolt, but she held me down, and when I'd almost gotten free, she used my shirt as an ashtray. The pain from that burn gave the man enough time to pull me up by my wrists, and then he hauled me—she *let* him haul me—into the bedroom. There was just a mattress on the floor, and he threw me on it before kicking the door shut. His breath smelled like rotten eggs, and he kept trying to pin me down, but I fought...I fought so hard. I could hear my mom beating against the door for me to shut up, but the guy had locked it, so I was stuck there, tears running down my face as I tried to get away."

"Please tell me you got away," Ace whispered, and when I met his gaze, I didn't even think he'd realized he'd said that out loud.

"There was a moment when I thought he'd get the best of me and I'd let him. Not because I wanted to, but because I couldn't physically fight against him any longer. So I stopped moving, stopped fighting. And you know what he did? He got up. He unzipped his pants. He took them off. And it was then that something inside me snapped. Some kind of fire ignited in my body, and I knew I was going to get away. No matter what it took, no matter if I died trying to get away...I was not living one more second in that place, and I was *not* letting the drug addict pedophile on top of me win. So when he got back down on the mattress, I let him lie on top of me. And when he moved in just the right position, I reached down between his legs and I crushed him in my fist as hard as I could. His eyes rolled in the back of his head and he screamed out in pain, and that only made me squeeze harder. I would've ripped it off, but that wasn't the end game. I needed to get away, so I let go, and when he curled into a ball on the mattress, I ran for the window. And once I was outside, I kept on running. I ran until I couldn't run anymore, and when I figured I was far enough away I could stop and catch my breath, I realized I'd stopped outside of a police station. I hadn't ever thought of going to the police before. I thought maybe I'd be able to crash at a friend's house, but when I saw the station that night, I was running again. Up those stairs, through the front door, and into a small white room, where I told the officers my story."

"Jesus Christ, Dylan," Ace said, his hand going to the back of my neck. "I had no idea."

"Why would you?" I asked, and then blinked, trying to bring him into focus. It wasn't until a tear fell down my face that I realized the reason I couldn't see him clearly. I was crying. I brought a hand up to swipe at the wetness on my cheek, but Ace got in first, brushing it away with his thumb. "I've spent every second of my life *since* that day making sure no one would ever know where I came from. I bounced around from foster home to foster home for a while, and at the time I thought I was lucky to be given a roof over my head for nothing more than the check the government would give them. Until the day my caseworker came to pick me up from the latest stopover. She told me that they'd found somewhere permanent. A family who was looking to adopt in the future, and she wanted me to go with her to meet them."

"Sunshine and Ziggy?" Ace asked, and I bit down on my lower lip and nodded.

"You can imagine my first impression of them." I gave a rueful smile, and when Ace returned it, the weight that'd begun to suffocate me seemed to ease. "I told my caseworker she was out of her mind. There was no way I was going to live with some *high as a kite* hippie types, I think were my exact words, and I remember her pulling me aside and telling me that she'd worked with Sunshine for years and there was no one who would be more open and understanding than the two of them. I thought she was out of her mind, but who was I to argue with her? She was the professional, right?"

I reached up to touch Ace's jaw line, and when my hand shook he took a hold of it and brought the pads to his lips to kiss them.

"Then what?" he asked.

"Then I moved in with the strangest, most unconventional family imaginable, and they turned out to be exactly what I needed." I shut my eyes and tilted my face up to the sun, letting the warmth of it dry my tears as I remembered those first years living with Ziggy, Sunshine, and Lennon, and a smile split my lips. "Those first few months were…odd, to say the least. Not only was I adjusting to living with a new family, but this family was much different to any that I'd ever been a part of. My own had been a piss poor example and all the stops in between had been relatively normal. But then along comes Sunshine, a woman who could brighten up the darkest day, and they made me fall in love with them."

I brought my attention back to Ace, and the acceptance and warmth in his eyes made me reach for him and loop my arms around his neck. His hands lay gently around my waist as I wriggled closer. "It wasn't easy. Sunshine and Ziggy helped me through years of counseling, and always encouraged me to be open with how I was feeling. As you've seen firsthand, they're sharers by nature, givers, and they helped me through the worst years of my life. They also taught me to take *control* of my life and the situations I put myself in. They're the best people I've ever met," I whispered, licking my lips and feeling more exposed than ever before. "Until you."

Ace pressed a soft kiss to my lips, and then shut his eyes as he took in a deep breath. I couldn't begin to imagine what he was thinking about everything I'd just told him. Hell, half the time I didn't even know what to think, and I'd lived it. But when those blue eyes reopened, the expression there stunned me. It was fierce, possessive, and so full of love and pride that I didn't dare speak for fear it would vanish.

"Dylan, I…" he started, and then brought both of his

hands up to cradle my face. "I have never met anyone like you. You're brave, and kind, and I'm not sure what I did to deserve getting to call you my own."

I swallowed around the lump that had lodged in my throat, and tried to calm my thumping heart, but there was no way. Not with Ace looking at me with such devotion.

"And I want that. More than anything else. I want every part of you. All of the good, the bad, and, yes, even the ugly. *That's* what makes you so unbelievably beautiful. The fight. That survival instinct that has driven you to be the best you can be despite the odds. You are so much more than a stunning face, Dylan. You're the man I've fallen in love with."

I brought my hands to the back of his head and crushed my lips to his with all of the passion and love that was dying to burst free. Ace kept his hands on either side of my face as his lips parted, and when I sank my tongue inside to taste him, I couldn't remember ever feeling safer and more at home than I was there in this man's arms.

"Ace," I said, and when I raised my head I let my gaze rove over his familiar features. I brought my fingers around to trace the angles and planes of his cheekbone and jaw, until I reached his lips. Then I traced a line around them, enjoying the fullness of them, before taking his chin between my thumb and forefinger so I could lean forward and whisper against his mouth, "I love you too."

19
MORE THAN
A DAYDREAM

THOSE THREE LITTLE words from Dylan's mouth sent a reviving jolt to my heart, bringing me to life in an explosion of color. I hadn't even noticed I'd been living in a world of grey. In that moment, it wasn't enough to have his mouth on mine, to have him straddling my lap. Never enough. My heart was so full I thought it would burst out of my chest, and the only way I knew to show him how much was to get as close to him as he would allow.

I lifted him off my lap and got to my feet, and then I took his hand in mine, leading him downstairs to the bedroom. Once we were inside, Dylan's warm front pressed against my back, and as he planted kisses from my neck down my shoulder, his hands roamed possessively over my chest. I reached up to the back of his head and craned my neck to the side to give him better access. His lips traveled up the length of my neck, and when he got to my ear and whispered, "I want to be with you," my knees came close to giving way.

Dylan gently trailed his fingertips across my shoulder blades as he walked around my side to stop in front of me, and when he reached for my hand and entwined our fingers, I felt the enormity of the touch, as if he'd just handed me his heart to hold—and essentially he had.

"Dylan, we don't have to do this. Not right now. We can just be here, together."

"I know," Dylan said, and then looked down at our joined hands before raising them up to his lips, where he pressed a kiss to my knuckles. "But that's not what I need right now. I want to feel *you* all around me." He drew my arm around his waist and planted a feather-soft kiss over my jaw. "That's where I feel safe. In your arms. And today, I want to be as close to you as another person can be."

My breath got stuck somewhere in my throat at his words, and when his eyes found and held mine, the love and trust shining in them swept away any lingering doubt that this was the right thing to do.

No longer able to deny myself the pleasure of touching him, I brought my hand up to cradle his face, and when he leaned into my palm and let his eyes flutter shut, I marveled at the long lashes sweeping against his gorgeous skin.

His full lips had fallen open on a sigh, and before I could stop myself, I took them with mine. Slowly, mindful not to jolt him out of the languid headspace I could see him slipping into, I brought our joined hands up between us to lay his palm over my heart and then lowered my head to touch my lips to his.

My eyes fell shut with that first contact; I wanted to experience the taste and texture of him without being distracted by anything other than the whimper that escaped him as I slipped my tongue between his lips. Dylan's fingers dug into my chest as he swayed closer to me, and I slid mine up through his hair. As I cradled the back of his head and deepened the kiss, I felt Dylan's other hand come down to rest on my waist just above the band of my shorts. *And God, this is sublime,* I thought, as Dylan continued to tease the naked flesh at my hip.

As we were caught up in the taste of one another, I couldn't have said how long we stood there sampling each other's mouths, and swallowing the sounds of pleasure escaping us. But when he pulled away and nipped at my lower lip, I had trouble focusing on him. My head was spinning, my blood was racing, and I'd never wanted to be with anyone more than I wanted to be with Dylan right then.

"I want you inside me," he whispered, and I didn't hesitate. Walking him backward, I took his lips with mine again, moving forward until his legs hit the edge of the bed. Before I could lower us, Dylan's hands were on my wrists.

When I stilled, waiting to see what he was going to do, his fingers went to the button of his shorts, flicked it open, and pulled down the zipper. Then he looked me in the eye and did the same to my shorts.

"Every time we're together like this, I swear I have to pinch myself that you're really standing here in front of me. But you are, aren't you?" he said.

"Yes, I really am. And Dylan?"

"Mhmm?"

"There's nowhere else I'd rather be."

Dylan tugged his shorts and briefs down his thighs and stepped out of them before sitting on the bed and angling his head up at me. With unhurried hands, he lowered my clothes down my legs, his fingers skimming along the sides of my thighs as he pulled them off. Then, as he came back up, his lips brushed the tip of my cock in the softest of kisses, and my hips jerked forward.

"God." I sighed and traced the rough stubble of his cheek. "I don't know how I got so damn lucky to have you in my life. But I'm so thankful to whatever brought you to me."

Dylan scooted back on the bed, and I crawled my way over his body, straddling his hips and leaning down over him so that my mouth was only inches from his.

"All that time I spent wanting you," I said, and grazed a kiss along his temple. "And now you're mine."

"All fucking yours." His voice was a low rumble in my ear, and as I brought my gaze back to him, I could see

the love swirling with the lust in those sea-green eyes of his.
I recognized that look now. It was one that had been there
for weeks, but I was only just learning what it meant. I
wondered if he could see the same in mine.

"Ace?"

My chest was rising and falling against his, and as he
widened his legs and I settled between his thighs, I ran my
fingers through his hair. "Yeah?"

"Help me forget."

I lowered my head to nuzzle into the crook of his
neck, and listened to the soft sound of him breathing—in
and out. In and out.

"Help me shut my mind off," he whispered.

"I can do that."

"I know. Because guess what I just found out?"

"What's that?"

He craned up and placed his lips by my ear and said,
"Ace Locke loves me."

When he laid his head back on the pillow and a shy,
impish grin curved his lips, it made one appear on my own.
"Does he, now?"

"Yep, he does," he said as he slowly wound his legs
over the backs of my thighs, and then wrapped his arms
around my neck.

I rocked my hips over the top of his and allowed
myself to sink into the sensation of having his erect cock
aligned with my own. Pushing aside the seriousness of our
earlier conversation and losing myself in the glorious

moment of lying down with him this way, the soul-searing connection I now felt as I stared into his eyes was not lost on me. With nothing more than our bare skin touching, I felt closer to him than I had to anyone else in my entire life, and I wanted to savor that for as long as I could.

* * *

MY HEART THUNDERED at the expression in Ace's eyes as they roamed over every one of my features, and when he braced his forearms on either side of my head and said, "Kiss me," nothing could've stopped me.

I crossed my ankles against his lower back and bowed up off the mattress, making sure to connect every part of my body to his that I could, and the low growl that emerged from his throat had me crushing my lips to his. Ace's mouth parted beneath mine and I bit and sucked at his lush lower lip as he used the arms he had anchored by my head to shift his entire body over the top of mine in a delicious body rub.

Jesus, that feels— "Again," I said, and Ace smiled against my mouth.

"What…this?" he asked, and again rolled all of his hard, warm muscles over the top of mine, including his thick cock, which was leaving a sticky trail all over me.

"Yes, exactly that," I said. "It feels— *Ahhh.*"

The groan that left Ace summed up pretty damn well

how good it felt, and when he brought a hand down to trail the backs of his fingers along my ribs to between our bodies, I gasped. Ace had shifted his body slightly to the side and wrapped his strong hand around our engorged shafts.

"Oh God. Please," I said as his hand flexed and my hips punched up, gliding my erection through the fist he'd made around us and against the tender underside of his.

"Dylan," Ace said as he began to move in perfect synchronicity with me. We continued to rock against each other as we watched every thought and feeling cross the other's face, and when I knew I was perilously close to exploding all over him, I braced my hands on his chest and halted him.

"Inside me," I said, panting. "I need you inside me."

Ace nodded and pressed a bruising kiss to my lips before he released the hold he had on us. I groaned at the loss, and the hungry light in his eyes made me clench my teeth and tell him, "Hurry."

Ace got off the bed, picked up his shorts, and grabbed what he needed from the pocket. With his focus locked on me like a tractor beam, he brought the square packet to his teeth and tore it open. I splayed my legs apart for him, and took a moment to check him out as he rolled the condom down his veiny cock. Then he tore open a packet of lube and slicked it all over himself, and picked up a second before climbing back on the bed, and I licked my lips in anticipation.

Resuming the exact same position, Ace hovered over

me with an arm by my head and my legs spread wide to accommodate him.

"Wrap your leg around my waist," he ordered, his voice raspy and deep.

I not only wrapped my right leg over his hip, I once again twined my arms around his neck, and Ace shut his eyes as his nostrils flared. I knew he was trying his best to take this slow and steady but was having as much difficulty as I was. Because right then all I wanted was him inside me, filling me until I didn't know where he ended and I began.

When he seemed to have himself under some modicum of control, he brought the second packet of lube to his lips and tore it open, and before I knew it the packet was tossed aside and his slippery fingers were sliding their way along my perineum to my hole.

"Ace—"

He pressed his mouth to mine, cutting off my groan, and as his tongue speared between my lips, his finger pushed inside me. My hips jacked up off the bed, and I tore my mouth from him. My body was so ready for this; it felt overly sensitized, as if I would shoot all over him with nothing more than a finger in the right spot and a smile from the sinfully handsome man working me over.

"I can't wait," I told him, and clutched at his shoulders. "Don't make me wait any more."

Ace removed his finger, and when his hand smoothed over my hip and around to the cheek of my ass, I tightened my leg on his waist. I could feel him line the head of his cock up with my firm entrance, and as he began to slowly push forward, I gnashed my teeth together.

As he filled me, I couldn't stop the groan that left my throat. And even when he was balls deep inside, our bodies as intertwined as they could possibly be, I still wanted more.

"Dylan," Ace said. "You feel…"

"I know," I said, holding him firm against me. "So damn perfect."

Ace's cheeks clenched beneath my hands, and then he began to rock, small movements at first as I adjusted to the size of him, then he pulled his hips back, inching himself out. As he tunneled back inside me, I took a hold of my cock, working it in time to Ace's thrusts. His blue eyes never left mine, and he stayed hovering over me, keeping our bodies connected, skin to skin. Every time I pumped my shaft, the tip grazed against his rock-hard abs, and the friction was almost too much to take.

One of Ace's hands came up and threaded through my hair, pulling my head back so my neck was exposed up to him, and then he licked a warm, wet path up my neck.

"Yesss," I said. "More."

And just as I'd asked, he repeated the move, sending a shiver from the top of my head to my toes. Then his voice was a soft whisper in my ear, and his words made my heart leap.

"You're so much more than just a dream…you're my reality, Dylan. Now and forever."

Forever…

That word, whispered in my ear, had my heart thundering, my body trembling, and the orgasm drawing my balls up tight as I gazed up at him.

Forever with this man? I wouldn't have taken anything less, and as he let go of my hair and my eyes met his again, he said, "I want to come with you."

I twined my arms around his neck, and my legs around his waist, and as he took me over I heard words of love, comfort, and need being chanted in my ear. I could feel Ace claiming every part of me. From the tips of my hair, to the soles of my feet, and when he whispered, "Forever," the climax ripped through us both.

We came holding one another. Rocking the other through the storm and emerging on the other side, stronger for the journey.

20
MOUTH FULL OF HOT WEINER

MY PHONE VIBRATED in my pocket again, and I sighed and pulled it out to check the screen. Not that I needed to. Martina had been calling all day, but now wasn't the best time. We'd just arrived at the beach to have a bonfire with a few of Dylan's friends on our last night in Sunset Cove, and I had no intention of being rude and taking a business call. She could wait.

Dylan came up next to me then, two plastic cups in hand, and nodded toward my phone, which I shoved back in my pocket.

"She's called about a thousand times already. Don't you think you should answer that? Might be important."

I took the drink he held out to me and shook my head. "If I do that, it's back to the real world."

"We've gotta go back there tomorrow anyway."

"Am I hearing you right? You *want* me to answer this call?"

"Might as well. I don't think she'll stop until you do. Just tell her to make it quick." He leaned over and gave me a kiss, and then backed away toward where his friends were setting up chairs around a circular pit.

I groaned as I watched him rejoin the group, and then I fished the cell out of my pocket. The phone connected almost as soon as I hit her number.

"Ace?" she said, sounding frantic, and as soon as I heard her tone, my shoulders tensed up. "Where have you been? I've been calling all day—hell, all week—trying to get in touch with you. I know you're on vacation in Florida, but you can't tell me that phone isn't attached to your hip."

Yeah, okay, she has me there. "So you know I'm in Florida," I said.

"You think just because you go off to another state that paparazzi can't find you? Not that they're swarming like they are here, so you probably haven't noticed them."

"Is that what this is about? Because I don't care what they get a picture of. I'm not hiding. I just needed to get away for a few days."

"I get that. I do." Martina sounded sympathetic. "But I hope you get back raring to go, because I got the best phone call this morning. Are you sitting down?"

I glanced over at where Dylan was shaking hands and giving hugs to Derek and an attractive man in the brightest pair of electric orange Bermuda shorts that I'd ever seen. "No," I said. "Not sitting down."

"You should really sit down for this."

That got my attention. "Is this good news or bad news? You said best phone call, right?"

"That typically means good, yes."

Looking around me, I didn't see anywhere but sand to plop down on, so I kept standing. "All right, I'm sitting. What's up?"

Martina took a big breath and let it out on a rush. "Carly Wilde wants you on her show. Carly *Wilde*! An hour-long, possibly two-hour, interview exclusively with you."

"That's the best news ever?"

"Ace! This is huge. You know when Carly Wilde has someone on her show, it really ups their profile."

I snorted. "Like I really need my profile upped any higher. I've got paparazzi sleeping outside my fucking gate, Martina."

"You know what I mean. America loves Carly. You win her over, you win the viewers over, and we're back in business, baby."

I opened my mouth to respond with something sarcastic, but then I paused. She had a point, but why did Carly even want me on the show in the first place? When my career was plummeting faster than a skydiver without a parachute, and my love life was splashed all over every tabloid in the world?

"What does she want to talk about? Why's she

calling now? Why not when things were going well, hmm?"

"Oh, Ace. You know she loves a good comeback story. So does the rest of the world."

"I have to make a *comeback* now?" I asked, my voice rising. I looked over at the group starting the bonfire; Dylan's friends hadn't noticed my outburst, but Dylan caught my eye and raised a brow. I waved him off so he wouldn't worry, and then lowered my voice. "I'm not about to go on national television to do an interview with a woman who wants to know how I feel now that all my career prospects are suddenly vanishing and to rub in my face why."

"It wouldn't be like that—"

"It would, and I'm not doing it."

"Ace—"

"No."

I could almost see the shock on her face as she said, "So...you want me to tell Carly Wilde *no*. As in absolutely, positively no. Am I hearing you right?"

"That's what I said."

"You're making a mistake with this. She could help you—"

"I don't need her help. I don't need *your* help. Let me just...figure out my next step, okay?"

Martina was silent for a long moment. "If that's what you want..."

"That's what I want."

"I'll pass along the message, then. See you when you

get back."

"See you then," I muttered, and ended the call, wishing I'd never called in the first place. I tried to keep my face neutral when I glanced across the beach to see Dylan's eyes on me, but some of the strain must've showed, because he made a move in my direction and I shook my head and instead headed toward him. There was no way I was going to ruin tonight for him. This could wait until later, tomorrow, when we were on our way home. But here, tonight, with the balmy breeze blowing and the fresh, salty air wafting off the waves, I planned to enjoy the night with my boyfriend and his friends.

* * *

AS DEREK SLUNG an arm around Jordan's shoulders, I watched Ace slip his cell phone into the pocket of his shorts and head in our direction. For a second or two there I was worried I'd made the wrong move in suggesting he call Martina, but now that he'd hung up he seemed to shed whatever they'd been discussing like a second skin, and relaxed into his stride as he headed toward us.

"Okay," Jordan whispered, as he leaned my way, aiming a dazzling smile in my direction. "Before he gets over here. Can I just say how excited I am to meet your boyfriend?"

When Derek rolled his eyes, I chuckled and nodded. "You can. I'm pretty sure he wouldn't mind if you told him yourself."

"Oh my God. I would never," Jordan said, clearly mortified by the thought.

"Jesus, Jordan. He's just a man," Derek said as if he hadn't tripped all over himself when he'd first met him.

"I'm well aware he's a man," Jordan said, and then looked in Ace's direction. "I mean, there's no mistaking *that*. What is he, Dylan? Six foot three? Five?"

When Derek groaned, I couldn't help my bark of laughter at his put-upon expression. "Actually, he's only six foot or so. It's the muscles that make him look—"

"Delicious?" Jordan asked, innocently enough.

"Oh for the love of— Where's the alcohol?" Derek said.

"What? As if you weren't thinking it too," Jordan said. "I kind of have a *thing* for muscles."

I glanced at Derek's ripped biceps, which were on display in his black tank top, and then shot a grin in Jordan's direction. "I remember. Relax over there, He-Man. You look like you're about to have a stroke."

"Yeah, yeah. Fuck you, Prescott."

I bit the inside of my cheek as Ace finally came to a stop in front of the three of us, each of us looking at him with what I only assumed was wide-eyed innocence, and when silence was all that greeted him, he glanced in my direction and I couldn't help it. I lost it.

I busted up laughing, and when Derek mumbled, "Fuckin' hell," I laughed even harder.

Jordan showed no hesitation then, stepping away from his man to extend his hand like he was the Queen of Sheba, and when Ace took it, Jordan took another step forward and glanced up at him, batting his lashes. Full-on sex kitten.

"Well, hello there, handsome."

As Ace's lips curled to one side, he looked my way, and I just raised my brow, letting him know he was all on his own with this one.

"Hi," he said, and then tracked his eyes down Jordan to his blindingly bright pants. "Nice shorts."

Jordan cocked his head to the side as if trying to decide if Ace was serious or bullshitting him, and then he gave him a coy smile and a once-over of his own before announcing, "Nice...everything."

"Okay, Jordan," Derek said, stepping forward and taking hold of Jordan's elbow. "Excuse him; he actually has a brain, just not around—"

"Muscles," Jordan ended, and then let go of Ace's hand to trail his fingers down his arm, which made Ace's eyes bulge and me laugh all over again. *Shit*, I had no idea how Derek had wound up with that firecracker, but damn if it wasn't amusing as hell to watch.

"Obviously my boyfriend has a thing for *your* boyfriend, Prescott," Derek grumbled, crossing his arms. "Yeah, yeah, just get it all out in the open there. Maybe add a bit of tongue."

Jordan's trilling laugh echoed in the evening air as he

turned back to his man, his eyes gleaming, and then threw his hands over Derek's shoulders. "You know I'm a sucker for a man with a possessive streak."

"And muscles, yeah, we heard," Derek said.

Jordan looked over his shoulder at us and said, "Anyone here know a guy by that description? Resting bitch face, tattoos, sexy fucking ass? Doesn't usually play well with others?"

As Ace and I began to laugh, Derek tried to bite back the smile that was playing on his lips.

"You're lucky you're cute," he said.

"You're lucky I have a thing for bad boys named Derek Pearson," Jordan replied, and then dropped his arms and faced us. "So while we wait for the others, let's get our drink on and you guys can tell us every little juicy detail about how you met, how you've been sneaking around, how that place we can't talk about but we all know about was..."

"Nice try," I said as we all took a chair and Derek stoked the fire a bit. It had been relatively mild weather the last few days, and we'd spent them relaxing on the beach, boating, spending time with the family, and generally unwinding. I couldn't say I was dying to get back to the crazy that would welcome us tomorrow, and I had a feeling Ace wasn't looking forward to it either. But it'd been a good trip, and I hoped it'd gotten his mind off everything for at least a little while.

"See, this here's how we treat fancy folks who come visit us in little ole Sunset Cove," Derek said, and held up a skewer and a packet of beef franks. "We make you cook your own wiener over the fire pit."

"We're classy like that," Jordan agreed, passing us both a couple of skewers and a separate package of hot dogs.

Ace laughed and leaned forward in his chair toward the fire. "I'm not complaining. It's a nice change."

"You know," I said, "if you wanted to really go all out, you could've brought the—"

"S'mores?" Derek held up a bag of marshmallows and chocolate bars, and I promptly shut my mouth.

"Jordan brought these. I don't do sweets," he said, tossing the bag of marshmallows my way. "I shouldn't think you would be doing too many sweets either, Prescott."

"Oh shut it, Derek. Just because you're weird and don't eat desserts—" Dylan said.

"Really?" Ace asked, looking over at Derek. "You don't like dessert? Of *any* kind?"

"See, weird." Jordan grinned in Derek's direction.

"If we're gonna talk about weird, how about we discuss the fact that the last time we sat around a bonfire with s'mores you managed to—"

"Derek Pearson, you shut your mouth," Jordan interrupted, shooting to his feet. His eyes were round and his lips were pinched together as he glared daggers at a chuckling Derek. "Oh, but what fun would that be, Posh?"

Ace leaned over to where I sat beside him watching the show playing out across from us, and pressed his lips to my temple, where he whispered, "Did he just call him

Posh?"

When I nodded, Ace laughed and turned back just in time to see Jordan's scarlet face. "Be careful, He-Man…"

That only seemed to encourage Derek, though, because his hand whipped out and he grabbed a hold of Jordan's wrist to pull him down onto his lap.

"Are you threatenin' me?" he asked, his eyes glued to his boyfriend's in a way that made it crystal clear to anyone watching the two of them that they were madly in love.

"Only within an inch of your life," Jordan replied, and smacked a kiss to Derek's lips. "Oh fine," he said with a wave of his hand. "If anything, this story makes me sound extremely…talented."

"That's one way to look at it." Derek settled back in his seat with his arms wrapped around Jordan's waist. And if the attentive way Ace was now staring at the two of them across the fire was any indication, he was just as eager as I was to find out what had happened the last time these two had sat down to eat s'mores.

* * *

SITTING ACROSS FROM Derek and Jordan was like sitting across from lifelong friends. Within seconds of meeting them I felt accepted, comfortable, and welcome. But more importantly, I felt as though I could be the exact version of myself I wanted to be—Dylan's partner.

Dylan had reached across to take my hand in his, as Derek began to relay his story, and I couldn't help but wish for a few seconds that this could be our life. This simple, easy, day-to-day routine we'd been living since we'd arrived in Florida. Because *this* life was as close to perfection as I had ever imagined possible.

"The story goes like this," Derek began, grinning like a devil as Jordan rolled his eyes in a dramatic way I was coming to associate with the effervescent man. "We'd gone over to Brantley and Finn's for a bonfire, just like this one. They'll be here a little later, and anyway, we decided to make s'mores. A decision that was made before we'd all had a few too many drinks, and when it finally came time to get out the ingredients, this one here picked up a marshmallow, looked at me across the fire, and bet me that he could fit more marshmallows in his mouth than I could."

Jordan was pretending to pay very close attention to inspecting his nails as Derek continued to tell the tale. I had to admit, I was curious now just how many it had taken to win, since Jordan now claimed this story made him sound...*talented*.

"So, never one to back down from a dare, I took him up on the challenge. Really, I should've known better, having been at the receiving end of watching him swallow a mouthful of—"

"Derek!"

Dylan placed my palm high on his thigh and

squeezed as he let out a laugh, and when I cut my eyes in his direction, he licked his lips. *The tease is flirting with me.*

"Oh please, now you're acting shy?" Derek said.

Jordan shot him a glare. "*Stick* to the story."

"Oh, fine. Anyway, we started to each put a marshmallow in our mouths, one at a time. Finn was out at four. You'd think a lawyer would have a bigger mouth than that. Though his professor got five inside, and that explained a lot as to why he held Finn's attention all these years. But Jordan," Derek said, smoothing his hands up and down the top of Jordan's thighs, making him squirm atop his lap. And Dylan chose that moment to slip my hand down the inside of his thigh, making me almost mirror Jordan's agitated move. "Well, he gave me and my big mouth a run for my money..." Derek chuckled and then bit at Jordan's ear before saying, "Then left me in the dust."

I rubbed the firm thigh under my palm, and then glanced over at the two telling the story, and couldn't help but ask, "So just how many marshmallows *did* Posh get in his mouth?"

When Derek and Jordan both froze and pinned me with equally shocked expressions, Derek's eyes practically twinkled with mirth, as if he couldn't believe I'd just called Jordan the name I'd heard earlier, and Jordan...well, to say he looked shocked speechless was a gross understatement. He'd gone all slack-jawed, and straightened on Derek's lap like someone had just zapped him in the ass. I had a feeling I was witnessing an anomaly, because this guy didn't seem the type to be speechless or shy in any way at all.

"You better watch out, Locke," Derek advised as laughter bubbled out of him. "This one takes issue with *that* particular nickname."

"I don't know," I said as I looked Jordan over. "I think it suits him. I've been called much worse, trust me, and that's a title you should be proud of. By the way, you still didn't answer. How many marshmallows?"

Jordan seemed to preen under the compliment, before he settled back into Derek's arms and said, "Twelve."

Now it was my mouth's turn to fall open as I glanced at the bag of marshmallows sitting on Dylan's lap. *How in the world...?* Those things weren't exactly small, either. When I raised my eyes to find Dylan's, he held the bag up at me.

"Think you could beat that, hotshot?"

I shut my mouth and looked back toward Jordan, who'd brought Derek's fingers to his lips, where he kissed them, telling me, "What can I say? There isn't much in life I prefer than having my mouth full."

"He ain't lyin' about that, either. Thank God," Derek said, and though he was clearly joking around with his boyfriend, there was an underlying affection there. A love that was obvious to anyone looking at the two of them, and that made me yearn for what they had. I wanted to be able to feel that free with the wonderful man sitting beside me. I *wanted* to be able to show the world that I meant what I'd told him the other day on the boat. That I loved him.

AN HOUR OR so later, Derek's buddy Finn and his partner Brantley arrived, and not too far behind were Dylan's parents. We spent the rest of the night telling stories around the fire and eating hot dogs and s'mores, and I felt more "normal" than I ever imagined I could. Not only did I feel like a person, rather than a celebrity, but the deep sense of acceptance I was experiencing was unlike anything I'd ever hoped to feel. Down here, with Dylan's friends and family, I could be me. The real me. A person I was finally starting to understand, thanks to the man I currently had my arms wrapped around.

Dylan was cradling a beer as he spoke with Sunshine about when we would next visit, and as he spoke he casually turned his hand over to entwine his fingers through mine, as if he'd been doing it for years rather than months, and I marveled at just how lucky I was.

Somehow through all the chaos that was my everyday life, Dylan had found me. And as I stood there surrounded by so much love and warmth, I knew there was no way I was ever going to let him go.

21
MONUFUCKINGMENTAL

"DYLAN, IS IT true you're moving to New York?"

"Why didn't Ace go with you on your trip?"

As I headed past the handful of photographers outside my apartment, I was surprised there were any there at all, considering I'd been in New York for a week for a few shoots.

"Not today, guys," I said, keeping my head down. Once inside the apartment, which was feeling a little less like my temporary home lately, I rolled my suitcase over to the counter and fished my phone out of my pocket. This had been the longest I'd gone without seeing Ace since I met him, and I was anxious to get together now that I was back in the same time zone. Other than missing him like crazy, it'd been an unbelievable week. It'd started with a group shoot for Provocateur on Rockaway Beach in Queens, before I'd headed back to the city for the individual photographs. I'd shot *GQ* in Central Park by the Bethesda Fountain. Then the Gucci shoot had me at the top of One World Trade Center, taking in the breathtaking views of New York City and beyond. And my favorite part—commandeering what was conveniently named Dylan's Candy Bar for a sweet shoot that I had a feeling Ace's friend Ryleigh would've enjoyed. I may or may not have ended up back in my hotel that night with an embarrassing assortment of chocolates, gummies, and cake pops. *Fuckin' hell, those cake pops...*

"Welcome back, Mr. Prescott," Ace said, cutting off my thoughts before I could drool too hard. "When the hell do I get to see you?"

A huge grin took over my face at the sound of his voice. "Now. Five minutes ago. As soon as possible."

"You should've come straight here."

"Nah, I need a shower and some fresh clothes before I tackle you. Plus, I knew you had that meeting today with your agent. How'd it go?"

A long silence descended before Ace blew out a breath. "Uh...you know, not great."

"Not great? What happened?"

"Just the same old lately. Deals have dried up. We've started reaching out about different projects, but no one's biting."

"Shit, Ace," I said, and closed my eyes in frustration on his behalf. "It's so unfair. This is all so—"

"Hey?" Ace said through the phone, and I bit down on my lip to stop the rest of the words I wanted to say. "It's okay. I mean, it sucks, but if losing out on a few roles and sponsors means I get to be with you and be happy, then I would do it again in a fucking heartbeat. Okay?"

It always amazed me how Ace had the ability to make me feel like I was riding the biggest high of my life, but at the same time wondering if I should be.

"Stop it," he growled, and my lips quirked.

"Stop what?"

"Stop feeling guilty."

Damn. The guy knows me too well. "It's just—"

"No, Dylan. You don't get to feel guilty about any of this. Not your career, which you more than deserve. Not the fact that people are closed-minded bigots, and not the fact that I'm madly in love with you. Enjoy your moment. You deserve it. I don't tell you these things to make you feel bad about what you're doing."

"I know that," I said, letting out a sigh. "But it's still not fair."

"Maybe not. But maybe it's time for me to look into other things."

"Other things?" I asked, sitting up and running a hand through my hair.

"Yeah," he said, and I could hear a smile creeping back into his voice. "I've always been interested in the indie world. Movies, startup projects. That kind of thing. It's actually how I got to know Shayne's boyfriend Nate. Maybe this is a sign."

"A sign?" I chuckled. "Since when have you believed in that kind of thing?"

And without missing a beat, Ace told me, "Since I met Sunshine Prescott."

That had me laughing loudly. "Right? She kind of has that whole flower child vibe happening, doesn't she?"

"Seriously, if anyone was going to make you a believer…"

"Oh, she will be pleased to hear it. Hercules, a total convert."

Ace's laugh rolled through me as I kicked my shoes off and wondered just how quickly I could get undressed, showered, and over to the man on the other end of the phone.

"So…did you miss me?" I asked, even though I already knew the answer. It was nice to hear sometimes.

"Fishing for compliments, Daydream?"

"Maybe. Would that be so bad?"

"Not at all," Ace said, his voice dropping a couple of octaves. "And if you could see me right now, you'd know just how much I missed you."

"Is that right?"

"Mhmm…"

"And why's that?" I asked, settling back into the couch. The shower could wait a minute. Maybe until after Ace had teased me to a throb-worthy erection.

"Well, I'm shirtless, to start with."

"Oh…I like that."

"I thought you might," he said. "And I'm down on my knees."

I sighed at that visual, and lowered my palm to press to my pants. "Don't stop there."

"Nope, not going to. Because I'm surrounded by…"

My mouth was parted as I waited for whatever he was going to say, but when all I got was his sexy, heavy breathing in my ear, I demanded, "Surrounded by what?"

Then he laughed and said something I did *not* expect. "DVDs, Daydream."

Huh?

"I've been so fucking pathetic without you I've resorted to rearranging my DVD collection. I need you to get over here—fast."

"Please tell me you're arranging them by size."

"Contrary to what you seem to think, I haven't seen all of Hollywood naked. So, no. Sorry to disappoint, but they're getting arranged by genre and then alphabetically."

My hand left my pants, and I screwed my nose up. "So let me get this straight. You miss me so much that you thought rearranging your home theater was a good idea? I would've preferred masturbation in the hot tub."

"I'd prefer *you* in my hot tub."

"That's more like it."

"Good. You'll be dessert. Want me to call in anything for dinner? A new Thai place just opened down the street."

My stomach growled at the mention of food. "Yeah,

that sounds great. If you'll call it in, I'll swing by and pick it up on the way. Anything and everything sounds good right about now. Fucking starving."

"Two of everything comin' right up."

"I feel like I'm a bad influence. You were all chicken and kale when I met you, and now I've got you sending out for Thai. Should I apologize?"

"Nah. I think I deserve a few cheat days."

"Damn right you do. Especially after a long, hard day of rearranging DVDs," I said, chuckling.

"All right, all right. I'm walking away right now. See? I'm not an addict. I can quit anytime."

That just made me laugh harder as a knock sounded at my door. "If you say so. Hey, I think Lloyd from down the hall needs quarters for the washer again, so let me run and I'll be over there in an hour."

"Can't wait."

As I ended the call, the knock sounded again.

"Just a sec, man, lemme get some change," I said, opening the jar of quarters I kept on the counter. Another thing I'd had to get used to in L.A.—sharing a washer and dryer with dozens of other renters. I pulled out a couple dollars' worth and then went over and unlocked and opened the door. "Here you—" My words died in my throat as I came face to face with a woman a few inches shorter than me.

"Oh, sorry," I said. "I thought you were someone else. Can I help you?"

The woman's lips curved into a sad smile. "You don't recognize me?"

The words *should I?* were on the tip of my tongue, but I stopped short when I saw the way her eyes, the same sea-green shade as mine, gave me a once-over. My hand went to the doorframe as I looked at her again. Light brown hair, the same shade as mine, and instead of the thick makeup and red lipstick that used to cake her face, she hardly wore anything now at all.

"Holy shit," I breathed, as I realized who the woman standing in front of me was. The one I'd escaped all those years ago. The same one who'd used me for money, who'd been verbally abusive, and who'd thrown me into the lion's den with a man three times my age just to pay her rent.

Brenda beamed. "You're so much taller than I remember, Dylan."

I gripped the door beneath my hand to stop it from shaking as I stared at the smiling face tipped up at me. *God...it can't be.* But as I stood there paralyzed, it was as if I was transported back to that old, grungy living room, with the orange couch and stale air.

"Aren't you going to invite your mom inside?"

I was pretty sure the words *fuck no* were on the tip of my tongue, but I'd be damned if I could work out how to get them out. Visions of my childhood with *this* woman were long buried under a shitload of hurt, denial, and self-loathing, and it had taken years to banish the memories that, until recently, I'd forgotten were lurking inside of me. But they were there. They did exist. And so did she.

As she took a step forward, I came back to myself, to my current situation, and I blinked her into focus and straightened off the door, blocking her progress. "How did you find me?" I had to know. There was no way Sunshine or Ziggy would've told her, so that only left—

"Why, the TV, of course. You've become somewhat of a celebrity these days. Every time I turn on the tube, there you are. And your apartment."

My stomach knotted, and then dropped like a bowling ball into my gut as I white-knuckled the wood. I gulped in a much-needed breath of air and felt it get stuck when it hit the huge lump in the back of my throat. *This can't be happening,* I thought, but no matter how many times I blinked, each time I refocused she was still there.

"Can't we talk inside?" she asked. "I just want to—"

"No," I said, shaking my head. If I could've screamed *no, no, no,* then I would've. But that one *no* had been a stretch in my current state. Anything else would've been monufuckingmental.

"Son, please. I just want to talk to you. I've changed—"

"*Don't* call me that," I said. The smile on her face dropped then as she reached for my arm, and I stumbled back, hitting the door in my haste. "You need to leave."

"Dylan—"

"*Leave.* I don't want to see you," I forced out as I took another step back to grip the door handle, and as I began to shut it, I added, "Ever."

Her face vanished in the sliver of the opening provided by the door, and then it disappeared as it slammed shut. I made sure to lock the latches, and then added the chain for good measure, before I turned around, leaned my back to the door, and then slid down it until my ass was on the floor and my knees were pulled up against my chest.

She can't hurt me, I thought, as I wrapped my arms around my knees and fought to hold back the tears blurring my eyes. *She's nothing. She can't hurt me.* But even as I said the words on repeat in my head, the fact that I was curled up, frozen in place, told me one very hard truth. And that was that I was a fucking liar.

22
CRAZY BITCH

AS THE SUN peeked up over the horizon and slipped through the shades I'd drawn the night before, I trailed my eyes along the man lying beside me. With the sheets drawn to his waist, and his head resting on the plush pillow, Dylan looked calm and peaceful as he continued to sleep beside me. A far cry from how he'd arrived on my doorstep the night before. His hair, which had grown back to the familiar longer strands I'd originally known him to have, were tousled where he'd worried it with his fingers all night.

God, last night had been difficult. I'd opened my front door to Dylan expecting one thing, and ended up getting a whole boatload of something else. The second his face had come into view, I'd known. Even if I wasn't as connected with him as I was, seeing the strain on his face, the bloodshot eyes, and the hard set of his jaw would've sent up all the red warning signs. And when I'd reached for him, he'd practically collapsed into my arms...

"'Bout time you got here, Daydream. I'm starving. For food and..." My words trailed off, and the smile I'd been sporting since Dylan had called to tell me he was back home slipped from my face to be replaced by a severe downturn of my lips. My guy looked as pale as a ghost.

"Dylan? What's wrong?" And it was blatantly obvious that something was wrong. Dylan had his arms hugging his waist, his eyes were glued to his feet, and there were no plastic bags containing the dinner he'd told me to order for us that he would pick up.

No, he was pulling a statue routine, right there on my front stoop. Mute and all.

I took a step forward, out the door, and that was when Dylan finally raised his eyes to mine, and the lost and vacant look inside of them matched the hollow feeling now growing in the pit of my stomach.

Without another word, I opened my arms, and Dylan stepped into them—practically crumpled into them.

"Hey," I whispered, running a soothing palm up his spine to the back of his neck, and when he trembled, I knew I needed to get him inside. "Come with me," I said, and then shifted to wrap my arm around his shoulders and draw him into the house.

Watching Dylan fall apart in front of me as he told

me the story of Brenda showing up on his doorstep was heartbreaking—and it also had me seeing red. The fucking nerve of that woman… How could she possibly think it was okay to approach him like that? To approach him at all? After everything she'd put him through…

Dylan stirred, his brows pinched together, as if he was seeing something he didn't like. I reached over and, with a light touch, smoothed the wrinkles from his forehead. When his eyes flitted open to focus on me, he gave a small smile.

"I like watching you sleep," I said, running my fingers along his jaw.

He gave a low chuckle. "Why? Because I drool?"

"Because you look so peaceful. Almost innocent. The exact opposite of you when your eyes are open."

"Smartass."

"Always," I said, grinning. "And you don't drool or I'd make you wear a bib to bed."

"Please tell me that's not a fantasy of yours."

"You're a sick man, Prescott. But I like that about you." I rested my head in my hand as I trailed my fingers down the scruff on his neck. When they came to a stop over his heart, I said, "I think…that you should stay here for a while."

Dylan's half-mast eyes fully opened then, and his forehead scrunched again. "You mean a while as in all day today, or…"

"*Or* several days. In a row. For"—I gave a one-shoulder shrug, trying to act nonchalant about what I was asking—"a while."

A shy smile crept across Dylan's lips as he rolled toward me and mirrored my position, elbow bent, head in hand, eyes on mine. "Are you asking me to move in with you?"

I opened my mouth to tell him *yes*, but before the word could get past my lips, he brought a finger up to hush me, and his smile vanished. His eyes turned serious then, as though another thought had just entered his mind, and then he spoke.

"Are you asking because it's something you want? Or because of what happened with Brenda?"

I reached for his wrist and drew his hand down to the mattress between us, and then I stroked his cheek and lips and said, "I'm asking you because I want to be with you. Morning, noon, night. I'm greedy. I want any spare time you have to be my time." I rolled to my back, staring up at the eyes focused on me.

Yeah, I probably sounded like a control freak. But that wasn't what I meant. I didn't want to be the *only* thing in his life. I just wanted to be in it in some kind of permanent capacity. I wanted to share the good times and the bad with him. "That sounds crazy, I know—"

"No," he said, scooting across the space between us. I extended my arm on the bedding for him to come closer, and the sheet slipped down the curve of his hip as he molded his naked front to my side, and then laid his cheek on my shoulder. "It sounds like a dream," he whispered in my ear.

I looked his way, and when that shy smile reappeared, I felt my chest close to burst with love for him. "It does?"

Dylan nibbled his lower lip and nodded, before leaning in to nuzzle into the crook of my neck. "I'm greedy too."

As he said that, Dylan trailed his fingers across my chest then mimicked my move from earlier, flattening his palm over my heart. "Thank you for last night."

"I didn't do—"

"You were there," he said, and then his lips brushed my cheek. "You listened to me. You held me. And Ace?"

"Yeah?" I asked, turning so our noses touched, and when I saw the glistening remnants of a lone tear on his cheek, I gently kissed his lips and he whispered, "You made me feel safe."

I rolled him to his back then, and as I hovered over him, I cradled his head between my hands and skimmed my thumbs over his cheeks.

I had no doubt as I gazed down at him that I was in as deep as I could be with another person. And as Dylan lay there looking up at me with such trust—which, if I wasn't out of my mind for him, would have me running for the hills—I took pride in it. I wanted that trust. And the fact that he'd handed it over to me, when I knew it wasn't something he gave lightly, made what we shared all the more sacred for it.

* * *

A COUPLE OF days later I was sitting in my agent's office as she showed me the proofs from the Provocateur fragrance photoshoot. Claudia was leaning back in her leather office chair tapping her bottom lip with the end of her reading glasses.

"Sexy, aren't they?" she asked, as I studied image after image, and she was right. With the waves rolling into the shore, the snapshots of me, Rochelle, and Lorenzo, the two models I'd worked with the other morning, were *extremely* sexy.

The images I'd taken with the two of them writhing around in the sand had come out in a stunning display of sensuality at its best. They were a tease of what *could* happen and what *might* have happened while wearing Provocateur.

Rochelle was positioned on her back, arched up on her elbows with her head tilted back to expose her throat and chest in her miniscule string bikini while the water rushed to shore, surrounding her feet and ankles. Lorenzo was on her right side dressed only in a pair of faded jeans, just as I had been, and was leaning down over her with his back to the camera, his mouth obviously heading for her chest.

And then there was me.

I was on the other side. Stretched out in unsnapped

jeans, with my fingers slipped into the band of her bikini bottoms and my eyes directly on the camera. My hair was slicked back, and my face was the only one front and center, my eyes inviting whoever was looking to come join us with our wet jeans and wandering hands. And my pouty, parted lips, which Ace always got a hard-on for, told the customer that what I was doing was just as sinful as they imagined.

"Yeah. It's sexy, all right," I said. "Good thing no one knows how cold the water was and just how uncomfortable these shots here, the ones draping ourselves all over the rocks, were."

Claudia sat up straight in her chair and reached for the final shot. "No one cares about that. They care about what you all did after this shot. They care that the perfume she was wearing made two hot men attack her on a beach. And they will all care that someone as sexy as *you* are inviting them to join in."

I couldn't help but laugh at that as I pointed out the obvious. "Even if they all know I'm gay?"

"Pshh, please," she said with a flick of her hand, her eyes sparkling at me. "Probably more so because of it. Wouldn't surprise me that that was why they cast two men. What woman wouldn't want to be the object of two men's affection, as well as—"

"Yeah, yeah Claude. I get it."

"Exactly," she said, jabbing the air with her finger, as if she'd just solved the answer to world hunger. "This campaign is going to sell millions of bottles of Provocateur, and they know it. The camera loves you, Dylan, and so did the photographer and Osare who called to tell me they would love a contract with you ASAP to lock in some more dates. What do you think?"

What did I think? *Wow*, was the first thing. The second was that the offer was a stroke to my ego. Osare was a big company, and for them to want me…it was exciting. But still, I didn't want to be anyone's exclusive property, shoot-wise. I didn't want to have the ability to say no taken away. That was very important to me. Actually, it was one of the original stipulations I'd put firmly in place when I'd entered into the world of modeling way back when. Because if I was going to use my face and body to make cash, then I was going to say who got the privilege to profit from it. That way, if I needed a break or I wasn't comfortable, I could get the hell out of Dodge. And I wanted to make sure that was still understood.

"That's very flattering, Claudia. But you know how I feel about exclusivity."

"Yes, but—"

"No," I said, getting to my feet. "That's a non-negotiable. I'm good to go on next week's shoot. Just let me know what time to be there."

"Got it. You're the boss," she said, getting up and rounding her desk. "I'll get you those details as soon as they call. I'd expect to hear something tonight."

"That's perfect."

"Oh, Dylan. You're the real deal, you know that?

Beautiful on the inside and out. Have you ever thought about being a spokesman for—"

"Claudia." I laughed, shaking my head. "One thing at a time, huh? My life has been kind of a whirlwind lately."

"I know, I know. But there's so much potential ahead for you. I just don't want to forget anything."

I gave her a soft smile, touched that she really was thinking of what was best for me. It was one of the things that had drawn me to her when she'd first approached. And I was happy that it hadn't changed, even with the rising volume of work and the increase in our paychecks. She still treated me as she had when I was making a hundred dollars for a catalogue spread.

I was about to head out, and then at the last minute remembered. "Oh, one other thing. This is my new address." I scribbled Ace's—well, *my* address down on the notepad and gave it to her. "If you need to send contracts or checks. That's where I'll be as of today."

"Oh, new apart—" She stopped short when she read the suburb and zip code, and then raised her eyes to mine. Yeah, nothing more needed to be said. It was more than obvious where I was packing up and going. "Congratulations."

"Thanks." I grinned, and then turned and headed for the door. I stepped out into the hall and then made my way down through reception and out onto the street. And when my flip-flops hit the sidewalk, I stopped dead in my tracks.

There, standing by the side of a beat-up beige truck,

was Brenda. She was leaning against the hood, and when she spotted me, she straightened up and stepped up onto the pavement.

This was unfuckingbelievable. How was she here? How did she even know where *here* was? And how had she known I would be here today?

Remembering what had happened a couple of nights ago, the way I had frozen and then basically fallen apart, I drew upon all of the strength and safety I'd felt when I was in Ace's arms and told myself to walk over to her and demand she get lost or I would take the matter to the police.

Firm in my resolve, I marched in her direction, and couldn't stop my hands from balling into fists. She made me feel helpless and violent all at the same time. When she dared to throw a *hey, how you doing* smile in my general direction, I glared and continued coming until I was finally towering over her.

"What are you doing here?" I demanded, not giving her the opportunity to spit out some bullshit pleasantry.

She stuttered a little, probably having expected me to freak out again and run away. But not this time.

"I asked you a fucking question," I barked.

Having located her lying tongue, she swallowed and took her sunglasses off to try giving me the puppy dog eyes, but really, did she think I was that stupid?

"How did you find this place? Find me?"

"I told you, Dylan. I've been following your career—"

"Bullshit," I said, crossing my arms for something to do rather than strangle her.

"I have. I looked you up. This company was listed as your agent and agency, and I thought if I waited here you might show—"

Of all the— "Are you *serious*? You're stalking me now? What is wrong with you? I don't want to see you. Not now, not tomorrow. Not ever."

I turned, ready to walk away from her. Ready to be *done* with her. But when small fingers with razor-sharp nails and a surprisingly powerful grip wrapped the width of my wrist and dug into my flesh, I whirled around on her so fast she was lucky the momentum didn't upend her. "Get your hand off me."

"Please, Dylan, just talk to me. I've changed."

That was the second time she'd claimed such a thing, but there was no way I was buying it. What a convenient bunch of horseshit. As I was about to express that opinion out loud, I caught sight of someone out of the corner of my eye. I glanced to the left and yes, right there, standing beside one of the palm trees planted alongside the road, stood a man with a camera held up to his eye, pointed in my direction.

Great. This was just what I needed. Just what Ace needed. Questions about the woman I was arguing with outside my modeling agency. I could see the headlines now. Not to mention what would happen when they worked out the truth.

Feeling my blood pressure reach its boiling point, I looked back to the woman oblivious to what had just happened and lowered my voice to a menacing sneer so any passersby wouldn't hear me.

"People like you don't change. Bottom feeders rarely surface to the light, and if they do, it's only to feed on the likes of others. I won't tell you again. Stay away from me or I'll call the police. And if you don't want me to do that right now, you'll get in your truck, and get the fuck out of my sight."

As she backed away from me, my hands shook. But I stood my ground while she got in the piece-of-shit truck and left, just to reassure myself she wouldn't trail me home.

* * *

I SCOWLED AT the television as I dragged the masking tape dispenser across the brown packing box between my legs. It had all the clothes Dylan owned folded up meticulously inside, and was one of the last boxes to be packed up.

It was the Saturday after I'd asked Dylan to move in with me, and we'd decided this afternoon would be a good time to come over and pack up his place so we could head out in the stealth of night just in case there were paps lurking and asking questions as to where he was moving.

They'd find out soon enough. They always did. Case in point: the current story being played on repeat over the entertainment news shows. It was one after another with them, and it always baffled me that they showed them back to back with nearly the—*actually, the exact*—same story on each. And today's breaking news was the same as it had been yesterday, and the day before.

Who's the dirty blonde with Prescott? A disgruntled ex?

Is trouble already brewing with PresLocke?

Christ, if anybody bothered looking a little closer at the grainy photo that had been snapped of Dylan and Brenda, they would see the uncomfortable posture, the rigid set of his jaw, and the disbelief stamped all over his face.

But they weren't seeing that, because they didn't know what they were looking at. As usual, they were merely speculating on the bugs under the microscope.

Shit. I hated that this was happening to Dylan. That once again Brenda had popped up when I hadn't been there to support him. But when Dylan had come home that night and told me what had happened, I noticed a distinct change in him. There'd been a determination that night that he wouldn't be ruled by her and his past fear that had made it a little easier to swallow. Until, of course, all of the news stories had started.

"Okay. I think that's the last of it for now," Dylan said, coming out of the bathroom and glancing around the tiny living room at all the boxes that were packed up and taped up, ready to be loaded in a couple of hours.

I reached for the remote and flicked off the TV just as Dylan came around the end of the couch and flopped down beside me.

"Perfect. We can get the rest next weekend."

"Yeah. That sounds good. Just the tallboy, couch, and we can give away the TV stand," he said, and then sighed. "I'm really going to miss this place."

"Me too," I said, settling back with my arm across the seat. Dylan took up the silent invitation and leaned into my side. "We had a lot of firsts in here."

"We did, didn't we..." he said, aiming a lecherous grin in my direction.

I nodded and couldn't help but lean in and press a firm kiss to that flirty mouth of his, and as his lips parted for my tongue, I dipped it inside and lost myself in the taste of him. He moaned and brought a hand up to touch my neck, and the sound and touch made a shiver run right down my spine to my cock. He was delicious.

"Mhmm, you seduced me in here," I said against his swollen mouth.

"Did I?"

"You did. You introduced me to your parents, then stripped out of your clothes, and seduced me out of my ever-loving mind."

Dylan gently sank his teeth into my lower lip, and as he pulled his head away, dragging the tips against my flesh, I groaned and was about to tumble him to his back when—

Knock. Knock. Knock.

—happened instead.

"Shh...don't answer," Dylan said, until the knock

sounded again. He groused and I laughed.

"It's probably just Lloyd, and you have all those quarters. You might as well give them to him," I said, and got up off the couch. I scooped up the jar of coins and glanced over at where Dylan had lain down on the couch, clearly having the same thoughts I was right then. "Don't you dare move."

I jogged to the door much quicker then, and when I pulled it open I drew up short because there, standing in front of me, was the woman from the grainy photo. The same woman Dylan had painstakingly described to me the first time he'd seen her a little over a week ago. And even without having seen and heard all of that, her eyes were the same as those of the boy she'd so carelessly tossed aside.

Yes. There was no doubt in my mind that I was finally face to face with Brenda.

"Oh." She gasped, a hand flying to her chest, her eyes wide. "I'm sorry. I was looking for—"

"I know exactly who you're looking for," I said, cutting her off right from the get-go. Dylan had made it abundantly clear that he wanted nothing to do with this woman. He'd told Sunshine, he'd told me—*hell*, he'd even told Brenda, but she kept coming back for more.

So if she wasn't going to listen to Dylan, if she didn't take *his* threat seriously, then perhaps it was time she heard it from another source. Someone who *wasn't* scared of her.

I stepped out the front door, the jar of coins still under my arm, and took great satisfaction from the way she backed up.

"Do you know who I am?" I asked, and I was sure to put on my most intimidating face. When she nodded, I opened my mouth to say more, but then I heard my name.

"Ace? Ace, who is—" Dylan's voice came to a stop, just as I sensed him arrive behind me. "What the fuck is the matter with you?" he shouted, and moved to charge forward.

I raised my free arm, planting a hand on his chest. Dylan was seething, his chest rising and falling, and I had no idea what he would do if he actually got his hands on the woman now glancing between the two of us, her eyes narrowing.

"I believe Dylan was very clear when he told you not to contact him."

"He was," she said, her voice having dropped the saccharine sweetness from a second ago and taking on an edge. A rough, sharp edge that had my fight instincts rising to the surface. "But you see, *this* is what I was coming for. What I've been waiting for."

"The fuck, Brenda? Get out of here," Dylan said, but it fell on deaf ears, because just like she'd said, she'd zeroed in on her target and it had nothing to do with her son. It had nothing to do with reconnecting with him. Or mending broken fences. *No.* It had everything to do with using him to get her next big hit. And I had a feeling that was—

"Ace Locke. My, my, Dylan. Your pretty face sure landed you in a pot of gold, didn't it? You always did aim higher than where you started. And thank God for that." She cackled, and the sound dripped with the poison she was dead set on trying to spread. "This will work out rather nicely."

"What do you want?" I snapped, but had a feeling I already knew the answer. I just wondered how much she thought she could milk me for.

"Two million dollars."

"What?" Dylan yelled, and muscled forward again, making me really put an effort into holding him back. "You've lost your fucking mind."

"On the contrary, *son*," she said, using the word as an insult. "I'm of very sound mind. What's a couple of mil to someone like him? Nothing."

This woman had another thing coming if she thought she was going to get shit from me. "What makes you think I'm going to give you a dime?"

Her eyes cut to the hand I had splayed on Dylan's chest, and the malicious quirk that curled her wrinkled lips made my skin crawl.

"Because I don't think you want the entire world to find out you're screwing a whore."

Blind rage distorted my vision then, and the jar of quarters that fell from my hands and smashed to smithereens on the concrete didn't even register. I charged forward and backed the bitch up until her back hit the rail so fast her feet barely carried her. Once we were toe to toe, I ground my molars together and growled. "I suggest you fuck off and crawl back to whatever hellhole you slithered out of. You won't get shit from me. And if I ever catch you sniffing around Dylan again, you'll have more than the police to deal with. Do you understand?"

Her eyes, the same ones I'd likened to Dylan's only minutes ago, were close to black, and I realized just how wrong I was. Hers were dead inside. There was nothing there. Just a bottomless pit of cruelty and malice.

"He must be a hot piece of ass for you to—"

My hand whipped out, shocking her into silence as I grabbed a fistful of her shirt, and that was when I felt a hand on my back.

"Ace."

Dylan's hollow voice barely registered through my fury, but when he spoke up a second time, he caught my attention.

"Ace, let her go. She brought an audience."

As if her shirt had burned me, I dropped the fabric and stumbled back, looking over the balcony for the first time since I'd stepped out on it. And sure enough, standing down on the lawn were several paparazzi with their cameras aimed up at the second floor. Aimed at me.

Brenda laughed, and the sound was so disturbing I stepped back into the apartment and reached for Dylan's hand, tugging him along with me. Then just as I turned to slam the door shut, I heard her speak.

"Aww, isn't love grand?" she cooed, making Dylan pivot to face her too. She ran a hand over her black blouse, then dug in her purse to pull out a little red square. "I think I said everything I wanted to. When you come to your senses and want to deal, lover boy, you can reach me here. You've got a week."

She tossed the cheap pack of motel matches our way, and the both of us let them fall at our feet on the floor, then, without a word, I followed through on my initial impulse and slammed the door in that bitch's face.

23
I HAVE CONFIDENCE

"OKAY, DYLAN, WE want these forty-two seconds to convey casual sophistication, effortless masculinity, and a polished confidence that every gentleman wants. We'll start with you lounging against the end of the bar, blurred out, with the bottle...here," the director, Gary, said. He was a tall, reedy guy with thick-rimmed glasses and long grey hair tied at the nape of his neck. He then pointed to the props master, who was positioning the whiskey bottle that sat on the bar top beside my left arm to face toward the cameraman. "Got it?"

I nodded. *Yep, got it.*

I'd been looking forward to this shoot all week. It was my first commercial on this scale and magnitude, and I was excited to see how it played out. Setup was much like a mini movie. When I'd arrived at the Edison, I'd been shown into a room for makeup, hair, and wardrobe, and once I'd donned the pristine Dolce & Gabbana suit I'd been ushered out to the bar, where a tight-knit crew was scurrying around to get everything into position for the first scene of the day. There were between twelve to fifteen people setting up equipment, as I listened to the directions being given to me.

The basic gist of the shoot was to make the alcohol appear to be the elixir that would turn any average Joe into a bold and suave man about town. Ace had told me to channel my inner Sinatra, and I had to admit, I was thinking about that bygone era as I stood there in the muted lights of the bar, with the smooth sound of a piano playing from somewhere off behind me.

"Okay, we're just about ready here, Dylan. You good?"

"Yes. Ready when you are."

"Perfect," Gary said as he walked backward toward the cameraman, boom operator, and producer. Two guys were up behind the lights, and when everything went quiet, I got my cue.

Yes. This right here was what I was born to do. I loved the quick no-nonsense, in-and-out—*usually in one day*—world of modeling. You came to set, were made up exactly the way they wanted you, and then you were shown where to stand and then the photographer, or cameraman in this case, positioned themselves, and you unleashed your magic.

Unlike moviemaking, this came naturally to me. Modeling was all about knowing your angles, the best light, how to use what God had given you to project the emotion the designer, producer, or company who had hired you were after. And luckily for me, I seemed to have a knack for that. No words were usually needed, no script to memorize, just the right twinkle in your eyes, the right cock of your chin, curl of your lips, or *come get me now* pout, and the photographer snapped, snapped, snapped, until he was shouting—

"Brilliant, Dylan! That was exactly what we wanted. Barely an extra take in there."

And only six hours later...*that* was a wrap.

I'd headed back to the small room I'd changed in earlier, and was in the middle of hanging my tailored slacks on the hanger when my cell phone started to ring on the small loveseat backed up to the far wall. I zipped up my jeans and glanced over to see Ace's name and number lighting up my screen, and when I picked it up I couldn't help the smile that crossed my lips.

"Aren't you supposed to be on your way to a meeting, hotshot?"

"I am," Ace said with a jangle of keys accompanying his voice, letting me know he was probably headed to his car as he spoke. "I just wanted to call and see how the commercial went today."

Uh huh, sure you did. More like he was calling to make sure a certain woman hadn't shown up, stalked me, called me, or popped out of a bush somewhere.

It'd been nearly a week now since Brenda had shown up at my apartment to blackmail Ace into keeping her silence about my past, and though it had taken me a couple of days to stop looking around every corner, paranoid that the boogeyman was going to spring out and ruin my life, I'd finally started to believe she'd listened to Ace's threat and fucked off for good.

That didn't make me feel any less guilty over what she'd tried to do. The memory of her demanding millions to keep from spreading her venom made me shudder every time I thought about it. But after much persuasion from Ace, I'd done my best to push it aside, and it finally seemed that things were settling down again.

"The commercial went great. Everyone here was wonderful, and you will soon see me sipping whiskey from a lowball down at the Edison." Ace's hum of approval came through the phone as I took my short-sleeved button-up off the hanger and slipped into it. "Oh and ahh…I may, or may not, have been given a few cases of the good stuff to take home with me. Soooo, can I persuade you with a bottle of Blue Label to come and help me move the rest of my furniture out tonight?"

"Hmm, I don't know…" Ace said as his Lamborghini's locks beeped. Then I heard a door open and shut and he was back. "Can I lick it off you?"

Yes, please. "I'm sure if you were available to help me, then that could be arranged."

"In that case, how about I meet you there after my meeting?" he suggested, just as he must've turned over the ignition. As the car roared to life, I groaned in his ear.

"I swear, every time I hear that car turn on I get hard."

"That makes two of us. You made this vehicle very difficult for me to drive, Daydream."

I leaned my shoulders back against the wall and grinned. "Are you complaining?"

"Fuck no. Best three million dollars I ever spent."

"Holy shit," I said.

Ace made a sound that was half purr and half growl, but one hundred percent animalistic. "Oh, there was nothing *holy* about what you did to me on this car."

I forced my eyes shut and lowered my hand to my stiffening cock. "Don't start something you can't finish."

"I know. I know. Give me a couple of hours and I'm all yours."

I nodded, and then switched gears, wanting to know how he felt about the meeting he was headed to today. He hadn't said much other than he was going to go.

"You excited?" I asked.

"About meeting with Ronaldo Mendez?"

"Yeah. I mean, you've never met him before, right? It was nice of Alejandro to set this up. He's a pretty big name."

"Try one of the biggest," Ace said.

"I'd be super nervous."

"Uhh, thanks—"

"No. No. I don't mean it like that. It's just he's *Ronaldo Mendez,* mega producer. That's huge."

I heard Ace let out a sigh, and imagined him rubbing his hand over the back of his neck. "It is. Honestly, though, I'm trying not to get too excited. Things haven't exactly been going my way lately, so I'll go and check out what he has to say. But I'm not going to stress about it."

I hated that. I hated that Ace was feeling that way. But it wasn't like he hadn't warned me this would happen, and most of the time it didn't even seem to bother him, especially when it was just me and him together. However, that didn't stop the stab of guilt I felt whenever someone called to tell him he was dropped from yet another movie or sponsorship.

It all seemed so unfair. Here I was doing better than ever *because* of Ace and my connection to him, while his career and life crumbled because of me. It made a person stand back and really look at their self-worth and what they had to offer, because in the end that *was* all I had to give him. And I hoped like hell every day that that was enough.

"Just see what he has to say—you never know in this town what's going to happen from one day to the next. And weren't you the one who told me it's all about who you know and your connections?"

Ace laughed. "Throwing my own words of wisdom back at me?"

"Yep. He wouldn't have called you and set up a meeting if he wasn't interested. So, go see what his project is.

See if it's something you're interested in or something-—"

"Ridiculous?"

"Ace…"

"Okay, okay," he said. "I'm going, and I'll approach the meeting with an open mind."

"Good," I said, happy to hear a touch of humor at the end there. "And Ace?"

"Yeah?"

"When you're finished, hurry home to my place. I'll be waiting."

After we said our goodbyes and ended the call, I checked my hair in the mirror and that my clothes were in order before I picked up my backpack and headed for the door. It was time to head over to my apartment and finish to say my goodbyes.

* * *

AS I SLOWED my car to a crawl, I made my way past the enormous houses located in the gated Beverly Park community and turned onto Beverly Park Lane.

God, the neighborhood in which I lived housed some impressive homes of the rich and famous, but some of these sprawled farther than the eye could possibly hope to see. When I found the number I was looking for, I brought my vehicle to a stop at the massive gate, which was flanked by two stone pillars, and illuminated by a Tudor light on each side. There was a camera mounted up top one of those thick columns, and one aimed in the general direction of my car's license plate. As I sat there, waiting to be screened or checked by whoever was at the other end of those security devices, I looked around at the dense foliage flanking the perimeter of the stone wall, which extended out to the left and right of each pillar.

Palm trees, ferns, and creeping ivy that was close to overtaking most of the exposed wall gave the home an extra barrier against anyone who might wish to camp out front and take photos of whoever was beyond the gates. In less than two minutes, *I would guess*, there was a clunking sound and then the wrought iron yawned open, inviting me to proceed forward.

Okay, so I'd told Dylan before I left that I hadn't been feeling the nerves. But, the truth be told, as I drove up the paved driveway flanked by a perfectly manicured lawn and thick-trunked palm trees, my hands were sweating and my heart was thumping.

This was a huge opportunity being offered up to me. Of this, I was aware. A meeting with Ronaldo Mendez was notoriously difficult to get, and when Alejandro had called to tell me his father had wanted a meet-and-greet, I'd barely believed it.

Life was always throwing you curves, new twists and turns in your journey, and in my professional life I'd been told from the get-go that sometimes it was all about connections. But this? This seemed crazy. Unreal, even.

Considering the way I knew *this* particular connection could never be discussed in a public setting due to binding contracts and the fear of being sued. It was still hard to believe that out of that sex-filled, fantasy-fueled night had come a "masked" opportunity I could never have seen coming...*or uh,* had *seen coming,* as it were.

Either way, Alejandro had really come through in getting me behind the famous gates of the Tuscan Vineyard Estate to see his father.

And now that I was here, I was determined to do everything in my power to make an impression.

I climbed out of my car, and as I shut the door behind me, I closed my eyes for a moment and let the afternoon sun warm me.

I can do this. I've done this a hundred times over. Just walk in there and sell Ace Locke, the action star. Right. The one thing tripping me up, though, was that lately no one had wanted Ace Locke the action star.

Trying to squash that train of thought, I adjusted my navy-blue sports coat and checked that I looked presentable. Matching pressed slacks, white open-collared shirt, and my brand new pair of black Ferragamo derbies. I was good to go.

I walked up the stairs and headed toward the double-wide glass and iron doors, and just as I reached them and would've rung the bell, a short, portly woman appeared and opened the door.

She was in black from her short, bobbed hair to her

leather-covered toes. Her complexion was olive, tanned skin, with wrinkles creasing the corners of her eyes when she smiled up at me, and I would guess she was in her late forties or early fifties.

"Ahh, welcome, Mr. Locke. Mr. Mendez has been expecting you."

"Thank you," I said, returning her smile and waiting to see if she would give her name.

"I'm Maria. I look after the home for the Mendezes and have for years. My husband tends to the yard and keeps the workers who tend to the vines in line."

"Well, you both do a wonderful job, Maria. This place is beautiful."

"Thank you. Come in, come in. Mr. Mendez is in the study. I told him I'd bring you straight through. So please, follow me."

And off she went. She turned on the heels of her flats and walked forward, leading me into a massive rectangular grand entrance where a wooden carved entry table sat with photos upon photos of the famous family who lived there. I stepped around it, and continued forward on marble floors so shiny they reflected the chandelier above. I couldn't help but look up at the huge white columns and archways to the second story.

Wow, this place was something else.

"This way, Mr. Locke," Maria said, taking the three steps up to the middle of the rectangular space that had a door all the way on the far side of it and two ramps that led up to the second level. She took the left, heading up the gradual incline, and I was quick to follow, not wanting to be caught gawking at the stunning spread.

When she reached the second level and walked toward the far end of the left side, she stopped at a closed door and knocked twice. I waited beside her, willing my pulse to slow down, because it was threatening to make me pass out, and then I heard a famously familiar voice call out, "Yes. Come in," and Maria pushed open the door and said, "Good luck."

Ohhh, yeah. I'm gonna need it, I thought, walking into a room that was much darker than the brightly lit entryway. As I glanced around the room, the rich cherry-wood-paneled walls automatically created a warm and inviting feel.

On every wall was a painting I had no doubt was worth more than most people made in a year, and littered around the room were antiques that were placed to look worldly and sophisticated, and had probably been painstakingly picked out by an overpaid home decorator.

I stopped and let my eyes adjust to the sunlight streaming through the window, and as my eyes traveled the room, they finally spotted a dark head of hair on a man seated on a couch facing the fireplace.

"Ace Locke. Come in and shut the door, son. We have much to talk about."

And without a moment's hesitation, I did just that, wondering where this next twist in the road would take me.

* * *

UGH, I WAS a nervous wreck. It'd been three and a half hours since I'd spoken to Ace, and I'd already exhausted the options on TV, showered, changed into the spare shorts and t-shirt, and still had time to bite all the nails on my right hand down to nubs.

Where was he? I was dying to know how things had gone. But so far I'd heard nada. No text, no call, no missed voicemail when I was showering. Hell, maybe these things always took this long; I didn't know.

I glanced at the time—it had just turned seven thirty, and I was hoping we'd be able to order in and have a final picnic of sorts to say goodbye to this place, but if he didn't get here soon, I was gonna go grab some grub and start without him. I was starving.

I was just getting up to start a new round of pacing when there was a loud knock on my door. With a huge grin on my face, I raced over to it and was sure to check the peephole after the whole Brenda situation, and when I saw the back of Ace's broad shoulders, my breath caught and I quickly unlatched and unlocked the door.

When I swung it open, he turned to face me with his hands in the pockets of his dress slacks, looking all cool and casual and sexy.

"Hey there, handsome," I said by way of greeting,

and as Ace sauntered forward, I noticed the proud set of his shoulders, the cocky swagger to his walk, and when he stopped beside me to brush his lips to mine, the confidence in his eyes had my knees close to buckling.

"Hi yourself, Daydream."

The husky timbre of his voice did all kinds of shit to my brain and cock, but it was the spark in his eyes that was really wreaking havoc on every nerve in my body.

"Come in," I managed, and Ace knew exactly the effect he was having on me, because his lips curved on top of mine and he raised his brows.

"Come in...where?"

I brought the hand that was resting by my side to his chest and chuckled. "How about we start with my apartment?"

"And then..."

Well...someone was in a mood. I shoved him back a little, and when he winked at me, I blushed. I actually fucking blushed. "And then you just might get lucky."

"I am feeling lucky today," Ace said, and slicked his tongue across his lower lip before he walked inside the apartment. I slowly closed the door and took in a deep breath.

Hot damn, he had my brain scrambled and all off kilter as I tried to remember what exactly I'd been dying to ask him. I relocked the door and rounded back to see him sitting on my couch with his arms spread across the back, his jacket hanging open, and his legs kicked out in front of him.

"Why don't you come sit over here with me?" he said, and I didn't know what was going on here, but a wave of shyness swept over me. "Dylan...come 'ere," Ace said, his voice dropping down to that tone that stroked all the right places, and I sank my teeth into my lip.

What was going on with me? I felt as though I was tripping all over myself. Clumsy. Totally off my game. And all because Ace was here? And that was when it clicked. *That* was the difference.

Ace was here. *Ace Locke.* The movie star. Mr. Confident. Mr. Blow Them Up, Sex on Legs, Save the Day was sitting on my old couch looking at me like he wanted to strip me naked and eat me for dinner.

And that was when I remembered exactly what I'd been going to ask him. How his meeting had gone. But judging by the man I was looking at, it had gone well. *Very* well.

"Good meeting today?" I asked.

Ace nodded and crooked his finger at me again. "Come over here and I'll tell you about it."

As I walked over to him, I took in a breath and marveled again that he was here with me. That he was mine, and when I finally sat down beside him and he pulled me as close to his side as he could get me, I laughed at myself.

"Why are you acting like you just met me all of a sudden?" he asked.

I angled my face up to him and gave a wry grin.

"You're throwing off that whole larger-than-life vibe, and it's—"

Ace leaned in and swept my mouth up in a delicious kiss that had me turning into his body and bringing a hand up to touch his cheek while he wrapped his arm around me. When he was finally done destroying any capacity to think, he pulled back and I blinked a couple of times to get him into focus.

"Fuck," I said, touching the base of his throat with my fingertip. "Just give me a minute to remember how to think."

That made Ace laugh. "You're seriously adorable right now, Daydream."

"Yeah? Well, when you come in all *Ace Locke movie star*," I said adopting my best movie announcer voice, "I tend to forget that I get to sleep with you each night. It makes me stupid."

"Not stupid...cute, sexy, and a little shy, apparently."

I rolled my eyes at him, and when that only made him laugh harder, I huffed. "Oh, cut it out."

"But it's so funny. The first time I met you, you weren't shy at all."

"Well, no. I was pissed off at you."

When Ace's fingers moved to the back of my neck to flirt with my hair, he asked, "Would you like me to piss you off then?"

"No...I want you to tell me how the meeting went."

Ace acted as though he was thinking about it, and then he flashed a smile so wide it almost stretched his entire face.

"It went great. Beyond great." Twisting his big body on the couch, he brought his arms down between us so he could clasp my hands in his. "Ronaldo told me about this new film he's producing. It's an adaptation of a book he fell in love with. A drama about a couple struggling to save their marriage after years together and only having been with each other. It's about love, betrayal, passion, and finding yourself before committing to someone else. It's got a low budget but an A+ cast, A+ producer, and, well, he wants me to be in it."

"Oh my God, Ace, that's—"

"I know," he said. "I can't believe it. That he wants me to be in it, and not just a secondary character—he wants me as the lead."

"What?" I shouted, and then I jumped to my feet, unable to contain my excitement. "That's amazing. Oh my God," I said again, as tears welled up in my eyes. I was so happy for him. So proud, and I could tell by the look on his face and the moisture gathering in his own eyes that he was just as overcome with emotion. Ace reached for my wrist and tugged me back down, and this time when I fell it was into his lap, and I kissed him hard. When I pulled back, he was shaking his head and tracing my jaw as he said, "You should've seen me sitting there in his huge study, in his Tuscan villa with its very own vineyard. I felt like it was the first time I'd ever gone to a meeting."

"Aww…" I said. "So you *were* nervous."

"Of course."

"Liar."

"Well, I try not to voice the nerves; that way they can't overwhelm me. But you know what, he was really nice. Before we even started talking about why I was there, he told me right up front he had no problem with my sexuality or who I was dating, and I was there in his office because he'd seen my body of work and wanted me to be there."

"Wow."

"I know," Ace said with a sigh. "After that I could breathe a little easier, and then everything just kind of came together. He gave me the script to read, and to see if I'm interested, but I…"

"Yeah?" I said as I stared into Ace's amazing blue eyes.

"I've wanted something like this for years."

"A drama? Really?"

"Mhmm…and with such a great cast and Ronaldo producing it, I can hardly believe this is serious."

I massaged my hand over his chest. "Well, believe it. You deserve it, and I'm glad he's smart enough to see what a fantastic actor you are no matter who you're—"

"In love with?"

I grinned. "Yes. That. But I have to say, now the idea of takeout and having a picnic here to say goodbye to the place feels a little underwhelming."

"No, I think it sounds perfect," Ace said as he glanced around my little rattrap. "This place needs a proper send-off. Why don't we order Chinese, and I'll help you load the U-Haul, and then we can—"

"Go out with a bang?" I whispered against his mouth.

When Ace groaned and ran a hand down to cup my ass, he said, "My thoughts exactly."

24
LEAVING
WITH A BANG

AFTER WE'D EATEN dinner, I lounged back on my "in the wall" bed and watched Ace move around the tiny kitchen throwing out the empty Chinese containers. I'd tucked two pillows under my head and was eyeing him with what I knew had to be a totally depraved smirk, because the entire time he'd been cleaning, I'd been devising the perfect way to say "congratulations on your new job," while also giving a proper, *or not so proper*, farewell to this place.

"What?" Ace asked, when he finally glanced up to see me eyeing him. He tied the end of the garbage bag, washed his hands, and then came around the counter to lean a knee on the end of the mattress. He'd taken his jacket off and unbuttoned his cuffs to roll them up his forearms, and as he stood there, all of my shyness from earlier flew out the window.

I gave an innocent enough shrug, trying to play off the fact I wasn't eye-fucking him—hard. "I didn't say anything."

His eyes cruised the length of my torso, down to my shorts, and I knew there was no way he would miss the distinctive bulge now on prominent display there. "No, your mouth didn't. But your body sure did."

I brought a hand down to press it over the zipper of my pants, and then bent my left leg to push up against it. "Is it?" I asked, grazing my teeth over my lower lip. "Hmm, and what's it saying?"

Ace's eyes had fallen to where I was curling my fingers around the erection now throbbing between my legs, and then they slowly crept their way back up to collide with mine.

God, the lust that was swirling in his aroused expression had my entire body close to overheating, and just when I thought he'd climb up the bed and connect that spectacular body of his with mine, he moved back and straightened to his full height.

When my mouth parted, and I was about to ask where he was going, Ace held a finger up and then gave me a smirk to match mine from seconds ago.

Oh hell, I knew that look. That look meant I was in for it. That look meant that the wicked flame of arousal had consumed all vestiges of politeness in the enormous man walking around the end of my bed. And the flush that now warmed the skin of Ace's cheeks meant that I'd successfully tempted the savage to the surface.

"It's saying that it wants me to look at it…"

I chuckled, as I stretched my leg back down the bed and tracked him to the mostly empty tallboy in the corner of my apartment, knowing what he was going for.

Condoms. Lube. Yes, I haven't packed that drawer yet. Get them—hurry.

"I think you might be right. I want to make an exit with a bang," I said, undoing the button of my shorts and lowering the zipper. Ace stopped to watch me, and then boldly adjusted the erection I could see straining against his own zipper.

"Take them off," he said, when I went to slip my hand inside. "I want it all off, Dylan. Now."

Fuck. When Ace got like this my brain just about melted out my ears. Controlling, sexy, and totally zeroed in on getting the both of us off. I knew whatever was about to go down in the next few minutes would most certainly leave me relaxed—and maybe, if I was lucky, passed out from pleasure excess.

With my eyes on him, I slipped my thumbs into my shorts and briefs and had them over my ass and hips and down my legs quicker than ever before. After I kicked them to the floor, Ace licked his lower lip and unbuttoned and unzipped his dress pants.

"The shirt too," he ordered.

Jesus.

"Now. Dylan."

I whipped it over my head, tossed it somewhere out of my way, and then lay back down and gripped the base of my cock. A groan rumbled through my chest at the pleasure of touching myself, and when Ace cursed, I turned my head on the pillow to see he'd shoved his hand into his pants to stroke his own length.

There was something to be said for being completely naked and under the hungry gaze of your lover. I'd always been a fairly sexual person, someone who enjoyed their past encounters, and I'd always thought myself to be a versatile partner, happy to be taken or be the one taking. But hell, if I wasn't always quick to hit my knees or back for this magnificent man. I had this insatiable craving when it came to Ace. There was no explaining it. But when he was around, I needed contact no matter which way he wanted to give it to me.

"So," Ace said, voice raspy, full of ramped-up lust as he dug his free hand into the pocket of his pants to pull out a square packet. "I'm not sure if this is a good time to mention it, but I want to stop using these with you," he said as his lids lowered and he continued to palm himself.

Sweet Christ. If my moaned "*Yesss*" wasn't answer enough, the reaction my entire body gave was proof positive that the idea of Ace orgasming deep inside my body, with no barrier in the way, was an erotic invitation I couldn't, and wouldn't, ever deny. My eyes shut, the soles of my feet hit the mattress, and my hips jerked up, as my fingers clenched around my cock so hard the veins in my forearm popped.

"I take it you like that idea," he said as he tossed the packet to the floor. "I'm glad to hear it, because the next time I'm inside you, you're gonna feel me when I explode."

Oh shit...so that isn't *going to be tonight?* Ace was obviously hellbent on torturing me.

"Tonight, however..." he said, turning away to rifle through the drawer, and when he rounded back, a light bulb went off.

How had I forgotten what *else* I kept in that drawer? Oh, that's right, he destroyed my brain cells. Chalk that up to one more thing I loved about him. The fact that he knew all of my kinks, all of my quirks, and all my secrets, and still loved me.

"I think we have time for one more *first* before we leave. Don't you?"

And fuck me, right there in his hand, was thirteen inches of wicked-hot fun.

* * *

I'D BEEN THINKING about *this* particular moment since the first time I'd spent the night in Dylan's bed, and consequently the first night I'd spent inside Dylan. Yep, I sure had, and before he moved out I was determined to have it.

Dylan was naked and laid out flat on his bed, with his dripping cock in his hand and eyes so full of fevered arousal I was surprised he hadn't set his bedding on fire with how amped up he looked.

I was finding it increasingly difficult to concentrate with the throbbing ache of my cock pounding out an insistent beat in time with my racing heart. But God, Dylan stripped of everything was a powerful lure to that side he always referred to—*my beast.*

Who knew I even had that in me? This man, apparently. The one now watching me stroke the thirteen-inch dildo like I was a hypnotist. But tonight I wanted Dylan to be the one to work his magic. He'd joked with me that first time that I shouldn't feel intimidated by the size of the sex toy, and I'd been quick to assure him that was certainly not the case when it came to the thought of him using this thick phallus. No, quite the contrary. I was eager to see it in action. And tonight was the night.

I arched a brow as if daring him to say no, but by now I knew Dylan and his sexual proclivities well enough to know that my man liked an audience. So I tossed the toy on the bed by his hip, and then turned to grab the bottle of lube. After I shut the drawer, I walked back around to the end of the mattress where the couch sat facing the bed, shoved my pants and boxers to my ankles, and then stepped out of them before taking a seat.

Dylan moved then, getting up on an elbow to look my way. "Uh—"

"Don't tell me you don't know what I want," I said, arrogant as ever, knowing that also flipped Dylan's switch.

Then I wrapped my hand around my dick and gave a long pull, groaning at the sensation.

Dylan picked up the dildo and looked at it before meeting my gaze across the sizzling, sex-filled air. "You want me to use this on myself."

The way he said it was not a question, because he knew he was spot-on, but I decided to give him an answer just the same. "Yes, Dylan. I want you to fuck yourself with it."

When his mouth fell open, I schooled my features to blank. *Oh yeah*, Dylan's erection, if possible, had become longer and harder with those words, and when he picked up the bottle of lube and opened it, the sound was like a gunshot ricocheting around the tense room.

I slowed my strokes as I watched him pour the cool liquid into his palm, and then he closed the lid, tossed it down, and snatched up his toy.

With his green eyes fixed on mine, he sat up then, with his back to the wall, and placed his feet flat on the bed. He then draped his arms over his knees, and the view he'd just given me was nothing short of fucking spectacular.

But the instigator wasn't done one-upping me. *No.* Because Dylan then angled the flesh-colored cock in his right hand, and proceeded to lube that fucker up good and well with his left. Once he was done, he laid the toy by his side, let his legs splay wide, and then lowered that left hand to massage the rest of the lube over his rigid shaft, heavy balls, and finally down to that tight little hole.

My eyes were zeroed in on his fingers as he teased and tormented himself, slipping the pads of his fingers over that dark pucker before pushing against it gently. When a moan splintered through the otherwise silent apartment, my eyes flew up to his, and the way Dylan then caught his breath had me giving a strong pull of my own dick, because surely that meant—

Yesss.

As my eyes lowered back down, I saw that his finger had disappeared inside his body and was slipping in and out. *Shit. Shit.* That was so hot. Dylan reached down to hold his balls up and out of the way so I could see exactly what he was doing to himself as he slid in a second finger and had me groaning.

"Dylan. Fuck."

But he didn't respond, other than to pull his fingers out and then push them back inside, over and over again. As his hand moved faster and those fingers began to twist and spread, he began to pant and curse in the room, and I was rendered speechless at the wanton display happening only feet away from me.

It wasn't until he pulled his fingers free entirely, and reached for the thirteen-incher, that I was aware how quiet I'd been through the exchange. Because when I tried to speak, my voice cracked.

Dylan looked over at me, his cheeks pink, his lips swollen from chewing them as he'd bumped over his prostate time and time again, and I tried again to speak.

"Closer."

When he narrowed his eyes, I got to my feet, dick in hand, and then crooked a finger at him, indicating that he needed to come the fuck closer to me. With a sensual curl of his lips, Dylan moved down the bed, dildo in hand, and then placed a pillow for his head before he lay on his back and bent his legs.

Yeah this is perfect, I thought, because Dylan was now so close, I could touch his bent knee.

* * *

NEVER *EVER* COULD I have dreamed this up. Ace was standing at the end of my bed, legs braced, milking his cock, looking down at my widespread thighs, waiting for me to pound myself with my thirteen-inch friend. Yeah, *never*. But fuck if I wasn't up to the challenge.

My erection was aching, it was so hard. Any blood that had been in other parts of my body was currently all located in the steel shaft that I couldn't quit stroking. Pre-cum had leaked all over my stomach and abdomen, and the sticky mess was helping with the glide and slide as I curled my fingers around the toy I was about to go to town on.

I licked my lips as I brought the dildo in between my legs, and I shut my eyes as I lined it up, because I knew if I watched Ace's face while I slid the fuck stick inside of me, it was going to be all over before I could pull it out and shove it back in.

"Fuck yes," Ace growled as I pressed the head to my entrance. "Show me how you take it. God, I've dreamed about this."

That had my eyes popping open. As I slowly eased the silicone past the first ring of muscle I groaned, and then clamped my teeth into my lower lip. Ace's eyes didn't rise from what was going on down below. So I started up again, adding pressure to the toy, pushing it in and then pulling it back, before repeating the move and going a little deeper. As I continued the seductive push and pull of it all, I added firm tugs of my dick to the well-choreographed performance I was putting on for Ace. My breathing was all over the place as my arousal increased, and finally, when the toy was lodged inside of me, Ace's "Stop" had me halting.

I found his gaze, and the look there should've frightened me, as I lay spread wide and vulnerable, but it didn't. Instead, that raw look made me want him to tear into me. It made the hand on my cock tighten and a whimper bubble out of me, and with no other words, just that one look, Ace had me begging him.

"Please," I said, needing his hands on me. His mouth. Whatever he wanted to give. "Finish it for me."

Ace kneeled on the small space I'd left at the end of the bed, and then reached down between my legs and gripped the end of the toy. As he slowly pulled it from me, a shout tore from my throat, shocking the two of us with the sheer volume, but it was when he reversed the action and burrowed it back inside that I was gone.

My body felt as though it was floating as I lost my mind under the man driving me out of it. The muscle of my arm pumped and flexed as I continued to give myself a feverish handjob in time to the quick jabs Ace was now delivering to me. And when I felt the hot jets of Ace's cum splash onto my chest and abs, my climax slammed into me, and I screamed the place down as I crashed from the best high I'd ever experienced.

Oh yeah, we sure as fuck would be exiting the building with a bang.

25
UNLOCKED

"I THINK THAT'S the last of it," Dylan said, grunting as he dropped his end of the tallboy onto the floor of my foyer.

Correction—*our* foyer. It was midmorning Saturday, and after dragging ourselves from his bed and moving the last of his furniture from his small apartment, he was officially moved in. Well, not including the stuff still sitting in his place in Florida, but he said he'd deal with that later.

Dylan's hand went to his lower back as he straightened, and my lips twitched in amusement.

"You okay there, old man?" I asked. "Not gonna keel over, are you?"

He held up a finger in response, and I couldn't stop the laugh that bubbled out.

"A little heavy lifting and the man is down for the

count—"

"A little?"

"It's not like we had a huge house to move," I said. "We might need to work on your stamina. I'm willing to go all night with you if that's what it takes. Work you hard and deep."

Dylan shot me a glare and shuffled down the hall. "Haha, you're hilarious, asshole. It's not the furniture; it's the fact that I worked my*self* hard and deep for you that I'm a little worse for wear this morning. Where do you keep the aspirin?"

"That's the drawer I know," I said as I walked past him into the kitchen and opened the drawer by the fridge. I took out the pills, grabbed a water out of the fridge, and then set them in front of him. "Ibuprofen's better for muscle aches. And I'm sorry, we should've waited—"

"No, we shouldn't have waited until we got back here. The whole point was to give it a send-off. And boy did we. You know, I don't even think Derek had me work some of these muscles—" He stopped and laughed when he caught the expression on my face. "I meant at the gym."

"I've never heard the bed called the gym before, but..." I grumbled.

Dylan swallowed the pills, and when he'd finished off half the water bottle, he grinned. "I have to admit, this jealous side is kinda hot."

I reached for the top of his jeans and tugged him forward, and when he was flush against me, I ground my hips against his.

"Does that feel jealous to you?" I asked.

"No...it feels amazing," Dylan said, and wound his arms around my neck. When he winced, I frowned.

"Aww, poor babe. You really are sore, aren't you?"

He pouted, and those delicious lips of his were more than I could resist. I took them in a hard, swift kiss as I wrapped an arm around his waist and kneaded my fingers into his lower back.

"Oh *God*," he said as he pulled his mouth away. "That feels—"

I did it again, and Dylan groaned in a way that made my dick hard.

"Good?" I asked.

"Yesss..."

I continued to dig my fingers into his back and then ran a firm line up his spine to his neck, where I massaged the tense cords there. Dylan let his head fall back as he rolled his hips against me, and I smiled at his obvious enjoyment. He certainly knew how to relax into a moment, and the taut muscles under my fingertips definitely needed to be worked out.

I looked past his shoulder to the TV that was playing in the background, and as Dylan's lips found the side of my neck, a familiar face flashed across the screen and I froze. The arms I had wrapped around Dylan tensed, and my jaw locked up like a vise as the headline popped up on the screen.

EXCLUSIVE: NEW INFORMATION ON ACE'S BOY TOY *UNLOCKED.*

But that wasn't what had me all rigor mortis. *No,* I thought as the show cut to commercial. It was the woman whose face they'd run that headline under. The woman who was seated in some studious-looking room, with her hair straightened, perfect makeup applied, radiating an innocence she certainly hadn't had a week ago when she'd been blackmailing me for a cool two mil. And fuck, the idea of what that bitch was about to say almost had me herding Dylan out of the kitchen and back to the U-Haul we'd just finished unpacking.

"Hey," Dylan said as he lifted his lips from my neck to look at me. He'd probably noticed my dick had flagged and my attention was elsewhere, and considering I usually had trouble focusing on breathing when he was near, I was sure he'd picked up on my change in mood. *Fucking great.*

"What's wrong?" he asked as he pulled away from me. When he caught sight of my face, his smile dropped. "Ace? What is it? What's the matter?"

I tore my eyes off the commercial playing, and when I found his gaze I opened my mouth to tell him, but in my periphery I caught the intro to the entertainment show and it was too late. Dylan had seen the direction of my stare and pivoted to take a look at what had stolen my attention from him, and as his spine straightened to the point where it looked painful, I wondered what was going through his mind.

"Sex, lies, and dirty secrets were unlocked this past week," the announcer said. "We've got all the details on the mysterious man in Ace Locke's love life. That's right. Dylan Prescott, the other half of PresLocke, has been an enigma up until now. With Locke and his camp staying quiet on the whirlwind romance, not much has been learned about the sexy Calvin Klein model, other than he looks *muy caliente* in a pair of briefs. But we sent Holly to sit down with a woman who knows all about this young man. After all, who would know him better than his own mother..."

Oh shit.

Shit.

Shit.

Fucking shit.

My eyes darted to the man standing an arm's length away from me, and as I went to reach for him, Dylan began to move. One foot in front of another, he tracked across the space between the kitchen to the couches like a robot with the single-minded focus of getting as close to the mounted screen on the wall as possible.

As the blasted show cut to another set of commercials, to no doubt draw out their thirty minutes of viewership, I watched Dylan come to a dead stop in front of the TV and wait.

Yep, they'd certainly succeeded in doing their job in this house. And while millions across the nation would wait, and sit through the ads for the top story they were keeping until those final few minutes, *we* waited through commercial upon commercial for them to come back and reveal just how deep they planned to twist the knife to get the top scoop.

There was no other sound in the house except the sales pitches of every item that flashed up on the screen, which I doubted either Dylan or I comprehended. Yeah, the two of us were like goddamn zombies. We'd zoned out on all that was around us, including one another, as we waited for the other shoe to drop.

26
I AIN'T SAYIN' HE'S A GOLD DIGGER

THIS IS NOT happening. This is not *happening.* But as I stood with my nose practically glued to the screen in Ace's—no, *our*—TV room, the urge to vomit told me otherwise. My hands had grown clammy as I'd crossed to the spot I'd now taken up residence on, and I was trying to remember if I'd taken a breath in the last five minutes, or if I needed to.

Before the commercial break, Brenda's face had been splashed across the screen in HD, but the image that had been broadcasted to millions was definitely *not* the Brenda I knew. It appeared that dear old Mom had gotten tired of waiting for a phone call that wasn't going to happen, and where we'd stupidly thought she had decided to take Ace's advice and leave, she'd made a phone call of her own.

My hands shook by my sides as I ran through all of the words that'd been exchanged between us since she'd resurfaced from whatever hell pit she'd resided in after being released from jail, and I wanted to scream. I couldn't begin to imagine what she planned to say next—who knew when it came to Brenda. But as my anxiety tried to chew itself free through the lining of my stomach, my gut ached at the thought of what was about to happen next.

I was vaguely aware of Ace moving behind me, probably coming closer, but I didn't turn for fear of what I would find if I looked at him. What was he thinking right now? What a colossal mistake he'd made? *Fuck. Probably.*

"And here's the story you've all been waiting for. Who *is* Dylan Prescott? Don't change that channel—this is the story that'll be talked about around the water cooler on Monday. And you don't want to miss out."

The too-thin brunette who'd delivered that nauseating introduction to the happy downfall of my reputation then turned toward the wall of televisions mounted behind her as the show's logo vanished and the camera switched to the interview.

There, framed within the confines of Ace's television, were two women. One I recognized as a reporter for the show. She had blonde hair, and I'd guess her to be in her mid-to-late twenties. I'd seen her before, relaying the latest gossip on the rich and famous and even—I hated to admit it—waited for the breaking story at the end of the show if it involved someone I was a fan of.

Well, I thought wryly, *how do you like that...* Felt a little different to be on the other side, didn't it? And wasn't that the truth. Again, there was that need to regurgitate the breakfast I'd eaten earlier with Ace, and the need only intensified when the reporter began to speak. "Brenda, thank you for agreeing to sitting down with us today. We can't tell you how delighted we were to receive your call."

The cameraman then zoomed in on the attractive lady in her early fifties wearing a pretty coral blouse buttoned demurely to her collarbone, where a string of pearls—*fake, I'm sure*—rested against her skin. Her messy hair from last week had been straightened and pushed behind her ears, and where she'd had two gaudy hoop earrings there were now pearls to match the necklace. *Isn't she the picture of motherly perfection.*

"Thank you, Holly. I'm pleased to be here."

As she aimed a smile at the reporter across from her, I knew the woman thought it was genuine, and I supposed it was. Brenda was probably thrilled to be starring in her own jacked-up reality show, but the sixth sense I had when it came to this woman had me searching every feature of her face until... *There it is,* I thought, as I took a step closer to the screen. I tilted my head to the side and zeroed in on the slightly narrowed eyes, and there, lurking in the green depths that were so like my own, was a calculation I knew was about to fuck me.

"First off, I have to point out," Holly said, "it's obvious as I sit across from you where Dylan gets his good looks from. You are absolutely beautiful."

Brenda let out a fake laugh and brought a hand up to her pearls to finger them. "You're very sweet. Thank you."

"No. No. I'm serious. While we haven't had the opportunity to talk to Dylan himself, that now-famous billboard of him in Hollywood, the national ad campaigns he's been featured in, and those delicious photos that have recently surfaced with none other than Ace Locke have given us a glimpse of your handsome boy."

Brenda nodded as she lowered her hand to place it on her lap atop the black pencil skirt she wore. "Oh, that's my Dylan—"

"Is she fucking serious right now?" Ace finally spoke up from somewhere behind me. But I held my hand up, halting him, and he fell silent. I wanted to hear every single word that came out of her lying mouth.

"From a young boy he's been a looker. A charmer, too…"

Brenda let the words linger in the air like bait, waiting for the fish across from her to bite. It took no longer than a heartbeat, or two, and then Holly was right there chomping down on that hook.

"A charmer?"

"Yes," Brenda said, her smile stretching, pleased no doubt that her crumbs were followed. "I mean, as a child he was always getting into mischief. The usual kid stuff, of course. Some stolen candy here, a skipped class there, but by the time he was eight…or maybe nine? He was a master at talking his way out of the little things. And then you add in those dimples of his, and who could resist such a face?"

"Who indeed?" Holly chuckled along with Brenda,

thinking she was getting a nice little scoop of a mother recounting her years with her young son. *Yeah, right.* "Not Mr. Locke, apparently."

"Apparently," Brenda agreed.

"So you know we have to ask: has Dylan brought Ace home to meet the parents yet?"

My hands balled into fists by my sides, and I clenched them so hard that my nails threatened to break the skin of my palms. God, Brenda was lucky she wasn't close by, because I seriously would've contemplated murdering her right then and there. Damn the consequences.

"Unfortunately, Holly, things have happened in my past that have distanced me and Dylan, and though I'd hoped we would reconnect now that I'm here in L.A. I'm saddened to say that thus far, he has refused to see me."

As one falsity after another rolled off her scheming tongue, the camera zoomed in on her face, and I was disgusted to see a sheen of moisture welling in her eyes. *No...she isn't...*

"Things," Holly said ever so gently—*because we wouldn't want to hurt her fucking feelings.* "You're referring to the time you spent in jail for drugs and prostitution?"

Brenda made a show of bringing the edge of her fingers up to under her nose, sucking back an elaborate sniffle, and there was Holly, leaning over with a tissue.

"Please, take your time. I know this must be difficult."

"Thank you," Brenda said, delicately dabbing her

nose. "It's been a long journey to get clean and where I am today. I've made mistakes in the past. Many mistakes. But you have to understand I was doing what I had to do to get by. To provide food and a roof over my boy's head."

"Of course. That's admirable. A mother's love knows no bounds."

If I hadn't been standing two feet from the television screen, I wouldn't have believed the shit I was hearing.

"It really doesn't, Holly. And that's why it's so heartbreaking that Dylan... He's..." Brenda stopped, sniffed, and then, yep, the crocodile tears started to fall down her cheeks. "He's refused to see me and has even gone so far as to convince Mr. Locke I'm here to come between the two of them."

"And are you, Brenda? Do you disagree with the relationship your son has entered into with Ace? Does it worry you that it's changed him in any way?"

"It already has. Dylan has always been overly ambitious. He used to tell me he would do *anything* to get out of our humble...situation. Even going so far as helping me by using his considerable charms to lure in clients back in the day."

Holly shifted uncomfortably on her chair, and I could tell she was getting ready to ask the million-dollar question. I braced myself for whatever was about to come, but never could I have expected the next words spoken between the two.

"So you're saying that Dylan helped you to sell

drugs when he was just a boy?"

The tears flowing over Brenda's cheeks miraculously dried up as she took a moment to compose herself, and then she blinked and shook her head.

I held my breath, praying for some kind of natural disaster to take place so the television station would lose signal, or be swallowed up by the earth, but no such luck. A second later, Brenda set off a bomb that blew all of the years I'd spent honing my happy existence straight to hell.

"Oh no, dear. He helped me with the men."

Even though Brenda hadn't come right out and said the words, the silence in the room where the live interview was taking place, and the dumbfounded expression on Holly's face, made it crystal fucking clear that the message had been received.

I could see tomorrow's headlines, or the ones that would pop up later tonight: ACE LOCKE CONNED BY GOLD-DIGGING FORMER PROSTITUTE.

"Like I said, Holly," Brenda said, and this time when the cameraman zoomed in on her, she turned to face the lens head-on, "Dylan was a charmer and always knew how best to use his *handsome* face."

As the blood roared through my brain, the ringing in my ears became so loud I didn't even hear what Holly said as she wrapped up the piece. It wasn't until the television shut off that I realized the seven-minute segment was over.

* * *

I HAD NEVER seen Dylan so quiet or so still. It was as if I were standing in the room with a statue. And his immobility terrified me. I had stood behind him, watching the train wreck on the entertainment show play out, and with each question that had been asked, and every answer that had been given, my rage had intensified.

I wanted to scream, to curse the fucking roof off my house, and then get in my car, track that bitch down, and teach her a thing or two about just how charming *I* could be. But the eerie lifelessness of the man an arm's length away from me kept my feet firmly in place.

Brenda's intentions and motivations here had been clear. If I wasn't going to hand over the dough, then she was going to go on air and tell a sob story to the first person who offered her a substantial chunk of cash for the goods. She'd laid the trap, and now she was going to sit back and wait for the first idiot dumb enough to pay her. And this town was not lacking in those.

I tried to bank my outrage on both my own and Dylan's behalf, and would call my lawyer Logan ASAP, but first…first, I needed to wrap my arms around Dylan and make sure he was all right.

"Dylan," I said, careful to keep my tone even as I took a step toward him. When he didn't answer, I tried again. "Dylan?"

I lowered my eyes down to the fingers he still had curled into fists, and that was when I noticed the tail of his shirt moving. As I walked closer, I saw shivers racking his taut shoulders, and cursed beneath my breath. If I'd been feeling a blinding anger, I couldn't begin to imagine the fury that must've been humming through Dylan's body to have him so strung out he was vibrating.

I swallowed, trying to think of the best way to approach him. I'd seen many sides of Dylan over this past week when it came to Brenda, but this—this was on a whole other scale. I walked around him, stepping in between the wall where the blank TV was mounted and the man staring at his feet with great intent.

"Dylan," I said, and I saw his nostrils flare, at least showing some indication that he had heard me. When he didn't raise his head or respond, though, I lifted an arm to touch his elbow, and that had him moving—away from me.

"Don't," he said, finally lifting his eyes to meet my gaze head-on.

Refusing to believe he meant that the way it sounded, I took a step forward, but when Dylan moved one back, I stopped and asked him the words I was having trouble comprehending. "Don't what?"

Dylan licked his lips and then said with a detachment I'd never heard from him before, "Don't touch me."

And Christ, that packed as much of a punch as I imagined a bullet straight through the fucking heart would. I wanted to demand why, but judging from the way he was holding himself, braced for a fight, I figured I should listen.

"Okay, I won't," I said, trying to temper my own heightened emotions. "I just want to talk to you."

"About what?" he snapped, and the arctic bite to his words made a crack of doubt splinter in what I'd always considered a rock-solid foundation between the two of us. "How my mother just went on the biggest entertainment news show and told the world she's spent time in jail for doing drugs and selling sex? Or the fact that she just announced that you're dating a gold-digging whore?"

"Dylan," I said, wanting to reassure him I didn't care about any of that, but he wasn't done. It was like the pin had been removed from the grenade he'd been holding, making an explosion imminent.

"Well?" he asked, his eyebrows flying up so high they almost hit his hairline. "What'll it be, Ace? Which one of those two would you like to discuss first? Because both seem equally entertaining to me."

"Hey, it's all going to be okay. We can—"

"Okay?" he asked, and the sound that followed was ugly and distorted. A strangled laugh. "How is this going to be okay?"

I was ready to explain the hundreds of ideas, spins, and scenarios that had run through my mind during the segment. But when he took the two steps required to bring him back toe to toe with me and his eyes creased, I lost my words.

"You know what I hate?" he said, and the fact that he didn't wait for an answer let me know he hadn't really thrown that out there as a question, more a statement of fact. "I hate that I'm the one ruining your life."

"Dylan—"

"What?" he said. "Don't try and deny it. Ever since we walked out of Syn, your career has taken hit after hit. Your life has become the circus you always told me you hated, and now this. Now everyone thinks you're sleeping with some crack whore's son and secretly wondering just how far my 'charms' extend…into the bedroom, maybe? Who knows what Brenda will tell people? At some point you have to stop and ask yourself, what are you doing with me? *Why* are you with me? Hardly seems worth it for you from where I'm standing."

I hated hearing Dylan talk about himself and us that way, but I could tell the words were being fueled by frustration and the inability to do anything about what had just happened. I'd been there many times over, and the best thing I could do for him was let him process this the way he needed to.

That didn't stop me, however, from reaching for his elbow now that he was close enough to touch, and Dylan shook his head and cursed.

"I need some space," he said, backing up.

I let him go and wanted to plead with him not to leave. But if he wanted to, I wasn't going to stand in his way. He turned and headed for the hallway, his shoulders now sagging, likely from the weight that had just been heaped upon them, and just before he disappeared, he glanced back at me and said, "I'll be upstairs. Just…think about what I said."

As Dylan vanished from sight, I knew I would think of nothing but. However, I was also aware that nothing was going to make me change my mind about the man who'd just walked upstairs to take some alone time in *our* bedroom.

27
SOME KIND
OF MAGIC

I DIDN'T KNOW how long I'd lain there in Ace's bed, but as the daylight was swallowed by darkness, the night crept inside the large windows and chased the sun into the shadows. Some time ago, I'd kicked off my shoes and rolled to my side, hugging the pillow under my cheek as though it was an anchor to reality, because what had happened today—that had to be some kind of horrible nightmare. *Right?*

Several times over I'd tried to shut my eyes and fall into the oblivion of sleep, but each time I did my brain rewound the interview from earlier, and replayed it on the inside of my eyelids. Then it followed up with a quick recap on me telling Ace to dump my pathetic ass before it was all too late, and the memory I had of his face as those words had tumbled from my mouth made me want to fade away all over again. It was hard to believe all of that had happened when just last night we'd been celebrating, but I knew from the dull ache in my chest that it had.

I had no idea where Ace was. All I knew was that he'd done what I'd asked and given me space. And now that the anger, embarrassment, and pain had combined to numb my body, I could think of only one person that could shock me back to life.

I rolled to my back and scooted to the end of the bed, intending to get up and track down the man whose room I had commandeered. But I stopped short of standing when I made out Ace's silhouette in the white wingback chair that usually sat in the corner of his large room. He'd moved the seat so it was situated at the end of the bed, dead center, and I wondered how long he'd been sitting there brooding.

"Hey," he said as I shifted so my legs were hanging over the edge of the mattress. I ran my palms along my thighs and tried to blink him into focus, but the room was too dark and Ace had chosen his position with care.

"How long you been sitting there?" I asked.

"Two hours."

Damn.

"I told you. I like to watch you sleep."

Yes, he had told me that, hadn't he? When was that? *This week, last?* It felt like years ago now as we sat there with all this weird distance between us. Distance I'd put there.

"Ace, I—"

"No. Don't. It's my turn, don't you think?"

I clamped my mouth shut and glanced over at the

windows, trying to swallow back the emotions that were threatening to pour out of me and make me drop to my knees and tell him how sorry I was. But before I could get down to the ground, he was talking again in a voice that demanded I face him and pay attention. So I did just that.

"I've been sitting here trying to think of the best way to explain to you how I feel about everything that you said to me downstairs today. But the more time that passed by and the longer I waited for you to come find me, my reasons for *why* I'm with you changed."

Oh God. That didn't sound promising. He sounded like a man who'd been sure one minute and then changed his mind the next. And considering I knew he loved me with all of his heart the night before, that didn't bode well for me now. But...I was determined to hear him out. After all, I was the idiot who'd issued the stupid demand that he think over all the reasons he was with me, so it wasn't like I could ask him to forget about it now. Could I?

"Here's the thing, Dylan. If I could change the world, if I could wrap you up in my arms and make sure nothing bad ever happened to you again, you need to know that I would do that in a heartbeat."

"Ace—"

"No," he barked, and this time got to his feet. "It's my turn."

I nodded in the dark, where I remained perched at the end of his bed, watching him close the distance.

"You asked me two very important questions earlier,

and you're damn well going to listen to my answers."

When he held his hand out to me, palm up, I slipped mine into his, and when he drew me to my feet, I went. Toe to toe and eye to eye, I could see him clearly now through the shadows playing off the walls and curtains of the room. His eyebrows were drawn together and his lips were pulled tight in a stern line, and while he looked as though he wanted to throttle me, I could also see compassion and worry etched in the lines of his face.

"The first thing you asked me is what I'm doing here with you." Entwining our fingers, Ace took a deep inhale, and when he let it out, it was as if it were the first full breath he'd taken since he'd last touched me. Then he whispered, "I'm living."

I could feel tears welling in my eyes, and when I shut them to stave them off, I heard him say, "Look at me, Dylan."

And when I blinked and refocused on him, I was shocked to see his own eyes were glistening. "The second was why. *Why* am I with you…" As Ace's voice trailed off, he brought his other hand to my cheek and asked, "Where else would I be?"

My mouth parted, but before I could get a word out, he swooped in and took my swollen lips in a kiss that was sweet and full of promise and had me placing my hands on his chest for purchase as I swayed into him. When he rested his forehead against mine, he said against my mouth, "I love you. Where you are, I want to be, and I realized that as I paced the length of this house for three hours straight. It didn't matter that you were up here and I was down there— you chose to stay even when you needed space. And that means everything to me."

I was *such* an idiot. But instead of saying that, I leaned in and kissed him all over again. Conveying without words that I felt the same and was sorry for saying what I had downstairs when anger and frustration had been riding me.

I lost myself in that kiss as we reconnected there in the intimate embrace of night, but when I thought he would maybe lower me to the bed and pull me into his body to sleep this horrible evening away, Ace once again did the unexpected. He pulled away from me and said softly, "I don't want you to worry anymore. I already called Logan so we can sit down and hash out what legal recourse the two of us have in this kind of situation, and…"

I was relieved to hear we would be able to chat with a lawyer regarding the whole Brenda situation, but there was something else going on here too. I cocked my head to the side and took in the wry grin I could see curving Ace's lips.

"And?" I finally said, letting him know I was more than fine so far with how this conversation was going.

When he nodded and took in another deep breath, he said, "I called Roger and Martina, and told them to get Carly Wilde on the phone and set up that interview she's been after."

When my mouth fell open, Ace put his pointer finger under my chin to help me close it.

"Why are you so shocked, Daydream? I think it's time that 'Ace and his camp' were a little more vocal about the mysterious new man in my love life. Don't you?"

"But...but...I know how much you don't want to—"

"I changed my mind," he said with a huge grin now that had me chuckling.

"Just like that?"

"Just. Like. That," Ace said, and punctuated each of his words with a kiss before taking my hand and leading me to the bedroom door. "Come on—we have some phone calls to make and some meetings to schedule, and then you and I are going to come up here and sleep in *our* bedroom."

As we headed downstairs, I couldn't help but wonder over the magic Ace held, because even on the worst of days he had the innate ability to make everything seem as though it would all be okay.

28
TIME TO
GET WILDE

"MR LOCKE?"

A hesitant female voice followed two light raps on the door of the dressing room that Ace and I had been ushered into around ten minutes ago. He'd just finished up with makeup and had slipped into his tailored Armani suit jacket, which matched his fitted black pants. "Yes. Come in," he said from where he was standing in front of the mirror adjusting the cuffs of his black shirt.

I was seated over on the plush two-seater couch that was pushed up against one of the walls, watching him get ready for his exclusive "Ace Locke with Carly Wilde" interview that was about to take place in—

"We'll be ready for you in ten minutes," Kelly, the assistant who had been helping us out today, said. "I'm here to take you down to the green room. Mr. Prescott can watch the segment from in there."

Ten minutes. *Oh man.* Ten minutes suddenly seemed so very close.

"Sounds great. I think this is as good as it's going to get," Ace said as he turned around to look my way.

I got to my feet and rubbed my clammy palms over my grey dress slacks, and then trailed my eyes up his long legs to his handsome face. When I noticed the slightly tense set of Ace's shoulders, I was clued in enough to the man I was looking at to sense the underlying nerves behind the smile. I walked over to stop in front of him and brought my right pointer finger to my lips, tapping it there in contemplation. "You look like this famous guy I know," I said, and then snapped my fingers before pointing at him. "Yes...big action star. Takes no prisoners. Sexy, too," I said, reaching up to smooth my hands over his shoulders. "*Very* sexy."

Ace's eyes shifted to the woman beyond my shoulder, and then he grinned. "Well, since his is the only opinion I worry about, I say we're ready."

"Very good," she said as I turned to head her way, and when I took a step, I felt Ace's hand take mine. I glanced over my shoulder at him, and when he took a deep breath I tightened my hold on his fingers as we headed for the door of the dressing room.

Today was huge. What Ace was about to do was monumental, life changing, and I couldn't believe he'd agreed to it, much less appeared genuinely excited, minus this small case of nerves.

It had been a little over two weeks since the night of Brenda's disparaging interview, and since then we'd had several conversations with Ace's friend and attorney, Logan Mitchell, who'd advised no contact with her, and no comments *about* her. The best way to fight this for the moment was with silence, and though Ace had adamantly told Logan he wished he could do a whole lot more than bite his tongue, Logan had advised him, *"For once, listen to me, Locke. That's what you pay me very handsomely for. Although I have been told that my mouth alone could be worth millions."* And, after much grumbling, we'd agreed with the bossy lawyer and followed instructions.

We'd remained quiet, and so had Brenda, but we knew her silence wouldn't last for long. But right now the only people who continued to speculate and talk about that sit-down with Holly and my mother were the entertainment magazines who had nothing else to gossip about, and *that* had been Ace's cue. Both Roger and Martina had agreed it was time to tell our story. It was time for Ace to step out of the closet and go public with an exclusive interview on the *Carly Wilde Show*, and now here we were walking down a corridor to her green room to wait.

As we were ushered inside, the first thing I noted was how nice it was. For some reason I'd expected a little room with a couch and a TV, but that was not the case at all. There was a bar along the back wall, the lights were low, and there were several couches facing a wall filled with televisions showing the program currently being recorded.

"Please make yourself comfortable," Kelly said. "There are drinks over at the bar and someone will be in shortly to fetch you, Mr. Locke."

"Thank you. You've been very helpful this afternoon," he replied.

"It was my pleasure. And it was lovely to meet you too, Mr. Prescott."

"You too," I said with a smile, before she shut the door and I walked over to one of the couches to take a seat. "This is nice."

Ace followed and unbuttoned his jacket before he sat beside me. I stretched my arms out along the back of the leather and then waggled my brows at him. "Too bad you only have a few minutes. We're all alone, fully stocked bar, you're lookin' all hot in your suit..."

Ace's lids lowered as he leaned in to lightly kiss my lips, and then he whispered against them, "Are you sure you want me to do this? There's still time to cancel."

I sucked my upper lip under my lower one and pretended to think about his question before my mouth curved into a grin. "Am I sure I want you to go out on public television and tell the world we're dating?"

"Well, it will probably be a lot more than just that."

"Hmm, yeah, I guess so. But...I'm not adverse to people knowing that you're off the market. And I trust what you'll say."

Ace brought a hand up so he could brush his thumb over my chin, and then he held my face steady. "Good.

Because I would never do anything to hurt you."

I blinked at the sincerity I saw in his eyes, and then nodded. "I know."

"Okay. And for the record, this is just as much about me telling the world that *you're* off the market too. So don't believe for one second that this isn't a purely selfish move."

I chuckled at that, but then sobered as I searched his blue eyes. "Are you nervous?"

I remembered him telling me once that he didn't like to voice his nerves, because if he acknowledged them they would get the better of him. However, this time, he didn't hesitate. The corner of his lips quirked and he said, "Yes."

"Yes?"

When he nodded and slid his hand up to cup my cheek, I raised my own to cover his.

"About which part?" I asked.

"About me not making a fool of myself over you."

My heart swelled at that and a relieved laugh slipped free of me. "Oh?"

"Mhmm," he said, running the pad of his thumb over my lower lip. "How am I supposed to answer calmly when she asks me how I feel about you, when all I want to do is..." Ace took in a shuddering breath and leaned in to steal a kiss, and when he sat back I said, slightly breathless now myself, "When all you want to do is what?"

Knock. Knock. Knock.

"Mr. Locke, we're ready for you," Kelly said when she stuck her head in the door.

Ace nodded and rose to his feet while I sat there sputtering, wanting to know what he'd been going to say. But I'd just have to ask him later. It was time for him to go and sit down with the most popular talk show host in America, and there was no way you kept her waiting.

"I'll see you soon," he said, and then bent at the waist to give me one more kiss. "Wish me luck."

"Good luck, hotshot. I'll be watching," I said, indicating the televisions on the wall.

"You better be," he said, and then shot me his movie-star smile as he turned and headed for the door.

As I watched him go, the broad line of his shoulders, the tapered waist and long legs eating up the space, I couldn't help the pride filling my chest. That man was mine, and he was about to go and tell it to the world.

* * *

IT'S SHOWTIME, I thought, as I followed Kelly, who wove her way backstage around props, people, and scaffolding to a side door. She instructed me to wait as two efficient men hooked me up with a battery pack that clipped to my belt under my jacket, and then they attached a tiny mic to my lapel. I could hear the excited murmurs of the audience through the door as the preshow entertainment wound up, and the nerves I'd confessed to Dylan only seconds ago slammed into me tenfold.

Jesus, I felt lightheaded.

"Excuse me, do you have some water?" I asked Kelly, who nodded and quickly dashed off, reappearing with a bottle. I took several gulps and then shut my eyes, trying to center myself as a loud roar went up beyond the door I was standing at.

Carly Wilde had just walked on stage, I heard muttered behind me somewhere.

Oh God. Oh God. This is really happening. I'm really about to do this.

I continued to look at the door only a few feet away from me, and knew that in less than two minutes it would slide open for me to step out on stage, where I would sit down and tell all of my secrets to several million of my closest friends. And though I wanted to do it, when I thought of it in those terms, I also wanted to pass out.

I shut my eyes and shook my hands out, and reminded myself why I was here. *What* I was doing here. And when I remembered the look on Dylan's face just before I'd left him there in the green room, my pulse steadied and my frazzled nerves calmed somewhat, because for once I knew the end game here, and that was to tell the world the truth and to *finally* be free and happy.

"All right, Mr. Locke," Kelly said, glancing at the door. "You're up in five, four, three—"

No more was said, the door just slid open and I heard, "Here's that moment you've all been waiting for. Please welcome Ace Locke," and the audience of approximately three hundred got to their feet and went ballistic.

There were screams, shouts, and wolf whistles, and several women at the front of the room were sobbing, as they hugged and jumped up and down with one another as I walked onto the stage and waved at the crowd. I stopped between the door and the couch to face the audience and gave a huge wave and slight bow, as I'd been instructed, and that sent up more whooping and hollering and had me relaxing into the excitable atmosphere and my role here today.

Today I was the celebrity I'd spent the past decade honing. I'd perfected that persona and character to a T, and as I aimed my famous smile out at the crowd and turned to head toward the woman whose show this was, I was shocked at the calm that overtook me. I knew this role. I could play this role, and I'd be damned if I didn't win this group over by the end of this interview.

When I reached Carly, her smile was radiant and sincere as she opened her arms to me for a welcoming hug.

"Ace, so happy to have you here today," she said by my cheek. Her black hair was cut into a chic bob that angled down to two sharp points in line with her chin, and her cream stilettos made her five-foot-four frame tall enough that she was eye level with me. She was dressed in a sleek black sleeveless dress that was cinched high on her waist with a cream sash, and then hugged her curvaceous figure to where the hemline hit just above her knees. She was gorgeous, and not only one of the most respected talk show hosts and entrepreneurs, but also a fashion icon.

I embraced her in a warm hug, which was surprisingly firm for such a petite lady, and when we pulled apart she turned to her adoring audience and announced, "He's really here!" And that set the crowd off all over again.

As they cheered and screamed, some even gasped when I looked in their direction. Carly took a seat on her famous crimson couch and I took my spot beside her. She grinned over at me as I adjusted my jacket and sat back to survey the crowd. The spotlights were bright, but not blinding, as I stared out at the anonymous faces all smiling back at me, waiting for whatever it was I was going to reveal today, and as the excitement mellowed to hushed murmurs, Carly let out a boisterous laugh and looked my way.

"Welcome to my show," she said, and I couldn't help but reciprocate with my own laugh.

"Thank you. I definitely feel welcomed."

She nodded and then scanned her fans before bringing her eyes back to mine. "They are quite exuberant today, aren't they?"

I clapped my hands along with the cheers that went up at that, and when I heard someone shout, "We love you, Ace," I looked to the left in the general direction the platitude had come from and gave a wave and a smile.

"And isn't that the truth," Carly said, recapturing my attention. "The world loves Ace Locke. They love watching your movies. They love getting to know you through interviews and press. They love speculating about the *special* man who's caught your attention. And in general, the world just can't seem to stop talking about the private man behind the larger-than-life movie star that you are. So, calm yourselves, people," Carly said good-naturedly. "We only have him for a limited time, and I know you want some answers out of this guy before he leaves. Am I right?"

When the affirmatives rang out around the studio, I leaned back into the couch, placing an arm on the back of it much like Dylan had in the green room. Settling into my seat, I placed an ankle on my knee and turned my body toward my host as she crossed her legs and faced me. Her blue eyes glittered at me as she reached out to pat my hand that was resting on the back of the plush seat.

"So, how are you doing today?" she asked.

I barked out a laugh at her simple segue into the beginning of the interview. "I'm doing just great, Carly. And yourself?"

"Oh, I'm fantastic," she answered as if we were at an intimate brunch for two instead of sitting down for an interview for over seven million. "But we aren't here to talk about me, mister. We're all here today to talk about you." She paused for a second and then added, "Well, you and a certain someone who goes by the name of Dylan Prescott."

God, I couldn't have stopped my smile if I tried. But as it was, I wasn't trying.

"Look at that smile," she said, patting my hand and leaning forward. "Just the mention of his name and your entire face lights up."

There was no denying that. "He has that effect," I said, and the crowd erupted into applause.

"Yes. I can see that. And I have to thank you for agreeing to come and sit down to talk to me today."

I nodded toward her, pleased that she was so easy to talk to. I'd always heard that about her, but having never interviewed with her in the past, I hadn't been convinced until this very moment. "Thank you for having me."

"Of course. You have to understand how happy I am to have you here. You're such an inspiration to many already through your acting and charity work over the years. And then there was your coming out, which I'm sure helped many young men, and women, feel that it was okay to be proud of who they are, just like you are. And now here you are, someone so private, proving once again what courage looks like. You've smashed through Hollywood stereotypes and stepped out of the closet in a most *public* way, and I for one am humbled to sit across from you right now and watch you smile at the mention of your boyfriend's— I can call him that, right?"

I chuckled. "Yes. He is most certainly that."

"Then to finish my thought, it's a joy to watch you smile over the mention of your boyfriend's name."

"Thanks, Carly," I said, and the crowd clapped and stomped their feet as I allowed my gaze to travel the entire length of the studio. The acceptance on all their faces, plus that of the woman opposite me, made it easy to open up with her and just be myself. "It hasn't been an easy road, especially these last few months. I've dealt with countless setbacks in my career, people who have decided not to risk working with me due to what is going on in my personal life, but I wouldn't change it. Dylan makes it worthwhile. And if me going through this publicly—sharing my story, and his, with all of you—makes the life of one person a little easier...then I'm happy to be here and talk to you about the man who has made *me* a better man."

As a chorus of *awws* echoed around the room, I gave a bashful shrug. "What can I say? He kind of makes me sappy."

"We're not going to complain about that. Are we, guys?" she asked her adoring audience, who shouted out *nos* and *hell nos* until she returned her attention to me. "Okay, so come on, you know I want some goods here. The juicy scoop on how you two really met. There's always speculation about these kinds of things, but we have to know. Was it romantic? Did you see him through a crowd and have to talk to him, like it was reported? Or did you call him up after spotting that hot billboard of him, you know, this one," she said with a gesture of her thumb over her shoulder to the massive wall screen behind us, and up popped that sinful Calvin Klein ad of Dylan. The one with the leather jacket, the briefs, and the come-hither stare that had started it all, and if I'd thought the wolf whistles were loud for me... The women that made up ninety-nine percent of this audience went crazy. They cupped their hands around their mouths and howled like they were at a strip show, and some even put their fingers in their mouths to whistle the roof off the building as Dylan's ad remained blown up center stage for their pleasure and, *oh yeah*, mine.

With a smug grin, I slowly brought my eyes back to the woman whose were wide and innocent as she said, "I don't know how you would ever look at him and *not* smile."

"That's a dirty play, Carly. How am I supposed to think when you have that photo up there?"

"Good point," she said. "We'll just pretend it's not there."

I looked out to the grinning faces, happy to see them enjoying themselves. "Sure. I can do that. Umm...what was the question again?" I joked.

Carly clapped her hands together, laughing. "How did you two meet?"

"Oh, that's right. Well," I started, and then scratched the side of my nose. "It's a funny story, actually. And he tells it a little differently to me."

"Does he?"

"Yes. I'm sure. But, uhh, I met him on our first day of *Insurrection 2*. I was driving to work and he was walking in the middle of the road, and, well..." I paused and gave the crowd my best *it wasn't my fault* look as I ended, "I almost ran him over."

"Wait, you almost ran him over?"

"Yeah." I laughed.

"But he ended up dating you anyway?"

"What can I say?" I said with an arrogant grin. "I'm that charming."

"Woohoo. We believe *that*. Don't we?" Carly said, encouraging the masses to vocalize their thoughts, and when they all shouted a loud *yes* in unison, she looked back at me and waited for them to settle down again. "I have to confess, Ace. Just like everyone in here and out there, I've been watching and reading what I can get my hands on about the two of you. I'm not sure what it is that's drawing us all in and wanting to know about this relationship but... Oh, who am I kidding? It's because it's *you*, Ace Locke, biggest movie star in the world, sex symbol, now telling us that you are an out and proud gay man in a committed relationship that has made this story explode. Then add in those sexy snapshots of you and Dylan in Vegas, and the amount of attention you two have received over the last few months is unheard of. How are you dealing with all of that?"

It was shocking to me that my chest hadn't tightened in fear and my face wasn't flushed at her words, but as I sat there thinking over Carly's question, I realized for the first time that I was finally comfortable talking about this, and *that* was a powerful realization. It was also one other thing I could thank Dylan for. Helping me accept who I was right down to my very core.

"Well, it hasn't been without incident, that's for sure," I said, and then shifted to put both of my feet flat and place my forearms on my knees. I steepled my fingers together and looked out at the crowd, who, I'd noticed, had gone eerily quiet as they awaited my next words. "For the last decade or so—longer, actually—I've chosen to live in the spotlight. That was a decision I made going into this industry, and one I would do over again if it meant leading me back to this exact place in my life, and this man. But I've made mistakes along the way—we all have. I spent years hiding who I was. But now that I've found Dylan, I don't want to have to hide that. I don't want to worry that someone will take a photo and wonder who he is. So, if that means coming out here and telling you all that I'm in love with him, then I am more than happy to do that. To share that."

"I think that's what's so captivating," Carly said. I cocked my head to look over at her, and she curled one of her legs under herself on the couch as if we were sitting in her living room, not her packed studio on live network television. "That you *are* being so open about this. I mean, granted, it's been some time since the Vegas photos surfaced, but for a man who never once publicly acknowledged any relationship before, to hear you talk about Dylan is fascinating. This man has really changed you."

I nodded and chewed on my lower lip. "You're right. He has. He's funny, smart, incredibly kind and self-aware, and"—I stopped and peered out at the enraptured faces staring back at me and gave a cheeky grin—"incredibly sexy, am I right?" One woman let out a "hell yeah," and I pointed up at her. "See, she gets it."

Carly chuckled. "Oh, I think we all get that."

"I can't describe him better than that. Our life is under a microscope. And there are days that are extremely difficult, and stories that are told that aren't true. But all relationships come with problems—ours are just up for public consumption, and we know that. We are aware, and as long as we both know what's real and what's true then we can get through each day with most of our sanity, which is one of the reasons I'm here today. It was time to give voice to this relationship in the true sense of it. To give an honest narrative to what we share and who we are. And I thank you for letting me do that and be here."

As the crowd erupted in applause, Carly laid her palm on my shoulder and squeezed. "You are fast becoming one of my favorite people in the world. Sit tight, everyone— we'll be back after this commercial with more from Ace Locke and his upcoming movie role and where he sees himself and his new beau, Mr. Dylan Prescott, in the future."

* * *

I DIDN'T THINK it was possible to feel as happy as I did right then while sitting in the green room of the *Carly Wilde Show*. But with every word and answer that came out of Ace's mouth, my smile extended farther across my face. From the second he'd stepped out on that stage, Ace had the audience eating out of the palm of his hand, and they loved

him. The tense line of his shoulders from earlier had
vanished, and as he sat beside Carly on the couch, he talked
to her and the crowd as if he were holding a casual
conversation with me. It was as if he'd known them all for
years, and every now and then just in case they forgot *who*
they were all conversing with, Ace would aim his megawatt
smile at them and toss out some of that movie-star
arrogance, and boy did they go nuts over that.

My guy was incredible. It wasn't as if I hadn't known
that before, but as I sat there watching people react to his
mere presence, I really got it. Ace was…well, he was a true
inspiration. When he spoke, these people in the crowd, and
no doubt all over the country, were hanging on his every
word. And it was easy to forget who he was when you were
with him—he was just that affable.

Over the past few months, I'd come to realize
firsthand that in regard to celebrities, the public viewed
them as their own personal property. Their every move was
up for grabs, their lives, entertainment for all us normal folk,
because as far as we—*and yes, I lump myself in there too*—
continued to put them up on pedestals, they would always
be under scrutiny. But it was what they did with that fame,
that notoriety and level of success, which really made them
be loved or vilified. And it was as I listened to Carly discuss
Ace's choices, his decision to come out publicly and tell the
world who he was and how it had impacted and helped
others, that I really thought of him and his reach in the
broader spectrum of things. In the world beyond just him

and me. And damn if that didn't make me proud to be the one on his arm.

I took a sip of the bottled water I'd grabbed from the bar, and then glanced up at the screen, where Ace was leaning across the couch and saying something in Carly's ear. They'd just cut to commercial and someone had rushed in to touch up their makeup, but they must've been close to going back live, because everyone had vanished from the stage, Carly grinned at him and nodded, and then the show's theme music rolled, the logo appeared, and they were back, the crowd clapping and shouting their excitement.

"Welcome back, everyone, and to those of you just now joining us, I'm here with Ace Locke, the star of *The Last Guttersnipe*, *Hard Throttle*, and *Original Bourbon*, to name just a few, and he's just wrapped up shooting the sequel to Ron King's blockbuster hit *Insurrection*. Coincidently, the set of his latest movie *Insurrection 2* is also where Ace first met the new man in his life, the man we're learning a little bit more about today from Ace himself. Isn't that right?"

"It is," Ace replied with an extremely satisfied smile, and my cheeks heated the same way they had when they'd plastered my billboard image on the massive screen behind him earlier. As the audience clapped and the camera zoomed back to encompass both Carly and Ace, I was amazed at how relaxed he was. He'd settled right into discussing his life and us, and that comfort and level of ease made my heart want to burst with happiness, because I knew how long a road Ace had traveled to get to that point.

"Okay," Carly said. "Let's cut to the chase and ask some of the questions I know we're all *dying* to know. How long did you wait before you and Dylan first got together? Did you ask him out on a date?"

I chuckled at Ace's expression then. His mouth opened once, twice, and then he laughed. A spontaneous burst of *oh shit* laughter, as he seemed to recall the first time we'd *gotten* together. He then settled somewhat and answered, "It was at my birthday party."

"Oh!" Carly said, clasping her hands together, delighted by the seemingly innocent enough revelation. "So you asked him to be your date?"

"No," Ace said, and shook his head. He then looked directly at the camera, and I knew that stare, that intense focus he'd just rediscovered, was all for me as he answered, "I wasn't that bold. *He* asked me to come with him, and I did."

Fuck, there is no way *he just said that on national television.* But the smile that curled his mouth was one I knew all too well, and so was the spark in those blue eyes as the crowd went wild. *That cocky bastard,* I thought, chuckling to myself. *He is in so much trouble later.*

"Ahh, so Dylan isn't the shy, retiring type?"

Oh God. I could only imagine what Ace would have to say about that.

"No," he said. "I would never accuse him of being shy. There's been a couple of occasions...but for the most part I would say, no. Not shy at all."

"So...he wouldn't mind if we got him out on stage with us today, then?"

Wait. What did she just say? I shot to my feet as if I'd just been pinched on the ass. My eyes were wide and I was convinced my mouth had fallen so far open that my jaw might just be hitting the floor. But Carly kept on talking.

"I understand he's here with you, waiting backstage. Do you think he'd mind coming out to discuss the movie you two are starring in together? It's his first, right? I'd love to get an outsider's take on what it was like watching *the* Ace Locke up close and personal." Carly made sure to add a whole lot of innuendo to that final word, and when Ace began to laugh and look around at the crazed people now cheering *my* name, he rubbed a hand over his face and looked over at her.

"Yeah, okay. Let's get him out here."

No. Way. This is not— He did not *just say yes to—*

The door to the green room flew open and my eyes darted over to see Kelly motioning frantically with her hand to *hurry, hurry*, but my feet were glued to the floor as she called out some words I couldn't quite decipher. As my brain tried to keep up, two men raced in to attach something at my waist under my fitted grey vest, then attached—*oh fuck, that's a mic*—to my black tie and Kelly was tugging on my wrist, saying, "Follow me."

And with a final look to the TVs I'd been watching, I saw Ace on his feet and looking over his shoulder waiting for me as the crowd roared, and there was no way I would keep him waiting a minute longer.

29
GOBSMACKED

DYLAN WAS GOING to kill me. That was the first thought running through my brain, but my second was that it would be one hell of a way to go, because there was nothing in the world I wanted more right then than to see his face. Even if that meant seeing it in a room full of three hundred strangers and however many home viewers watching.

Talking about him for the last ten minutes had made me want to be near him again, to touch him, and knowing he was backstage waiting for me now made getting him out here the number one thing on my priority list.

I could hear the clapping and stomping of feet as the audience chanted, *"Dylan, Dylan, Dylan,"* and I got up to head over to the door I had emerged from earlier. It all took less than two minutes, and then the door slid back and there he was. *And damn,* he was gorgeous.

He looked exactly the way I had left him in the green

room. Perfectly put together in his pressed charcoal dress pants, a snug matching vest, and a light blue shirt with sleeves that were rolled to his elbows, and knotted at the base of his throat was an immaculate black tie. His light brown hair that had started to grow out up top had been highlighted with blond and styled back, and he didn't have one ounce of makeup on his stunning face, but nothing could've been added to make him any more attractive than he was right then.

"Hi," I said, and I knew my smile had to be big and foolish because I had an urge to wrap my arms around his waist and spin him around like an idiot, and when his lips curved and he said, "I'm going to kick your ass for this," he might as well have said he loved me, as happy as it made me.

I reached my hand out to him, and as he slipped his fingers into mine I winked and turned to the studio full of people, who for several seconds there had completely disappeared, and they all got to their feet and greeted Dylan in the exact same way they'd welcomed me earlier.

We walked across the stage hand in hand, and when we got to Carly, her smile was enormous as she took a step forward, and I let go of Dylan for her to embrace him. Dylan returned the hug in true Daydream style. He wrapped his arms around her and kissed her cheek, and when she took a step back, Carly brought her fingers to her skin as if to test that he really had put his lips there, and I got it, *boy did I ever.* Dylan's pure aura and energy was infectious. He radiated happiness and warmth to all those around him, and it was a true testament to Sunshine and Ziggy that their boy had the ability to be so open and loving with everything he'd gone through before them.

"Dylan Prescott, ladies and gentlemen!" Carly announced, and turned toward the audience. "The other half of PresLocke."

When Dylan faced our adoring onlookers, he took a step toward me and our shoulders bumped. He then turned to look at me, and the grin he let loose had me recapturing his hand in mine just to remind myself that he was real.

"Please, guys. Take a seat, take a seat," Carly said.

Dylan licked his top lip, and then looked behind us to the couch, where Carly had taken the same position as earlier, and I moved to sit back in my corner, leaving Dylan to settle in between the two of us. As I angled my body toward Carly, Dylan automatically scooted in closer to my side to also face her, and that sent up another frenzy of whoops. He laughed good-naturedly as he patted my knee, and then Carly raised her hands, indicating everyone needed to hush if they wanted to hear more. But the air in the studio was thrumming with electricity.

"Woah... That's quite an entrance there. I think it was even bigger than yours, Ace," Carly joked, and Dylan glanced over his shoulder at me.

"I think you might be right, but look at that smile," I said as Dylan's dimples appeared. "Who wouldn't get excited over that?"

Dylan laughed, and it lit his entire face as he shook his head. "Stop it," he said, but there was no real threat there as I raised my brow, letting him know I wasn't about to stop anytime soon. This coy side to him at my very obvious affection was so damn adorable that I couldn't have stopped even if I wanted to.

"Dylan," Carly said, recapturing his attention, and when he looked over at her it was all I could do to keep my hand on the back of the couch where I'd now put it. "How are you today?"

"A little overwhelmed." He chuckled. "Not gonna lie."

"Overwhelmed?" she asked. "I find that hard to believe. How can this little group overwhelm you when you're used to dating this guy?"

Dylan stroked my knee and looked back at me. "Good point. He is...larger than life sometimes."

"I can imagine," Carly said. "Yet Ace tells us that *you* were the first to make a move on him. That takes some courage, no?"

"Oh my God," Dylan said, and laughed, and I could tell he was fighting against a healthy dose of nerves and embarrassment as he brought both of his hands to his face. The longer he seemed to lose it and laugh, the more endearing he became to the crowd. Then, when he finally had himself under control, he lowered his hands and nodded slowly. "It's true. I did ask him out. I also asked for his number several times. I'd been a fan of his for a long time."

I couldn't help myself then—I preened at Carly and brought my fingers to Dylan's shoulder to squeeze it. "My number *one* fan, right?"

Dylan scoffed, and then indicated with his thumb over at me and said to Carly, "See what I have to deal with?"

That had the crowd chuckling right along with their host, and relaxed Dylan into the groove of things as he settled back into the couch and the crook of my arm.

"You two are just adorable together. It really is such a pleasure to talk with you like this."

"Thank you," we said in unison as she brought her legs up under her and said, "So, *Insurrection 2.* The place you both met. What can you tell us about it?"

"Not much," I said, giving Dylan his cue, and he nodded.

"Mhmm, our lips are sealed. But as a huge fan of the first movie," he added, looking out at the audience, "I can say without bias that you won't want to miss the sequel. This guy is one talented actor. And he looks *very* nice in dress whites, too."

As everyone clapped, I tugged Dylan closer to my side and felt my heart thudding at the moment we were sharing right now, at the perfection of it, and I knew what we were doing here was right. It was exactly as it should be. Every minute that had brought us together and led us to this point here, on this couch talking to Carly Wilde about our lives, my upcoming projects, and Dylan's modeling gigs had

been worth it. Because this man sitting beside me was my
future, he was my everything, and I was never surer of that
than when Carly reached over to pat Dylan on the knee and
ask, "Okay, young man. We've all watched this guy on the
big screen and imagined what it might be like to meet him,
and know him. But we have to ask you…what's it like to
date Ace Locke?"

As the question lingered in the air, the audience went
so quiet you could've heard a pin drop, and then Dylan
shifted in his seat to look at me, and the love in his eyes
made my breath catch in my throat, and my reasons for
being here today all solidified and came together in total
accord.

"It's everything you would expect it to be…and so
much more." Dylan placed a palm over my chest and smiled
at me before turning his—soon-to-be million-dollar—face
out to the people watching this intimate moment between
us. And then he told them with conviction and pride, "Ace is
the most extraordinary person I've ever met. His capacity to
give to others of himself and yet remain humble in the face
of all that he has truly astounds me. And even when
everything in his life has been turned upside down, he is
right there with a supportive hand or word to encourage
you to strive higher, and harder, for your goals. He is the
man you see in all of your movies. The man you fall in love
with because he's brave and saves the day. And I count my
lucky stars that he almost ran me over in the studio lot of
Warner Bros. that first day."

As Dylan's words came to an end and everyone in the studio's heart melted as they *oooed and ahhed*, I knew it was my turn, and before Carly got in with any more questions, I was off that couch and down on one knee.

* * *

WHEN ACE MOVED beside me, I turned to watch him— *holy mother of God*—get down on one knee beside me. I wondered if it was possible for eyes to fall out of one's head, because in that moment I was pretty positive mine were so wide they were close to doing just that.

What is he… I looked to Carly, whose beautiful smile was in full effect, and when I met her eyes I noticed they were glassy from moisture as she brought her hands to her mouth, and then dropped her gaze back down to—

Ace.

Ace, who was down on one knee, looking up at me with those gorgeous blue eyes full of love as he reached into the pocket of his black jacket and pulled out a small velvet box. I blinked several times as he became blurry, and realized I had tears in my eyes. The studio, that only moments ago had been a chorus of swoon, had turned to a hushed whisper of expectation, until Ace smiled at me—and then everyone and everything else in the world vanished.

I brought a hand up to swipe the tears from my eyes and saw Ace's Adam's apple bob as he swallowed, took in a breath, and said, "Dylan, I can't begin to explain all of the ways you have changed my life. You literally stopped me in my tracks the first time I saw you, and no, I don't mean at the studio lot. I mean the first time I *saw* you. And then, by some miracle of fate, you stepped out in front of my car that day, and if that isn't a sign, I don't know what is."

I heard the muted sound of gasps all around us, but it seemed far off in the distance, because right then the only person who existed was the one looking at me exactly as Sunshine had once described, as if I'd hung the moon. Ace's lips curved into a breathtaking smile as I sniffed back my tears, and then he reached up to smooth a thumb across my cheek.

"Every day you teach me something new about myself, Dylan. And every minute that I'm with you, I find another reason to love you."

My hand shook as I reached for his, and when Ace entwined our fingers I tried to stop myself from totally losing it as he continued to say every single word I'd ever dreamed of hearing him say.

"I know our relationship so far has been quick and a little unusual compared to most. But I know what I want. I've known since the moment you sat down across from me that first day on set. I want you. I love you," he said as I sat there on the *Carly Wilde Show* utterly gobsmacked.

I gazed down at the man who'd released my hand and opened the velvet box he was holding, and it was my turn to gasp then, because nestled inside were two exquisite rings of white gold, and when Ace pulled one out, my hand flew up to cover my mouth at the sheer beauty of it. At first glance the shine of the polished finish was magnificent, but as Ace lifted it from its cushioned home, I noticed the round black diamonds, channel-set, alongside the front and back of the band, and I lost my ability to think.

"Dylan *Daydream* Prescott," he said with a handsome smile as he drew my hand away from my mouth and held it in his. "If you can put up with everything that comes along with me, *nothing* would make me happier than if you would marry me."

The studio remained silent and still, awaiting my reply to the man looking up at me with his heart in his hands, but there was no doubt there, no question from him. Ace knew how I felt, he could see it in my eyes, and when I nodded—because that was all I could seem to manage—tears flowed freely down my cheeks, and I tried to find my words.

The crowd exploded around us in cheers as Ace slid the band onto my finger, and then he reached for my face, cupping it between his hands as he leaned forward and kissed me on stage in front of the ecstatic crowd and the millions watching us, and I lost myself in him.

Right there on national television, I cradled the sides of Ace's face and kissed him back as though we were in the privacy of our own house. I closed my eyes and poured all of the love and emotion I felt for him into that connection, and when we finally pulled apart, I said, "Yes," and the microphone picked up the word and carried it around the audience who had quieted down to hear whatever else I was going to say.

"Yes, I will gladly put up with it and deal with whatever comes our way. It would be my honor to marry you. I love you, Ace."

Ace took my mouth again in a sweet but fierce kiss, and as applause rang out all around us, I heard Carly off to my side saying, "I am so in love with these two, I just might have to have them back once a month to catch up. And that's all we have time for here today, but I think we got more than we expected. If you're just catching the tail end of this, then you're reading that headline down at the bottom right—Ace Locke and Dylan Prescott are officially engaged. Now the question on everyone's tongue will be when and where these two will tie the knot. Thank you all for joining us, and I'll see you next time on the *Carly Wilde Show*."

ACKNOWLEDGMENTS

Thank you to Jay Aheer of Simply Defined Art for the utterly stunning cover design for Locked. We are still so blown away by this one. You are beyond talented, and we're so lucky to work with you.

A huge thank you to Wander and Andrey of Wander Aguiar Photography. The gorgeous photo of Allen IS Ace Locke, and we knew as soon as we saw it that this book had to happen. Thank you for being such a pleasure to work with. We look forward to many more projects with you!

Arran McNicol - our (long-suffering) editor who never fails to tell us like it is. Wouldn't trade you for all the lollipops in Dylan's Candy Bar. The chocolates and gummies, maybe, but not the lollipops.

Jenn Watson & Social Butterfly PR - Thank you for helping to make our lives easier! You and your team over at

Social Butterfly are always there to help spread the word, create a gorgeous graphic, put together a last-minute note to bloggers when one of your authors winds up in the hospital (**cough cough they passed the test, Brooke**). We really couldn't run this half as smoothly as you do, and we thank you for working with us.

Judy's Proofreading - we appreciate you looking over Locked and catching all those nitpicky details our tired eyes can no longer see. Tackle hugs to you and thank you so much!

Carly Phillips and Erika Wilde - A special thanks to these two wonderful ladies who we are lucky enough to call friends. You are true inspirations in the writing business and a true testament to what hard work and dedication can help you achieve. Sometimes we still have to pinch ourselves that we get to call you friends and we thank you for letting us steal your names to combine you into one kickass talk show host in our book. A special shout out to that WILDE name (aka one of Ella's all time favorite contemporary romance series).

The Naughty Umbrella - We love you guys like our sisters and brothers from other mothers! You guys are total troopers, through sickness and in health...okay, this is starting to sound like wedding vows now, BUT in all honesty we thank each and every one of you for your love, support, patience, and understanding. It is moments like what took place during the writing of this book that let us know we're surrounded by true friends, and we count you all as those and can't wait to meet you guys.

Special thanks to all the fabulous bloggers and readers who continue to support us and take chances when we throw different genres/cliffies/non-HEA's at you. Thank you for trusting us to bring you a story you'll enjoy even if it hurts.

And, finally, to Brooke's gallbladder—good riddance you pain in the ass motherfucker. ← (Ella seconds this statement.)

We hope you all will stick around for Ace & Dylan's happily ever after, because it will be an affair to remember!

Xoxox,

~Ella & Brooke

ABOUT THE AUTHORS

About Brooke

You could say Brooke Blaine was a book-a-holic from the time she knew how to read; she used to tell her mother that curling up with one at 4 a.m. before elementary school was her 'quiet time.' Not much has changed except for the espresso I.V. pump she now carries around and the size of her onesie pajamas.

Brooke is a *USA Today* Bestselling Author and enjoys writing sassy contemporary romance, whether in the form of comedy, suspense, or erotica. The latter has scarred her conservative Southern family for life, bless their hearts.

If you'd like to get in touch with her, she's easy to find - just keep an ear out for the Rick Astley ringtone that's dominated her cell phone for years.

About Ella

Ella Frank is the *USA Today* Bestselling author of the Temptation series, including Try, Take, and Trust and is the co-author of the fan-favorite contemporary romance, Sex Addict. Her Exquisite series has been praised as "scorching hot!" and "enticingly sexy!"

Some of her favorite authors include Tiffany Reisz, Kresley Cole, Riley Hart, J.R. Ward, Erika Wilde, Gena Showalter, and Carly Philips.

Made in the USA
Middletown, DE
11 October 2018